# FISH FOR FRIDAY
### and other stories from *Collection Two*

Frank O'Connor was born in Cork in 1903. He had no formal education worth speaking of and his only real ambition was to become a writer. At the age of twelve he began to prepare a collected edition of his own works and, having learnt to speak Gaelic while very young, he studied his native poetry, music and legends. His literary career began with the translation of one of du Bellay's sonnets into Gaelic.

On release from imprisonment by the Free State Government for his part in the Civil War, O'Connor won a prize for his study of Turgenev, and subsequently had poetry, stories and translations published in the *Irish Statesman*. He caused great consternation in his native city by producing plays by Ibsen and Chekhov: a local clergyman remarked that the producer 'would go down in posterity at the head of the Pagan Dublin muses', and ladies in the local literary society threatened to resign when he mentioned the name of James Joyce.

O'Connor's other great interest was music, Mozart and the Irish composer Carolan being his favourites. By profession he was a librarian. He died in 1966 and will be long remembered as one of the great masters of short-story writing.

Frank O'Connor

# FISH FOR FRIDAY
## and other stories from Collection Two

Pan Books in association with
Macmillan London

First published 1964 in *Collection Two* by
Macmillan and Company Ltd
This edition (which forms Part II) published 1971 by
Pan Books Ltd, Cavaye Place, London SW10 9PG,
in association with Macmillan London Ltd
2nd printing 1976
© Frank O'Connor 1964
ISBN 0 330 02636 4
Made and printed in Great Britain by
Cox & Wyman Ltd, London, Reading and Fakenham

# INTRODUCTION

Eleven years ago 'The Stories of Frank O'Connor' was published. By the time it was finished I had to see a specialist who took a poor view of my condition, but the book itself was a success. More important, it was a book which I could, and still can, take for granted.

This was my downfall, because I agreed to publish a successor. I worked at 'More Stories' during emotional and financial troubles, and I have never been able to take it for granted. All I could do was to refuse to allow it to be published in England until I could tackle it as I felt it should be tackled. Off and on, this has taken the best part of ten years.

'Forgery' is how an eminent Irish writer has described this method of editing one's own work, but 'forgery' is not a term of literary criticism, and is, I think, an unnecessarily harsh one to describe what at worst is a harmless eccentricity. Literature is not an aspect of banking. It is true that a number of my stories have been re-written a score of times – some as many as fifty times – and re-written again and again after publication. My wife has collected copies of 'The Little Mother' she found in the waste-paper basket, but has lost count of her total, which is distributed over three countries and ten years. This is a great annoyance to some of my friends, particularly my publishers and editors, who would prefer me to write new stories instead; I am afraid it shows a certain lack of respect for one's own public image ('after all, old man, you are a professional or you aren't'); but simply as a forger I must be the greatest failure who ever lived because I forge only cheques that have already been cashed and spent.

The only criticism of this eccentricity, if I may so call it, that ever shook me was that of the editor of *The New*

*Yorker* in which so many of these stories have appeared. He asked, 'But *can* you remember the story you set out to write?' and it is a question I still cannot answer. I believe I can remember. I believe the essence of any story can be expressed in four or five lines, but I cannot prove it. All I could possibly do would be to refer the reader to a text-book of the short story in which the earliest and latest versions of one of my stories are printed together. But this would mean taking myself a great deal too seriously, which, from my point of view, would be hardly less objectionable than not taking myself seriously enough.

For the British and Irish reader the book has split up accidentally in a way I had not planned. Exactly half of it might possibly be familiar to him, the other half should be new. It consists of stories from my first book, published thirty-two years ago, and stories I have not yet published in book form, side by side in an ideal ambiance that will be shattered by the time the book itself appears. I have lost, or never known, the confidence of the Irish poet who wrote over a thousand years ago –

> God be praised who ne'er forgets me
>   In my art so high and cold,
> And still sheds upon my verses
>   All the magic of red gold.

FRANK O'CONNOR

*Dublin 1963.*

# CONTENTS

*A Sense of Responsibility*     11

*The Little Mother*     31

*The Sorcerer's Apprentice*     70

*The Old Faith*     90

*Vanity*     100

*A Brief for Oedipus*     110

*Father and Son*     122

*Private Property*     131

*Fish for Friday*     144

*Androcles and the Army*     157

*Achilles' Heel*     166

*The Wreath*     177

*The Weeping Children*     191

# FISH FOR FRIDAY

# A SENSE OF RESPONSIBILITY

The first time Mrs Dwyer saw anything queer about Susie's boy, Jack Cantillon, was when his brother, Mick, was killed in a motoring accident. Mrs Dwyer was the mother of a large, loud-voiced family. Her husband was a carpenter, known to his wife as 'poor Dwyer', whose huffy shyness had never permitted him to make anything of himself. In spite of the fact that she was twice his build and had ten times his brains, he lectured her as if she were an idiot, and she put up with it as if she were. She was a bossy, bosomy, handsome woman; very devout and very sarcastic She had three boys who were spoiled and three girls who were not, because Mrs Dwyer never had the least regard for women's rights. 'Let them give me the money and they can have the rights,' she said, and she only voted to humour her husband, who naturally attached great importance to his vote.

Jack Cantillon had come to the house originally, courting Annie, but after he had been doing it for some time the three girls held a conference and decided he was too slow for Annie and would be better off with Susie, who was slow as well. In return, Susie gave Annie her best blue frock and a pair of new ear-rings. If Jack noticed anything queer about the change he didn't say much. He never said much anyway.

He lived with his mother in a terrace house up the road. She was a thin, ravaged, actressy woman who, according to herself, had come down in the world a lot. She was the widow of a manager in one of the big stores in town, and Jack now worked there as well. He was the elder and steadier of her two sons, but he and his mother had never got on. Her favourite was Mick, who married a girl called Madge Hunt, a good-natured, stupid, sentimental girl. Madge, like his mother, adored Mick, who was easy-going and light-hearted, and she was very shocked at the harshness of employers who expected him to work even when he wasn't feeling up to it and the unreasonableness of creditors who wanted him to pay back what he owed them, whether he had it or not. She never objected when things got bad, and Mick had to transfer herself and the child back to his mother's. But a couple of years of marriage improved her sense of reality enormously, and by the time Mick was killed, not too gloriously, in an accident, and she had to go out to work, she was as hard as nails, cold and knowing.

Jack took Mick's death hard, considering that the pair of them had never been very friendly, and began calling regularly on Madge, who lived with her little boy on the road. To begin with, Mrs Dwyer saw nothing wrong in this: a decent grief is a respectable weakness, and she was nothing if not respectable. But it went on too long, till it bordered on insincerity – insincerity, or what was worse, lack of common sense. And it didn't stop there. Babs, the oldest of the Dwyer girls, who heard everything, heard from the woman who employed Madge that Jack had made her give up the daily work and paid the difference himself. What Madge's employer said was: 'There's a good brother-in-law for you!' What Babs in her loud, humorous way, said was: 'How well I wouldn't find an old fool to do that for me!' What her mother, a woman of remarkable judgement, said was: 'That's queer behaviour in a man that's supposed to be marrying our Susie.'

She wanted Susie to have an explanation with Jack, but Susie flew in a panic and said she'd be too frightened. In some ways Susie was a judgement on her mother; a dreamy, good-natured girl, but too fond of 'them old novels' to have any self-respect. Mrs Dwyer did not read novels and had plenty of self-respect. So far as the boys went, she would defend them with or without justification, but her daughters were the exclusive product of her own intelligence, and could be defended on every reasonable ground. They were personally trained, and if they failed in any particular, she would repair them without charge. Without going into difficult questions of moral theology, one might say that at a pinch she would replace them. She would certainly not let an occasion like this pass without an explanation from Jack.

'I hear you're very good to Madge Hunt, Jack,' she said one evening when she got him alone in the sitting room.

'Ah, Madge is a fine girl, Mrs Dwyer,' he said. 'And I don't think it's very good for a child of Michael's age to be left with strangers while she's out at work.'

' 'Tis hard, Jack,' she agreed, pleasantly enough. Never having thought of the world but as a vale of tears, she felt no responsibility to defend its inequalities. 'But won't it make it harder for you to settle down yourself?'

'Begor, I suppose it will – a bit,' he admitted cheerfully.

'And you don't think it's a long time to ask Susie to wait?' she asked reproachfully.

'It's longer than I like to wait myself, Mrs D,' he replied with a grin. 'I don't want to stay at home any longer than I can help. Of course, I may get a raise, and if I do, it will nearly cover the few shillings I give Madge. At the same time I can't be sure of it. I've told Susie already that I may have to wait, and if she gets a better offer I wouldn't stand in her way.'

'I hope she doesn't, Jack,' Mrs Dwyer replied with the least shade of pompousness. 'As you say, if she does, she'll have to take advantage of it. A girl has only one life.'

Mrs Dwyer was not pompous, but she had a mortifying feeling that Madge Hunt, who wasn't even intelligent, could get round Jack Cantillon when she failed.

'I'd have nothing to do with that fellow, Susie,' she said dryly when she spoke to her daughter later. 'He hasn't enough manliness to make any girl a good husband. The Cantillons all take after their mother.'

She could hardly have said worse than that, but Susie was not the sort to drop a fellow merely because her mother told her to. 'Them old novels' had her ruined, and when she grew alarmed at the idea that Jack didn't appreciate her, her only notion of maintaining her self-respect was to make him

13

jealous with another man. In the novels, that always showed them, usually too late.

Now, the only way she could do this in a way that would even be noticed by Jack was by flirting with his friend, Pat Farran, and Pat was anything but a good choice for that delicate office. He was tall and handsome, quick-witted and light-hearted. He was delicate. Having been brought up in a household of women and sent to work in an office full of women, he seemed at times to be half a woman himself. He could cook, he could sew, he had an eye for clothes, and never seemed to feel with women the embarrassments most normal men feel. With a girl he was just another girl, so understanding, sympathetic and light in the touch that it never struck her until later that this was the only feminine thing about him. By that time, it was usually too late, and the girl's affections were engaged. Women were always trying to telephone him, and some of the things he said about them were shocking. Of course, he didn't mean them that way, but a man has enough to do trying to think as well of women as the conventions require without getting inside information, and as a rule, men didn't like him much.

Susie didn't really like him either: he didn't seem to fit into any novel that she'd ever read, but she did want Jack to see that others appreciated her, and for a shy girl it isn't easy to find an attractive man who'll make love to her at the drop of a hat. Any other man would have withdrawn from a situation of such delicacy, but Pat lacked all real niceness of feeling. He saw through Susie, was delighted with her profound satisfaction at her own guile, and full of curiosity to know how far she would take it. When he met her with Jack he pretended to be dying of love for her.

'You'll come home with me, Susie,' he would say, embracing her. 'I can't live another day without you.'

'I can't, sure,' Susie would cry, half pleased and half terrified.

'Ah, why can't you? It isn't that fellow you're afraid of?'

'But you don't know what he's like!'

'I don't? I know him since he was ten. The coldest fish in Ireland! Never cared for anyone only himself.'

'Go away, ye whoors of hell!' Jack would say, helpless with laughter as though it were all a scene from a play.

But it wasn't. Not quite. The Dwyers had a cottage in Crosshaven that summer, and as Pat spent a lot of his time there, the flirtation continued, and Susie even began to enjoy it. The cliffs at night, the noise of the sea and the company of an attractive young man who knew all about love-making gave her a certain sympathetic understanding of other seductions she had read about. Perhaps poor Tess wasn't as much to blame as she had thought! She had the idea that Pat was beginning to respect her, too, and her mother, who admitted that she liked a fellow who had a bit of the devil in him, was friendly. But of any effect it might be having on Jack, Susie couldn't see a sign, and she could only wonder if her mother wasn't right and if there wasn't something lacking in him.

All that summer Pat was unwell, and after he returned to Cork he had to be operated on. Susie had never seen Jack so depressed. Every evening he was out at the hospital. Susie discovered from Pat's mother that Jack had offered to guarantee a loan so that Pat could get to Switzerland. When she told her mother Mrs Dwyer sniffed and said, 'That fellow will be supporting half Cork before you get him to the altar.' 'But they are great friends, Mummy,' said Susie, and her mother replied, 'Friends or not, he has other responsibilities.'

But it was too late for Switzerland. In the week after Christmas Pat died as he had lived, lightly, swiftly and making passes at the nurses with a sort of desperate gallantry that went to Jack's heart. After the funeral he took to visiting Pat's parents as he visited Madge Hunt, and busied himself with the tying up of Pat's small business interests. He was the sort of man whose sympathy could be best expressed over a set of books. But Susie realized that this was something very different from his behaviour after his brother's death. He kept a picture of Pat on his mantelpiece, and a couple of times when she called she caught him staring at it.

As time went on, and she saw it had become a sort of

fixation with him, she became more concerned. Women are more jealous of men than they are of other women, though Susie would have been horrified to be told that she was jealous of Pat. She put it all down to concern for Jack: his attitude was morbid, and she must try to change it. But whenever she belittled Pat he either looked pained and changed the subject or else told her that she didn't understand. This was really too much for Susie, because, after all, it was she whom Pat had made love to, and if she didn't understand him, who did?

'Ah, you're very foolish, Jack,' she said wearily. 'You let people influence you too much. I suppose it's the effect your mother had on you. I'd never let anybody influence me that way. Of course, I was very fond of Pat, but I could see through him. You never saw how shallow he was.'

'Now, Susie, don't let's argue,' he said pleadingly. 'Pat was not shallow. He had a very fine head.'

'He was very insincere, though,' said Susie.

'Everybody has his own way of being sincere,' said Jack. 'Pat was sincere enough, only it wasn't in your way or mine.'

'Ah, for goodness sake!' she said, laughing at him. 'You never knew where you were with Pat. He'd be ridiculing you as soon as your back was turned.'

'Of course he'd be ridiculing you,' Jack said almost angrily, 'but there wasn't any harm in it. He was the straightest man I ever knew.'

Then Susie realized that her only remaining hope of shaking Jack was to show him what Pat was really like. She knew from novels the effect that always produced.

'And I suppose you don't know what Pat was up to with me when you weren't there?' she asked quietly, trying to keep her voice steady.

'I know damn well what he was up to, whether I was there or not,' Jack replied with a positive grin.

'And you don't even mind that he was living with me?' she asked, beginning to sniff.

'He was what?' Jack shouted, delighting her with his

16

furious air even though it scared her into sobs and tears. 'You bloody little bitch!'

It was the first time he had ever spoken rudely to her, and she was scandalized at the injustice of it. Anything she had said, she had said only for his sake, to help him to see things better.

'Oh, it's all very well for you to criticize,' she stormed at him through her tears. 'It's all your own fault, you and your blooming old responsibilities. I suppose you have no responsibility to me. You knew the sort he was, and you threw me at his head. Any other girl that was kept dragging on the way I was would do the same.'

'Not making you a saucy answer,' he said, rising and glaring down on her like the wrath of God, 'I don't give a damn what you did, but I'm not going to have you going round, telling lies about a dead man.'

'Lies?' she exclaimed aghast, clutching her hands on her bosom.

'What the hell else is it?'

'It is not lies,' she said, springing to her feet, really furious now. She didn't mind accusing herself of being an abandoned woman, which is what all the interesting women in fiction are, but to be accused of making it up was the final indignity.

'Of course it's lies,' he said contemptuously.

'Oh, the conceit and vanity of you!' she screamed in a tone of outrage. 'You're so smug that you think a woman couldn't do it to you. You think Pat couldn't do it to you! Well, he did, he did, and I don't blame him. I don't blame him a bit. You're just like your mother, rotten with conceit. You're not natural. My mother said it herself. You don't even know the temptations people have.'

'And as I said before, I don't care,' Jack replied, squaring up to her, madder than she'd ever before seen him. 'But it could cause great pain to Pat's family to have stories like that going round about him, so don't do it again, like a good girl.'

Susie realized with stupefaction that, whether he believed her or not made no difference at all to Jack. He would still continue to think more of Pat's parents' feelings than of hers. It was no use at all practising scenes from novels on him because no novelist had ever met anyone as unnatural as Jack Cantillon. And there was no hope of sympathy at home, because her family never read novels anyway, and they would either think she was telling the truth and be ashamed of her or that she wasn't and think she wasn't right in the head. She went home in a state approaching hysterics and told her mother only that Jack was a most appalling man, a most unnatural man. 'Well, girl', her mother replied complacently, 'you can't say but that you were warned,' which was about the most useless thing she could have said, for the more Susie was warned, the more curious she became about Jack. She couldn't help wondering what worse there was to know about him, and that meant she was tied to him for a long time to come. When a girl ceases to be inquisitive about a man she is really through with him.

2

It was five years before he was in a position to marry her, and by that time Susie's spirit was broken. He was worse to her than cigarettes to another girl. She frequently thought how wonderful it would be to be married to a western islander, and to be made love to on the shore in sight of the waves, but the western islands were far away, and she would be shy about making advances to an islander, and besides, she would probably catch her death of cold.

Mrs Dwyer was not too pleased with the marriage. She had sized Jack up, and was not a woman to change her mind about people that easily, but she was prepared to tolerate him for Susie's sake. And, from the worldly point of view, he was rather a better match than the husbands the other girls had got. He was now chief clerk, and in time would probably be manager, like his father. He bought a fine dilapidated old house off the Wellington Road, with tall rooms and wonderful views, and a lavatory somewhere up in the roof that would put the western seacoast in the shade. There the two children were born, Pat and Molly. Of course, the boy had to be called Pat.

It seemed as if things were running smooth for them at last. Too smooth for Susie's comfort. Jack was all right in a pub with a few men, but he did not care for society, and he refused to dance. After his day's work, all he mostly wanted was to change into old clothes, and read, or play with the children. And she had never really got over the way he had made light of her great revelation. According to her mood, she had two entirely different versions of her relations with Pat, whose picture still stood on the mantelpiece as though nothing had ever happened between herself and him. The first and commoner version was that nothing had – which was perfectly true; the second was that something awful had happened, which was equally true, according to the way you looked at it. When she was in good humour – which was most of the time – there had been nothing between Pat and herself only what she called 'old cod-acting', but when things went against her, she looked at the photograph and scowled at the child, and realized that she was no better than a woman of the streets all because of Jack's monstrous selfishness; and when she felt like that she made him a thorough good, old-fashioned scene in which she wept and screamed and called him an old molly. Jack, staring gloomily out at the grand view of the city, tried to soothe her, but that only made her worse. Finally, when it got too much for him, he would dash down whatever he was reading, say 'F— you!' in a thick voice, and go out to get drunk. People who saw him in town at such times brought back reports of a Jack Susie had never seen – impudent, witty and scandalous. The first time it happened she was thrilled, but she soon discovered that his emotional vocabulary was limited to one word, and that when he had used it, he had no more to say for himself.

Then, trouble caught up with them again. His mother, having managed to exhaust her small means, had entangled herself in a labyrinth of minor debts that could somehow never be subjected to the ordinary processes of accountancy. Mrs Cantillon considered that sort of accountancy common, and she traced Jack's weakness for it to his father. All Jack could make out was that even if he paid her rent and as many debts as he felt should be paid, it would still be only a matter of months till she was in court again. Jack had his father's mousy horror of the courts: Mrs Cantillon couldn't see what was wrong with them. She found district court judges very understanding and very ready to sympathize with her problems.

This presented Jack with a horrible alternative. He went up one evening to Madge Hunt to ask her advice. Curiously, Madge, who had begun as something of a nightmare to him, was now his only adviser.

She opened the door and instantly put on her best party airs. You could see at once that she was a parish priest's niece. Oh, my, the kitchen was in such a state! He'd have to come into the parlour. She was sure he'd never forgive her. Michael was out at the School of Commerce. He must be dead after the walk. A drop of whiskey was what her uncle said was the only tonic. Jack put up with it good-humouredly. She was a small woman, flowery in manner, and not as well-educated as you'd expect from a parish priest's niece – in fact, you could easily mistake her for the proprietress of a country shebeen; but he knew that under the silly convent-school airs there was a cold, clear intelligence and great integrity.

'Well, Jack,' she said candidly when he had told her his troubles, 'it seems to me you'll have to be a bit of a bastard for once in your life.'

'Tell me, Madge, would I have to take lessons?' he asked with a grin.

'I'll give you free lessons, and you'll find they'll save you a lot of trouble,' she said without answering the grin. 'Put your mother in a home.'

'That's what I find so hard to do,' he admitted.

'Well, there you are!' she said with a shrug and a laugh. 'If you were the sort of man that found it easy to be sensible, I wouldn't be sitting as comfortable as I am. Whatever I say will only reflect on myself, but that's the way life is, Jack. She'll make a wreck of your home. You know that your-self.'

'I fancy she'll try,' said Jack.

'Don't fool yourself at all, Jack,' Madge said sharply. 'There won't be any trying about it. She'll do it. You're not the man to handle her, and I'm not criticizing you. There's only one way to handle her and that's to put her in with someone who could. You could put her in with me. I don't like the woman, but I'd take her for your sake, though 'twould mean more expense to you, because I haven't the room. But if you ask my opinion, she'd go to the poorhouse first. I'm not saying it to criticize your mother, Jack, because she's more to you than I am, but there's only one thing in the world she cares for, and that's her own way. You'll excuse me saying so?'

'I'll overlook it,' he said affectionately. 'Thanks, Madge. I'll talk to her about it, and see what she says.'

At the doorway she kissed him, and looked after him as he went back down the road, thinking to herself in her un-sentimental worldly way that he was probably the only man in the world she could have been happy with. There weren't many women who felt that way about him. Perhaps that was why he went to her for advice.

She had seen through Mrs Cantillon though, for that was exactly what she felt about Jack's cruel proposal. First she looked at him with a timid, childlike smile as if she were wondering if he was in earnest.

'You mean the woman who killed your brother?' she asked reproachfully.

'I thought they said it was a truck,' Jack replied mildly.

'They were being charitable.'

'Then what will you do?' he asked.

'Don't ask me, Jack!' she begged with the air of a tragedy queen. 'I'll promise I'll be no burden to you.'

Then Jack, seeing she was false all through, became gloomier still, remembering how she had exploited Mick and himself, and realizing that Madge was right and that he could never, never deal with her.

Mrs Cantillon, for all her silliness, was a woman of infinite perception. She saw that in the matter of getting her own way, which as Madge had said, was all she cared about, Madge, a hard, sly, cynical woman, would see through her little dramatizations before they even took shape, while Susie, as well as being a much better cook, would be putty in her hands.

Mrs Dwyer, a woman of small silliness and excellent perceptions, saw that too. She warned Susie on no account to agree to Mrs Cantillon's living with them, and, seeing Susie's complete lack of gumption where anything you could read about in a novel was concerned, she had it out with Jack himself. This time there was no pleasantness about it. She was fighting for her daughter's happiness and security.

'I don't think you realize the dangers of in-laws in your home, Jack,' she said severely.

'I think I do, Mrs D,' he said wearily.

'I don't think you do, Jack,' she said, her voice growing hard. 'If you did you wouldn't offer your mother a home with Susie and yourself. I saw more of that sort of thing than you did, and I never yet saw it come to any good. People may mean no harm, but just the same they make mischief.'

'Mrs Dwyer,' he replied with mournful humour, 'even my mother's best friend wouldn't accuse her of meaning no harm.'

Mrs Dwyer smiled, but the smile didn't last.

'That's all the more reason why she shouldn't be in the one house with you and Susie,' she said. 'When you married Susie, you took on certain responsibilities, and they're not easy. Young people have to have their disagreements, and they have to have them in privacy. I never interfered between ye, good or bad, because I know only too well what it leads to. Marriage is something between two people, and when a third person comes into it, mother or father, priest or lawyer, there's an end of it.'

'If you think I'd be likely to let anyone come between me and Susie!' he said almost with a groan.

'You mightn't be able to help it, Jack,' she said dryly. 'Your mother is your mother, whatever anyone might say.'

'If that day came I could always cut my throat,' Jack replied with one of his outbursts of violence. She had never seen him like this before, and she watched him with interest.

22

'I never got on with her,' he added candidly. 'I blamed her for the way she spoiled Mick. After my father's death I blamed her for the way she turned us against him. I knew then he was a fine man.'

'He was,' she said unemotionally. 'That's true. He was a fine man.'

'She told us lies about him. She doesn't know what the truth is. But she worked hard, and she was generous to those she liked. Old people have to live too, Mrs Dwyer.'

'They have, Jack,' she said without expression, 'but they haven't the same claims as young people. For everyone's sake, your mother would be better in a home. I have to think of Susie.'

'And I have to think of Susie and my mother,' he said gloomily.

'You may have to choose, Jack,' she said quietly.

'There are certain things you have no choice about, Mrs Dwyer,' he replied, and again she realized with irritation that this intolerably weak man, who allowed himself to be imposed on by his calculating mother, had a sort of doggedness that made him safe from being influenced by a woman of character like herself.

'Well, don't blame me if you wreck your home,' she said with finality.

'I wouldn't blame you, anyhow,' he replied.

'And don't expect me to go into it,' she added severely. 'I'm sure what you're doing is wrong, and that it will come to a bad end, and I won't make mischief, but I won't go where mischief is being made.'

With characteristic determination she kept her word. She did not visit Jack's house again, though the children came up regularly to see her, and Jack himself came every Sunday after Mass. She always received him with especial cordiality. She had too much pride to let herself be flouted, but it pleased her that he could take her rebuke in that impersonal way. 'God knows he's not natural,' she said to her daughters, 'but you can't help liking him.'

And that, from a woman of Mrs Dwyer's calibre, was a real concession.

It must be admitted that she had miscalculated Mrs Cantillon's style though not her content. She made hell of the home all right, but not in the straightforward way Mrs Dwyer expected and could have partly countered. She made no attempt to make Susie's life difficult and contented herself with making a hell of Jack's. The silliness of Mrs Cantillon had an aspect that was not far removed from genius. She knew his weaknesses in a way that Susie had never known them, because they had been largely created by herself, and she remembered with attachment childish humiliations he had endured. She knew that though a married man and a father, he had always remained something of a bachelor; had lived all his life in the one small suburb of Cork, knowing no more of his neighbours than was necessary for the small courtesies of life – weddings, christenings, and funerals – while his mother boasted that she knew everything about everybody. After his day's work he liked to change ceremonially into old trousers, but his mother began to jolly him into taking Susie out. On the surface it was all the height of good nature, and Susie, who found long-extinguished aspirations for society reviving in her, took it all at its face value.

'Sure, it's all for my own sake, girl', her mother-in-law said. 'What other chance have I of getting the children to myself, and, what other chance have you and Jack of enjoying yourselves?'

The worst of it was that she could not keep from tinkering with money, which seemed to have a sort of fascination for her. Jack didn't mind the occasional bet, though she started Susie betting as well, but when he discovered from a solicitor that Susie's savings were being put into house property he lost his temper. Susie screamed at him that he'd sooner let his money rot in the bank than put it to some use, and he replied that if his mother had done the same she might have been able to pay her rent instead of living with them.

The queer thing was that as the home grew more wretched Susie came to depend more on her, and even had arguments with her own mother about it. Susie argued eagerly with her that Mrs Cantillon wasn't so much to blame as Jack. In all their disagreements it was Jack with his monstrous egotism who had been at fault. He had always been that way, even as a boy – self-centred and cold – unlike Mick, who was sunny and generous and warm. If Madge Hunt had decided that she had married the wrong brother, Susie was well on the way to believing the same.

But finding herself on the same side as Mrs Cantillon about anything was something Susie's mother did not propose to let pass.

'Ah, for goodness' sake, child!' she said. 'As if the whole road didn't know what Mick Cantillon was like.'

'He was terribly misjudged all the same, Mummy,' Susie said tragically.

'He was, I hear!' her mother retorted coarsely. 'Don't be fooling yourself at all now, Susie. Your husband may be foolish, but his brother was never any good, and his mother is downright bad, and let nobody persuade you otherwise.'

And, on the day that Mrs Cantillon was found unconscious and dying at the foot of the stairs, Mrs Dwyer walked in to look after the children, and the quarrel was over. In fact, as nobody but herself realized, the quarrel had been over for a long time. Mrs Dwyer had been impressed by something which also would have occurred to no one but herself. His mother had shaken Susie, but she had not shaken Jack. A man who could resist the influence of a bad woman was something Mrs Dwyer had never encountered before.

Mrs Dwyer was facing troubles of her own at the time. 'Poor Dwyer' had been dead for several years; Jim, the last of the boys, had married, and she was living on her own. Characteristically, this, instead of making her brood, gave her a new lease of life. What to anyone else would have been the end of a way of living was to her the beginning of another. She plunged straight into a life of dissipation, travelling to Blackrock and Douglas to visit old friends, playing cards, going to the pictures and refusing to mind her grandchildren. 'Wisha, aren't I right?' she said to Jack with a shrug. 'Aren't I fussing round them long enough? God knows, you have no notion, the comfort it is not to have anyone but yourself to look after.'

But she had left it a bit late before taking her fling. Soon afterwards she developed arthritis, and Susie came to nurse her. But it looked as though her independence was over. She couldn't be left alone in the house, and would have to go and live with one of the boys – a bitter humiliation for a strong-minded woman.

Tim, an easy-going fellow, would have had her readily enough, but easy-going fellows get easy-going wives, and it was most unlikely that Mrs Dwyer, who boasted that she had never seen the day when a properly-cooked dinner wasn't served in her house, would put up with Nora and her per-petual round of sausages. Ned's wife had six children, and there was no room unless they took a bigger house. Jim, be-ing only just married, hadn't enough furniture, and it would take a lot to make the house liveable-in. It wasn't that the boys didn't love their mother or wouldn't have died for her if the occasion arose, but they were all in difficulties themselves.

Susie, who had a heart for everyone's troubles, understood this perfectly, and her heart bled for each of them in turn, but her sister, Babs, told them roundly that they were a bloody pack of wasters and then went upstairs to tell her mother the same. 'How often did I say it to you?' she shouted, with her arms folded like a market woman. 'How often did I tell you you were ruining them, and you wouldn't pay a bit of attention to me? One of them wouldn't eat a slice of bread unless you buttered it for him, and none of us could get anything, and that's the thanks you get for it.' Babs was a forthright girl who could be counted on to make everything as difficult as possible for everyone else. Her mother listened with amusement.

'The Lord lighten their burdens!' she said dryly. 'As if I'd be under an obligation to any of them!'

'Well, what are you going to do, woman?' asked Babs. 'You can't stop here.'

'I'm going up to the Little Sisters where I can be properly

26

looked after,' said her mother. 'I have it fixed this two years past. Did you think, after all my years, I'd go into another woman's house to have her telling me what to do? What a fool I am!'

The whole family realized when it was put to them, that, regrettable as it was, it was only what they had always anticipated. A woman of strong character like their mother could never become an encumbrance in the house of a daughter-in-law. She would have to die as she had lived, saucy and strong and independent.

The only one who didn't take it that way was Jack.

'I suppose they know it's going to kill her?' he asked Susie.

'Oh, Jack, you don't think that?'

'I don't think it at all,' said Jack. 'I know it.'

'But, sure, she couldn't get on with any of the wives!'

'And do you think she's going to escape other women by going into a home?' he asked sarcastically.

'I suppose she isn't,' said Susie, who was sufficient of a fretter to be easily cast down. 'But what else can you do with her? You know what she's like when she has her mind made up.'

'I wonder if she has her mind made up,' he said lightly, and then talked about something else. But Susie could see he hadn't stopped brooding about it at all.

Next evening, after a long walk up Montenotte and back by Mayfield, he called at the Dwyers'. The walk was part protocol, part technique: to call without the excuse of a walk would have made the visit official. Babs was in charge, and her mother ordered her out to make tea for Jack. Marriage made no difference to the Dwyer girls. Inside the door, they instantly reverted to a position of dependence and would do so while she had a roof over her head. And Jack's bread would be buttered for him the way 'poor Dwyer's' bread had been buttered because men liked it that way.

'I hear you're going up to the Little Sisters?' Jack said with apparent amusement as they sat over the bedroom fire in the dusk.

'Sure, of course I am, boy,' she replied lightly. 'You know what I always thought of in-laws. Can you imagine me

27

turned loose on one of them? Not, between ourselves, Jack Cantillon, that I'm not a better woman than any of them, as old as I am.'

'I'd put my money on you anyway,' he said, amused that even in her hour of defeat she had kept her vanity.

'God knows, Jack,' she said, leaning forward with her hands on her knees and staring into the fire, I don't know what sort of women are they rearing. They're good for nothing only drink and gossip – not but I always liked a little drop myself, in reason. That wife of Tim's – I don't care to be criticizing, but I don't know is she ever right. If I was a man and a woman offered me sausages for my dinner two nights in a row I'd crown her with the frying-pan. I declare to God I would.'

'You wouldn't come to Susie and me?' he asked, dropping his voice so as not to be heard by Babs. 'You'd be no trouble. The room is there since the mother died.'

'Was it Susie suggested that?' she asked with apparent pleasure that didn't take Jack in at all. He congratulated himself on observing protocol. Mrs Dwyer might just be prepared to discuss such an offer from a man, particularly a man who had only just dropped in casually on the way from a walk, but to have it made by a daughter would have been a derogation.

'Oh, I didn't discuss it with Susie,' he said hastily. 'It only just came into my mind. Of course, Susie would have to have the last word.' The last word, not the first. That had to come from a man.

'Wisha, Jack, boy,' she said, dropping protocol, 'I'm easy where I go. I had my day, and I must only be satisfied. At the same time, mind you, I'm glad to be asked. 'Tis a fright to feel that nobody wants you. I suppose vanity is the last thing that dies in us.'

'Oh, vanity!' he said. 'You never told me you were that way. Tell me, will you come to us?'

'I will not, Jack, thanks all the same. Ye had enough of in-laws to last ye the rest of yeer lives – not criticizing your poor mother, God rest her, whatever I might say while she was alive. 'Tis often I thought since how right you were, in spite of us all. I suppose 'tis only when your own turn comes that you see who was right and who was wrong. Besides,' she added, 'I wouldn't give it to say to the boys.'

'I thought of that,' he agreed seriously. 'I thought you might let me ask them. I feel sure they wouldn't stand in the way if they felt you were going to be more comfortable.'

She searched his face to see if he was smiling. He wasn't though she had too much respect for him to take his words at face value. As a card player she knew it was small use studying expressions.

'To tell you the God's truth, Jack,' she said, 'I'd hate to be in an institution. God forgive me, I could never like nuns. I don't think they're natural. But I warn you, you'd be a fool to take me in. I'd be no acquisition to you. I'd promise the earth and I wouldn't mean a word of it. Old people are a mass of selfishness We're like babies. You have no idea. You'd be waiting here for someone to bring you a cup of tea, and if your nearest and dearest died while you were waiting for it, you wouldn't care. And isn't it only natural?' she added, cocking an argumentative eyebrow at him. 'Sure what else have we to look forward to?'

'I'll talk to Susie about it,' he said, as though there was anything poor Susie could say that would make any difference. But once they got used to the idea, it seemed to the whole family that this was how it was bound to happen. Their mother would be impossible in an institution unless she were made matron at once. Jack was steady; he had a good job; he was the born burden-carrier, and in the matter of money would never be able to embarrass them as a real member of the family could have done.

But, as things turned out, Mrs Dwyer was anything but a liability. Maybe it was the thought that she had escaped the home that gave her a new lease of life. The first evening Jack came home from work she had his old trousers warming before the fire, and told him to change there. 'At my age, as if I couldn't look at a man with his trousers off!' she exclaimed. 'Do you want me to go out?'

'I do not,' said Jack.

'Wisha, why would you?' she replied cheerfully.

But in some ways she was a great trial to Susie. She looked after him as if he were a child, trying to anticipate what he really liked – never an easy thing with a man who never seemed to express a preference for anything. She started cooking special dishes for him; things she hadn't cooked for thirty years, and then lamented that 'her hand was out'. She was so pleased not to be treated as an imbecile, as 'poor Dwyer' had treated her, that she even started to read papers and books so as to be able to talk to him. 'Pick out some books for me there, Jack,' she would say modestly. 'Not one of them old love stories. Something sensible.' And then she would read for an hour with great concentration and say dryly: 'He got a queer one all right when he went about it. A wonder he wouldn't take a stick to her!'

When Susie started her first big row with Jack, her mother lowered her book and asked sharply: 'Susie, what way is that to talk to Jack?' and Susie broke down and went upstairs to weep. When Jack went to follow her in his usual way, Mrs Dwyer said firmly: 'Stop where you are, Jack. You only make her worse.' She put down her book and slowly followed Susie upstairs. She knew Jack didn't like it; she knew he remembered her warnings against permitting outsiders to interfere, but she also knew how her own daughters should be handled, which he never would.

'The trouble with you is that you don't know a good man when you meet one,' she told Susie, who was lying on the bed, weeping, and waiting for her husband to comfort her. the way any married woman would. 'I only wish to God that I'd had a husband like him – not criticizing poor Dwyer, God rest him.'

'God is good,' said Susie between her tears. 'I mightn't last long between the pair of ye.' As her mother chose to ignore this, she called defiantly at her through the closed door. 'Oh, ye'd be well-suited, the pair of ye!'

She mightn't have been too far wrong. On her death-bed Mrs Dwyer asked Jack and herself to see that she was buried with them. She did not ask it with any particular eagerness, but even then, she surprised Jack, because she was a woman

30

who had always despised sentiment, disliked anyone who professed to ideals above money and security, and expressed complete indifference about where she was buried.

That caused real friction in the family, but Jack suddenly turned obstinate and even cold. Years later, Susie, searching through a few old papers in his desk, found the undertaker's bill. It came as a shock, and she wept bitterly for a few minutes, and then began to wonder why on earth he had kept it. There were still one or two things that puzzled her about him. There was no escape for her now; a woman who had not ceased to be inquisitive about the man she had married.

# THE LITTLE MOTHER

## I

Joan lived in a little terrace house near Cork Barrack with her parents and her younger sisters, Kitty and May. Mick Twomey was a builder, honest, hard-working, unbusinesslike and greatly esteemed. He was small, slight and quick-moving, with a clear complexion and red hair and moustache. Joan worshipped him, because whenever she got into some childish scrape she didn't want her mother to know about she went to him, her eyes popping, her voice a thrilling whisper, for the 'loan' of a shilling. 'And you won't tell Mummy, will you, Dad?' she would ask, and he would say indignantly: 'What business is it of Mummy's? This is between you and me, girl.' What was more, he said it in a way you could believe. It was wonderful to have someone you could trust the way you could trust her father.

Her mother was a beauty; slight, attractive and sentimental, who mourned over the wrongs of Ireland, romantic love and the sufferings of the poor, and seemed to get a great deal of pleasure from them. Her husband, who had been a revolutionary in his youth, had come to the age of being sarcastic about all three, but Mrs Twomey remained faithful to any cause she once took up. She said prayers for the success of the Republicans at elections, dreamed in a most undemocratic way of titled romances for her daughters, and entertained beggars in the house. Mick would arrive unexpectedly to find some old shawly beggar woman eating her dinner in the kitchen and slam into the sitting room in a wild rage, but in secret he adored his wife and told his daughters that they'd never be a patch on her. He knew how to take advantage of her sentimentality as well, for whenever he got in wrong with her he had only to drop a gruff remark about somebody from Killarney – Killarney being where they'd spent their honeymoon – and sure enough, in no time she would be going about the house, singing in a sweet cracked voice *By Killarney's Lakes and Fells*. It was so easy it was mean, and it went to Mick's heart to do it, but he was old enough to value peace in the home.

The three girls were spoiled and from the time they reached the age of twelve you could find them round the gaslamp in the evening, or slinking up dark laneways with boys who were wilder than themselves. Joan had a broad, humorous face, a gay and dashing manner and a great flow of gab. She was big round the bosom and rear and walked with a roll that her father said was like a drum-major's. Kitty, the second girl, was taller and had a better figure. She dressed better, too, because she had a passion for dressmaking and couldn't see an old frock without realizing its possibilities. She was an untidy, emotional girl who took after her mother and was, accordingly, her father's favourite. May, being only thirteen, couldn't really be very wild, but with her miniature features, she promised to be the best-looking of the three, and there was something about her quick wit and quick smile that indicated she would take full advantage of it.

Mrs Twomey, being nearer their age than her husband's, couldn't control them at all. She would fly into a rage and go for them with whatever came handiest, and then remember some identical occasion in her own girlhood and her own mother's indignation until, forgetting all about the cause of her rage, she went round singing *Mother Machree* and the girls, forgetting their sore bottoms and injured dignity, would join in. Sometimes Mick, coming home from work in the evening, would hear them singing from the road outside, and, when he threw open the kitchen door, see the four of them sitting in darkness round the range and the fresh tears shining on their cheeks. 'Name of God, are ye at it again?' he would growl, striding over to light the gas. 'I suppose none of ye thought about supper?'

Sunday was Mrs Twomey's favourite day because after chapel in the evening the girls brought home their friends and their friends' friends. The gaslamp was lit at the foot of the little square outside; the gasjets hissed at either side of the fireplace in the front room, and the oil-lamp on the round table gave light to the piano. Kitty, the hostess of the three girls, made the tea and Joan played. Dick Gordon, Joan's fellow, usually started things off by singing *Toreador* or *The Bandolero* in a weak baritone. He was a tall, handsome young fellow with a long clear face, and while he sang Mrs Twomey smiled fondly and discussed himself and his family in what she thought was a whisper.

She was very glad of him for Joan, though there was something missing somewhere which she attributed to a Protestant streak, way back. He wasn't interested in republicanism and was even less interested in religion. He didn't go to the Sacraments, or even to Mass, unless it was to meet somebody at it. He was a well-read boy, and, seeing that both his own family and the Twomeys were mad on religion, he had out of pure kindness of heart studied the Bible and several other religious works, only to find them all filled with people rising from the dead or ascending into the sky without any means of locomotion – things no practical engineer could credit.

'And you mean you don't really believe in God, Dick?' Mrs Twomey asked wonderingly.

'Afraid not, Mrs T,' he replied quite cheerfully, as though he were not afraid at all.

33

'You don't believe in anything?'

'On the contrary, I believe in everything – everything I can put my hand on, that is.'

'You will, Dick,' she said solemnly. 'One of these days when all the things you can put your hand on are no help to you, you'll see God as plain as you see me.'

'That'll be the day,' he said with cheerful irreverence.

2

Each winter Mrs Twomey, who had a weak chest, suffered from bronchitis. She had ceased to pay much attention to it herself and treated it almost like an old friend. Besides, it was an ordeal for her to stay in bed or even at home, because she liked her trips into town and her gossips with old cronies on the way.

The winter after Joan became seventeen she had one of her usual attacks and recovered, and on the first sunny day went into town to Mass. She came back, feeling weak, and that night her bronchitis was worse. By the following evening she could scarcely breathe and sat propped up on pillows. Old Dr Mulcahy, who had been in gaol with Mick, thought it best not to remove her. In the early morning she had an attack of breathlessness and became so violent that it took Mick and Joan to hold her down. Mulcahy came and gave her an injection which put her to sleep. Then he took Mick into the front room.

'We're very old friends, Mick,' he said. 'I think I'd better prepare you for a shock.'

Mick drew himself up.

'Is that the way it is, Peter?'

'I'm afraid so. Even if she gets through this I'm afraid she'll be an invalid for the rest of her days.'

'I don't care what she is, Peter,' Mick replied violently. 'So long as they leave her with me.'

'Oh, I know, I know,' Mulcahy said gloomily. 'There aren't many like her. Send the elder girl into me, Mick. I want to talk to her.'

That evening Dick Gordon came and sat in the front room, talking quietly to Mick and the girls. Now and then the gate creaked as some old neighbour came to inquire. Mulcahy had been again and gone, leaving a morphia syringe behind him. The attacks of breathlessness had become so violent that there was no other way of controlling them, and the breathing was so terrifying that none of them could stay in the bedroom for more than a few minutes.

Instead, Mick would open the door softly and tiptoe up the stairs for a few minutes at a time. Dick interjected some quiet remark that was only intended to ease the strain. Coming on to morning, Mick jumped up and rushed up the stairs, and it was only then that they realized the breathing had stopped.

'Joan! Joan!' they heard him scream in an unnatural voice. 'She's gone! Your poor mother is gone!'

Joan gathered herself up to scream as well but Dick grabbed her firmly by the shoulders. 'Quiet, now, Joanie!' he said in the low voice one might use to a child, and he smiled at her as one might smile at a child. She put her head in her hands and began to sob with the others. When they went upstairs Mick was kneeling by the head of the bed. Their mother's head had fallen feebly forward and the jaw was dropped in an expression of utter weariness.

'Take Daddy downstairs now, Dick,' Joan said, gaining control of herself. 'I can manage.'

'I'll stay, Joanie,' said Kitty.

'No, Kitty,' Dick said firmly. 'Let Joan handle this'.

They returned to the front room and Dick led Mick Twomey to an armchair by the window and then poured him out a drink. He nodded acknowledgement but when he tried to raise the glass he could not bring it to his mouth. Dick took his hand and held the glass for him. Then Dick drew the curtain and daylight came in through the drawn blind. He raised it and stood for a few moments looking out at the still square where the gaslamp was still burning and at the fields and trees on the hillside above. 'Oh my!' he sighed with a curious boyish air and drew the blind again just as Joan entered. Her father rose with an erect and soldierly movement

35

and drew the other girls up with him by the hand. Then he turned to Joan and presented them with a curious air of formality.

'You must be a mother to them now, Joan,' he said with a firm voice. 'They have no one else only you.'

3

That little scene made an extraordinary impression on Joan. She was over-wrought, and it seemed to her to have something of the quality of a religious dedication, as though it were a taking of vows.

When she stood with her father and sisters by the grave on a hillside over Cork Harbour, she promised the dead woman that she would try to be everything she had been to them. She had no illusions about herself. She knew her mother had been a creature apart, whose innocence had kept her emotions always fresh and beautiful. Joan felt sure that she had no such innocence, but she thought that maybe she might have character, and the thought filled her with a certain mournful pride. It was as though within a few days her whole nature had changed: as though she no longer had a father and sisters, only a husband and children; as though, in fact, her girlhood had suddenly stopped.

For months their little house was gloomy and dark. It had something to do with the deep vein of sentimentality in them all. Suddenly one of the girls would forget herself while washing clothes in the kitchen and start to hum some song of their mother's and as suddenly stop in the middle of a bar. Then would follow a few intolerable moments of widening comprehension that would end in tears.

But it couldn't go on like that. However Joan's thoughts might wander, meals had to be cooked, laundry had to be done, bills had to be paid. And though the house and furniture were now all that was left of her mother, they too were responsibilities, and Joan knew that they would have to be changed.

The house was old, and it was old-fashioned, and nothing

36

in it had been altered in the twenty-odd years of her parents' marriage. There was still only gas in the front room, and the furniture, bought second-hand at auctions in houses three times the size, was a joke. Joan was ashamed that they didn't have a bathroom. It struck her as all wrong in a family of girls that fellows would always be walking through the kitchen, seeing things they shouldn't see and coming in with big bumps on their foreheads after finding their way to the lavatory. Above all, she wanted to get rid of the range from the kitchen and make it into a comfortable living room. Mick did wire the house for electricity, but he made excuses about the bathroom and the kitchen, and she knew she must go slowly with him because every change would seem to him like a betrayal of her mother. He wanted to die among the things that had been hers. Joan wanted to make a new life for them all.

Besides, there was a change in herself. The excitement in her blood when dusk came and the last light lingered on the fields and trees opposite the house was no longer the same. It had used to be like a fever; the cows lowing in the fields behind, the children shouting from the gateways, the pool of light round the gaslamp at the end of the square and the intimation of mysterious embraces; but now it was all touched with sentiment for poor human creatures whose voices would soon be stilled forever.

It was part of her new gravity that Joan took to going to Mass every morning. Wet or fine, she plunged out after her father had left for work, and soon became familiar with the other women who did the same. If one were missing she would call on her way home to ask if there were any messages she could do. Usually there were; it was extraordinary how helpless people were when they were in trouble, and in the evening, when she had given her father his supper she would explode on him with: 'Daddy, I don't think anyone knows what goes on in a place like this.' At times like these she was very like her mother; more self-conscious, more melodramatic, but with the same absorption.

And it had a silvery sort of poetry of its own, thin and sweet and clear as if it were a world renewed. The neighbours, who only saw it from outside, admired the way a flighty girl of eighteen turned gradually into a mature, responsible young woman. But it couldn't be expected that her sisters should see it that way. Now, when Kitty was out with some fellow, Joan actually worried about her. She didn't expect anything unreasonable, only that Kitty shouldn't be out too late, but even this Kitty resented. One night there was almost a scene.

'What kept you out till this hour, Kitty?' Joan asked, quite politely, but Kitty started back as though she'd been struck.

'What's wrong with you?' she asked angrily. 'Who do you think you are?'

'Oh, just the new housekeeper, Kitty,' Joan replied with a nervous laugh. 'Who did you think?'

'I don't know,' Kitty replied coarsely. 'Whoever you are, you're getting too big for your boots.'

That night Joan wept as she so often did nowadays. Children never understood the responsibilities of guardians. And it wasn't only Kitty, of course. She remembered how often and unjustly she had blamed her mother for the same sort of thing.

But Kitty and May soon realized that they had lost a sister and caught a tartar. It was true that Joan always had a touch of Reverend Mother about her, and had attempted to make up in knowingness for the affection that had been diverted from her to her younger sisters, but that had been mainly swank. In essential things she had remained part of the juvenile conspiracy, treating parents as enemies, raiding their stores and smashing up their intelligence system. Now, she had real authority and harried them mercilessly, particularly poor Kitty, who had been disorderly from birth, and left a litter of dirty clothes and pots and pans behind her. Her mother had been content to clean up after her, knowing poor Kitty had other things on her mind, but Joan didn't see why she should do it. Of course, she was always polite, but then, it seemed to be the politeness that got on Kitty's nerves.

'Kitty!'

'Well?'

'In the hall, dear,' Joan would sing out. 'That thing on the floor.'

'What about it anyway?'

'Nothing, Kitty, only it looks like your good coat. I wonder if you'd mind hanging it up?'

'Would you mind?' Kitty would mutter to May. 'Would you please oblige by removing your noxious presence from the premises? That one!'

Joan realized that none of them had been taught orderly habits, and that even in their school work it came against them. May was brilliant but her marks were shocking, so she had to stay in for an hour each evening and do maths and French with Joan who rapped her knuckles with a ruler and scolded her in a shrill voice for neglecting her irregular verbs. As if the life of any pretty girl were affected by irregular verbs!

And, having deserted to the enemy, Joan was worse than any parent because she had their whole intelligence service broken up from within. She would be waiting for them at the door, her arms folded, looking up and down the road for them till she trained them to scout first. Kitty would put her head quickly round a corner and say in a despairing tone: 'Christ on a bicycle! That one is there again!' May thought this was cowardice, and said so, but even she knew that Joan was a problem. It was no good telling her you'd been dress-making up the road when you'd really been out Mayfield with a boy because she'd done it too often herself and would be bound to find out the truth next morning at Mass from some old Biddy like herself. They had to tell the truth but they did it with bitterness in their hearts, not so much because they were afraid as because it derogated from their femininity; and in the intervals of wheedling and scolding they lapsed into mute and sullen conspiracy.

All the family learned from the new situation, but Joan, who was at the centre of it, learned most. She found it was far from being the romantic change of parts she had first imagined and not at all a matter of her father and herself on the one hand, and 'the children' as she liked to call them on the other.

At first, when she discussed money matters with Mick she was flattered by the grown-up tone of mournful candour in which he replied, but in time she began to suspect that the candour was fallacious – the accounts varied too much. It was hard to believe, and she hated to believe it, but her father was not always truthful.

One day, when she was worried about bills, she saw Kitty with a handful of silver.

'Where did you get all the cash, Kitty?' she asked lightly.

'Cash?' Kitty retorted with an attempt at brazening it out. 'What cash?'

'You needn't bother to tell me any lies, Kitty,' Joan said in an off-hand way. 'I can guess.'

'You can guess what you like,' said Kitty, now thoroughly alarmed as she saw her source of independence threatened. 'I got it from Aunt Molly, as you're so inquisitive.'

Joan was too digusted to argue with her. Her father, thinking she kept them short deliberately, had been supplying them in secret. That was his gratitude! She could see it exactly as though he were some man who had been unfaithful to her and imagine the mockery of her rivals. Mick was horrified when she challenged him with it.

'For God's sake, girl!' he exclaimed. 'I gave her a couple of bob. What harm is that?'

'You gave it to her behind my back,' said Joan.

'Well, would you want her to know what I gave you?'

'Ah, 'tisn't alike,' she said with an angry shrug. 'I suppose you know what they think themselves – that I grudge it to them?'

'Ah, don't be silly, girl!' he said. 'How could they think anything of the kind?'

He argued, pleaded, even lost his temper with her, but she was remorseless. He had been unfaithful to her, and, like every other deceived wife, she knew her disillusionment was a weapon. Never again would he betray her. Even later, when she went beyond the beyonds and challenged him about his drinking – a thing her mother would never have dared to do – he endured it patiently. Now she had three quivering victims, a thing that might have gone to the head of a less emotional girl than she was.

4

But Dick Gordon got the worst of it, and he did not understand it at all. Joan had always been what he thought of as a good girl, but she had also had her share of devilment. A couple of times when they stayed in Crosshaven she had slipped into his bed, and Dick, who understood that part of her very well, knew that she was only trying it out. It merely meant that she felt perfectly safe with him, which she was.

But those days were over. Now, when she thought of it, Joan merely wondered how she would feel if Kitty were to behave like that with some young fellow of Dick's age, and at once it ceased to be attractive. Even Dick himself was not very reliable – a young fellow who didn't believe in God, or eternal punishment, or marriage or anything. Even if she married him, there would still be endless arguments about what children should and should not be taught. So far as he was concerned they would grow up like heathens.

It was a real problem to her and caused her a great deal of worry. She realized that in her own way she loved him, and often in the evenings she forgot herself and stood at the door with her arms folded bending forward to look down the road for him. It was only when she saw him, coming towards her with his self-confident air, that she remembered the Protestant grandmother, and in her perturbation picked a quarrel with him. No, she couldn't go to the pictures that evening. She couldn't go for a walk. She couldn't even ask him to stay because she had arranged to coach Kitty for her Civil Service exam. And then she went into the front room and bawled again.

One night, Mick opened the door and walked in with a puzzled air.

'What the hell is wrong with you, girl?' he asked crossly.

'Me?' she asked, sniffing back tears. 'Oh, nothing. Why?'

'Are you having a fight with Dick?'

'No, Daddy. It's not that.'

'Well, don't. Dick is a fine young fellow.' Long ago Mick had promoted Dick to the position of the son he lacked, and since his wife's death this attitude had become fixed in him. 'Look! Don't sit here in the dark, moaning. Put on your hat and coat and go out after him. Tell him you're sorry, whether you are or not. He won't mind.'

Whether it was that he knew her father was on his side or not, Dick had a curious thickness that made him incapable of recognizing when he wasn't wanted. There were times when she thought him the thickest man in the world. He wasn't easy at home with a respectable family who thought the Twomeys were frivolous and unstable. He had been coming to the house for years until it meant more to him than his own. The old gate that squeaked, the flower-beds and lilacs, the little front room were Dick's romance, and he was prepared to fight for them. This, she saw, was something she would have to have out with him, and it alarmed her because she was not very good at scenes. And when this one came, it was worse than she expected because she made no impression at all on Dick. It was a spring evening and they were lying in a field over the harbour – an old haunt of theirs. Dick had his hands linked behind his head, and when she told him that they must see less of one another, he merely turned to look at her with an air of pity and amusement.

'What makes you think that?' he asked mildly.

'Well, things have changed so much, and I have so many new responsibilities, I wouldn't like to keep you hanging round,' she said, getting nervous.

'Oh, I have a few responsibilities of my own, you know,' he said with a smile.

'But this may be a matter of years, Dick.'

'Well, since we suit one another, we may as well put up with a few delays,' he replied blandly.

'But, Dick, we don't suit one another.'

This time he raised his eyebrows. Dick was an engineer and tended to treat people as though they were complicated bits of machinery. Something went wrong; you opened it up and fixed it, and then it worked perfectly again. She could almost see him working on her now.

'Don't we?'

'I don't honestly think so, Dick. Not any longer anyhow.'

'Since how long?'

'Oh, a long time.'

'Exactly,' he said blandly. 'Since your mother's death.'

(Joan could almost see it as though it were evidence at the inquest – 'She had not been the same since her mother's death.')

'Ah, Dick, it's not only Mummy's death,' she said impatiently.

'No, of course not,' he went on in the same bland tone. 'But that is the most important thing. You've had a shock, and you must wait for the effects to wear off.'

'Listen, Dick, I wish you'd talk seriously for once,' she said angrily. 'I know I was young and giddy, and I didn't understand how much certain things meant to me. I suppose it's only when someone you care for dies that you do know.'

'And that is part of the shock,' he said positively.

'It isn't part of the shock,' she cried. 'That's what I'm trying to explain. You just think everything is caused by something else and it isn't. I'll get over the shock, as you call it, but I won't get over things I believed in all the time, only I didn't pay enough attention to them. You don't believe in any of the things I believe in – that's the real trouble. You want me to marry you, and God knows I always wanted to marry you, but you don't even believe in marriage. You don't believe in sin. You could go off with another girl tonight and there would be nothing to prevent you.'

'Or to prevent any of your pious believers,' Dick said with cold anger.

'At least they'd know that what they were doing was wrong,' she said.

'Oh, if it's only a feeling of guilt you think I'm lacking in, I'll do the best I can,' he said wearily. He got up and brushed himself, but he was a man who could not keep his anger at boiling point. He looked down at her and smiled.

'Give yourself time, Joanie,' he pleaded. 'You've lost a wonderful mother, and it seems like the end of the world to you, but don't exaggerate. People don't get on in marriage because they have the same taste and the same ideas. Your mother didn't get on with your father for that reason. You and I didn't get on for that reason. We got on because we had respect for one another's feelings. That's all.'

It wasn't all, and she knew it, but it was hopeless to argue with him. He came back to the house every evening just the same, though each evening he seemed a little more despondent. He was. From his limited, logical, liberal point of view her breach with him made no sense even if he was wrong about religion. Sometimes in his liberal way he assumed he must be, and that there was probably an essential flywheel missing that would enable him to enjoy ascensions, assumptions and apparitions just like anybody else. But he knew the wild side of Joan better than anyone else, and he could not understand how the laughing girl who had pushed her way into his bed in Crosshaven could disappear like that, leaving behind nothing but a soured, censorious old maid.

He even discussed it one evening with Kitty when he accidentally met her outside the office – it did not occur to him that she had arranged the accident – but her explanations only mystified him more.

'It's all just pride, Dick,' she said coldly. 'Just rotten pride and vanity. All she wants now is a man she can boss the way she bosses Daddy and us. You're too independent for her altogether.'

That evening he asked Kitty to come to the theatre with him, Joan having already refused. It was Shaw's *Saint Joan* and during the last half Kitty wept almost without ceasing.

'God, Dick,' she sobbed, 'I always wanted to be a saint.'

He was amused and touched, amused by her emotionalism, touched by her resemblance to her mother. 'What an astonishing family!' he thought. After the theatre she insisted on walking home, swinging from his arm and stopping before shop windows. Finally she detained him for half an hour under the gaslamp at the end of the square. She knew she was in full view of Joan but this neither deterred nor incited her. She wanted to talk about the play.

'Do you think I'd let myself get burned the way she did?' she asked.

'I don't know,' Dick said with amusement, leaning against the lamp post, his feet wide and his hands behind his back. 'Maybe you would after changing your mind a few times as she did.'

'Twelve months ago I'd have been certain of it,' she said.

'And what made the change?' he asked without realizing what she was speaking of.

'You known damn well,' she said softly.

'I'm sorry, Kitty,' he said with real concern.

'Why would you be? You weren't rotten to her.'

'And if you'll forgive my saying it, neither were you,' he said with his gentle smile.

'I'm the best judge of that, Dick,' she said without rancour. 'And now, what do you think I'm going to do? Say I'm sorry and hope for another chance? Fat hope I have! It's all bloody cod, Dick Gordon, and you know it better than anyone.'

Suddenly she rushed away from him, and as she plunged up the hill he heard her sobbing as if her heart would break. There were tears in his own eyes. It was clear that Kitty had grown up with great rapidity.

5

For different reasons the same idea occurred to Joan. Next day it was obvious that Kitty had fallen head and ears in love with Dick, and Kitty in love gave off an atmosphere that simply could not be ignored. She was hoping to see Dick again the following evening, and when Joan detained her, she burst into tears and said that Joan was doing it for spite.

'What on earth do you mean, child?' Joan asked with an astonishment that was not quite sincere.

'Who are you calling "child"?' retorted Kitty. (It was the one word that was sure to madden her.) 'You pretend you don't want him, but you're mad jealous if he looks at anyone else.'

Joan gaped. It was only now that she was beginning to notice the change in her own character. Six months before, that skinny, pasty-faced little brat would not have dared to suggest that any man would look at her rather than at Joan, without Joan's showing her how wrong she was.

But Kitty continued to ignore her, and Dick, who seemed to have the hide of a rhinoceros, continued to call as though nothing much had happened except a slight change of object. From Kitty's rapt look when she had been out with him, Joan could see that he did to Kitty the sort of things he had done to herself. At a sign of approval Kitty would have broken down and told her, and Joan had no doubt at all that she told May. How could she bring up two children with that sort of thing going on?

It came to a head one Saturday afternoon when Kitty packed her bag for the weekend. Joan felt despairing. It was bad enough, having to stay at home and get everything ready for the Sunday while her mind was on something else; it was too much to be imagining a bed in Crosshaven and Kitty slipping into it beside Dick.

'Where are you going, Kitty?' she asked in her casual way.

'To Crosshaven for the weekend,' Kitty said, growing pale – casualness was something she still could not affect. 'Why?'

'Who are you going with?'

'The Caseys. They asked Dick and me. We're going in their car.'

'And did you ask Daddy's permission, Kitty?'

'No,' said Kitty, who always grew impertinent when she was frightened. 'Did you?'

It was really too much for Joan, who had no faith in her sister's capacity for keeping out of trouble and she complained to her father. He was a bad man to complain to, because he was full of pity for humanity in general and young fellows of Dick's age in particular. He, too, thought she was jealous – it was really extraordinary, the number of

46

people who got that impression – and of course, she couldn't really tell him about the sort of thing that went on – not without convicting herself.

'Ah, look here, girl,' he said irritably, 'wouldn't you make it up with Dick, whatever he did to you?'

'But honestly, Daddy, he did nothing to me.'

'Whatever ye did to one another, so.'

'We did nothing to one another, Daddy. I give you my word. It's just that we weren't really suited. You see, Dick has no religion.'

'Ah, religion my ass!' her father said furiously. 'Do you think I had any religion when I was his age? What the hell do you want him to do with you – say the Rosary? You make me sick!'

'It's not the same thing at all, Daddy,' Joan said obstinately. 'Your generation didn't have any religion, but there were good reasons for it. It's different with Dick. He hasn't any proper sense of responsibility, and Kitty hasn't either. Neither of them knows where to stop.'

'Ah, Christ, Joan,' he said, 'leave me alone with that sort of talk! I was the same when I was his age. He's only knocking round with Kitty to spite you. It only shows how fond of you he is. Damn it, didn't I nearly marry your Aunt Molly after one row I had with your poor mother, God rest her? And where would you be now if I did? Answer me that! You should never take things like that to the fair.'

All the same, Mick felt there should be something he could do about it. After an attempt at talking to Kitty who got up in her dramatic way and offered to leave the house next morning, he decided that that wasn't it. It was only when he ran into Dick Gordon accidentally one evening on Patrick's Bridge that he decided to confide in him. He was like Dick in this, that both found it easier to talk intimately to men. Men did not drop into blooming sentiment, and anyone listening to Mick would have thought he was only telling an amusing story. But Dick thought otherwise, and when he went away he already felt that he owed it to the man he would have liked for a father-in-law not to make any more trouble for him at home.

When he next met Kitty he suggested that they should give up meeting till she had got her exam and was independent. She agreed, reasonably enough as he thought, and, indeed, she settled down to work with a deliberation that surprised Joan. Though Kitty gave the impression of being frivolous and unstable, there was a streak of determination in her that was very close to desperation. Unfortunately for him, it was months before Dick realized that it was desperation rather than reasonableness, and by that time it was too late. He had lost the second of the Twomey girls without even knowing quite how he had.

6

For some months Joan had been seeing Chris Dwyer off and on. She had been astute enough to realize that he had fallen in love with her, all over a remark she had made about a concert, but that he would do nothing about it as long as she was seen round with Dick Gordon. Chris was not a dashing type at all, like Dick, and had never except inadvertently cut in on anyone.

He was a tall, good-looking young man with a long, pale face, clever eyes, a long, rather suspicious nose, and a weak, gentle mouth. He spoke in a Sunday's Well accent, swallowing half his words; dressed accordingly and even carried an umbrella. 'I really don't see what the objection to it is,' he said with his nervous laugh. 'I mean, it's so practical.' You could see that the umbrella meant something special to him, like a holy medal. Young May, who thought he was a queer, called him 'I mean'.

He came of a good family that had descended in the world, and devoted himself to the care of his mother, a woman of such invincible refinement that she didn't even understand what had happened to her income. The first time Chris asked Joan to come to a concert with him he told her the whole story of his life so that there could be no question of his inability to marry her, and Joan, who understood him perfectly, was very amused because she had no doubt of her

48

ability to marry him whenever she wanted to.

After that, he took her out on the same evening each week, umbrella and all. He was an orderly young man who liked to know exactly where he stood. He was also in his own way a clever one, conscientious and kind; and out of his great responsibilities he made up funny little stories which he told with an air of intense gravity that made them funnier still. When Joan laughed he grew quite hysterical, and his face became that of an ingenuous boy.

Joan confided in him her troubles with her father and sisters, and Chris – after a period of meditation – responded with a new version of his life story that contained admissions about his elder brothers, Bob and Jim. Bob gambled, and Jim, who couldn't be kept out of a church had broken out in *very* peculiar ways. Joan could not get out of him exactly what they were, but they were obviously a great trial.

Between family confidences and music, Chris and herself seemed made for one another, the only difficulty being that each had so many responsibilities that there was no hope of their ever being more than friends, but even this formed something of a bond, and they were genuinely happy in one another's company. Joan had at last got rid of the range, and had the kitchen done up in bright simple colours so that she didn't mind asking him in, even if they hadn't a bathroom. Her father, of course, didn't like the living room, and had retreated to the sitting room where things were still unchanged, but Joan had ideas for that, too. Or she would have, when she had got him to install the bathroom. She felt she would never be able to deal with a man as an equal until she could say: 'Don't you want to go to the bathroom?'

All the same, she still had troubles with her family. By the time Kitty got her job and left home, May was seventeen and a handful, in some ways worse than Kitty. Kitty had a temper, and wept and used dirty words, but May was a girl of extraordinary sweetness, with a disposition as clear as her complexion. She was a slight girl, cool, resourceful, and insinuating, with a smile that seemed intended merely to reveal her tiny front teeth, and she had some extraordinary ideas. For instance, she didn't believe in class distinctions, and only smiled tolerantly at Joan's insistence on a bathroom. It seemed she didn't think bathrooms were natural. She was a great believer in Nature, and Nature to her did not mean a summer bungalow in Crosshaven but a primitive cabin in West Cork with no bathroom at all. 'Do you want to go out to the haggard?' she would ask, with no consideration at all for the embarrassment she might be causing a visitor.

It was Chris, who seemed to know everything, who told Joan about May's friendship with Timmy McGovern and his crowd. Timmy represented several Dublin firms and was in line for the Dublin management of one. He lived on the College Road with his wife – one of the Geraghty girls from Glenareena (of course, Chris knew about them as well) and two kids. According to Chris, he was very popular, but not steady; definitely not steady. Even his best friend, Tony Dowse, said he was an imaginative man, and everybody knew what Tony Dowse was like!

Joan went straight upstairs and searched May's bedroom for letters. There were plenty of these, mostly from Timmy McGovern, and Joan and Chris read them together in the new living room with a sense of utter incredulity. Joan knew of old that all love letters were silly, but these were mad. They would go on for a paragraph in a jerky, spasmodic style like a broken-down car, and then soar suddenly into rhetoric about the long winding roads of Ireland or the world's not existing any longer for them when they were together.

'My goodness!' Chris said with a giggle that sounded like a cry. ' "The winding roads of Ireland!" Do you know him?'

'No, Chris, why?'

'He must be a ton weight, and his feet are so bad he can hardly walk a hundred yards.'

'And a married man!'

'That's the worst of it, of course,' Chris said, sobering up.

'What am I going to do? If Daddy knew he'd go mad.'

'You'll have to talk to her,' said Chris.

'Talk to her!' cried Joan. 'Wait till I'm done with her!'

But even talking to May was not as easy as it sounded. She was too well-guarded.

'May,' Joan asked dramatically, 'what's all this about Mr McGovern and you?'

'How do you mean – all this?' May asked sweetly.

'May, it's no use talking like that,' Joan said sternly. 'I read his letters to you.'

'Then you know as much about it as I do,' replied May.

'You should be proud of them,' Joan said bitterly. 'A married man!'

'They suit me all right,' May said with a shrug and a splutter. 'And married men are much the same as other men from the little I see.'

That was typical of May. She couldn't even understand that a few words in front of a priest changed a man's whole nature – or should.

'Aren't you forgetting that they have wives, May?' Joan asked sternly. 'A lovely time his wife would have, getting those letters read out in court!' She paused to see if the word 'court' would scare May, but she wasn't as easily scared as that. 'May, where is this thing going to end?'

'We didn't decide yet,' May replied with a guilty smile as though she blamed herself greatly for letting such opportunities slip. 'I dare say eventually I'll have to go and live with him.'

'You'll what, May?' Joan asked, wondering if the girl were really sane.

'Oh, I don't mean in Cork, of course,' May said apologetically. By now she seemed to be blaming herself for a certain weakness of character. 'I mean when he gets to Dublin. It might even have to be London. People in this country are so blooming narrow-minded,' she added with indignation. 'They get in a rut by the time they're eighteen – any of them that weren't in a rut before.'

At any moment now Joan felt that May would start quoting Timmy's letters to her and tell her that Ireland didn't exist either.

'May,' she said despairingly, 'where do you get these terrible ideas from?'

'Now, Joan, it's no use talking like a schoolgirl to me,' May said with unusual sharpness. 'You should have got over that with the measles. Timmy made a mistake in his marriage, that's all. Lots of men do, actually,' she added in a worldly-wise tone that made Joan writhe. 'Either he has to put up with Eily Geraghty for the rest of his life or make a fresh start somewhere else.'

'Well, he's making a worse mistake if he thinks he's going to make a fresh start with you,' cried Joan. May only shrugged and pouted a little. The matter was obviously one she could only discuss on a high plane of abstraction. Apparently she thought that Joan probably didn't exist either.

But Joan showed her. First, she complained to her father, and as usual he behaved as though she were the guilty party. Then for ten minutes he thundered at May in the manner of an angry Jehovah, and she was quite genuinely upset, but it was obvious to Joan that she was upset on his account rather than her own. It saddened her to see a man of such independent character reduced to talk about what the neighbours would think.

But Joan had no intention of letting herself be flouted. One afternoon she went to the Grand Parade where Timmy McGovern had his office. She disliked him from the first moment. He was a fat, big-built man with discoloured teeth, a long lock of dark hair that tumbled over his left eye, small merry eyes, and small, unsteady feminine feet that seemed as though at any moment they might give up the ghost. She could see what Chris meant about the improbability of his travelling the long winding roads of Ireland in anything but a large car.

Obviously, he was scared to death and gave her a wistful smile as he led her into his private office. In fact, he had only just arrived there himself in a series of roundabout routes. He had heard talk about himself and May, and Timmy was sensitive that way. Whenever he heard talk about himself he went into hiding. He did really mean it when he said the rest of the world didn't exist for him when he was with May, but when he wasn't it could be quite alarming.

His office was a small room with a window opening on the vent, a stationery press, a table, and a couple of chairs. On the table was a photograph of May, sitting on a rock over a mountain pool, and the sight of it made Joan mad. She opened her pocket-book and put the photograph in.

'If you won't protect my sister's reputation, I have to do it, Mr McGovern,' she said. 'Now, if you wouldn't mind giving me her letters!'

'Her what?' Timmy asked in consternation.

'Her letters.'

'I have no letters,' he said, growing sullen.

'Well, I have,' she said grimly. 'Letters from you to her. And, what's more, Mr McGovern, I intend to use them.'

'I'm sorry you feel like this about it,' he said nervously, fumbling with the spring of his pince-nez.

'And how do you think I should feel? You should be ashamed of yourself! A married man with two children, writing like that to a child – a schoolgirl!'

Nothing would ever persuade Joan but that the few words pronounced in front of the priest must produce some sort of change, but with Timmy they didn't seem to have taken. His eyes clouded with tears.

'I can explain that,' he said brokenly. 'I don't think you'd be quite so unreasonable if you knew the sort of life I lead. Mind, I don't want you to think I'm complaining of my wife! She was always a good woman according to her lights, but there was never any understanding between us. Eily is a peasant, and she hasn't an idea beyond the house and the children. When I met May I knew she was the only girl in the world for me. I love May,' he added with manly simplicity. 'I'd die for her this minute.'

'Thank you, Mr McGovern,' Joan said curtly. 'She doesn't need anyone to die for her. She needs someone to look after her. I didn't come here to discuss your disagreements with your wife. I came here to get my sister's letters, and to warn you that next time you see her or write to her, I'm going straight to your wife and then to the priest.'

Joan was bluffing, and she knew it. Timmy, like everyone else in Cork was vulnerable, but he wasn't as vulnerable as all that. If he had told Joan to take a running jump for herself there was very little she could do that wouldn't make as much trouble for herself as for him; but Timmy, a romantic man, lived in an atmosphere of crisis, and he was scared by the hysteria in her voice. That is the worst of out-and-out idealism; it so rarely stands up to a well-played bluff.

'You wouldn't do that to us?' he said reproachfully.

She knew then she had him on the run. She rose and went to the door.

'The child has no other mother,' she said. 'I have to be a mother to her.'

That did it. Timmy grabbed her excitedly and closed the door she had just opened. His dark hair was ruffled, and he was scowling and dribbling. As Tony Dowse said, he was an imaginative man. He begged Joan to be reasonable; he would respect May if she were his own daughter. It was just that life was impossible without her.

'If I don't get those letters today I'm going straight up to your wife,' she said.

Timmy looked at her and sighed. It was a terrible sigh as though at last the wickedness of the world had been revealed to him. Then he opened a drawer and took out a bundle of letters. Without looking at them Joan pushed them into her handbag and went silently down the stairs. She was full of triumph. At last she felt she had grown up and spoken to a man twice her age as an equal. She was so pleased with herself that she went straight to Chris' office.

'I got them,' she said, patting her bag, and Chris smiled.

'Splendid!' he said, a little too enthusiastically. 'Wonderful! Now, if only you can keep her away from him for a week or two, everything will be fine.'

'Oh, that's all arranged, too,' she said bitterly. 'He won't see her again.' And then something awful happened to her and she burst into wild tears.

'Oh, darling!' Chris said, forgetting himself. 'I knew I shouldn't let you do this yourself. I should have seen him. Look, wait a minute and we'll go out for a cup of tea. Or a drink? Maybe a drink would be better?'

'No, thanks, Chris,' she said, dabbing her eyes and trying to smile. 'I'll be all right. It's just the strain.'

But it wasn't the strain, and she stamped through Patrick

54

Street, shaking her head and drying her eyes. She had suddenly found herself turned inside out, and instead of feeling triumphant, she felt like death. Instead of denouncing Timmy as a vile seducer, she wanted to go back and denounce him as a bloody old pansy. She knew if any man had been devoted to her as Timmy was supposed to be to May – even if it was sinful, and mortal sin at that, and even if he did have a wife and two children – and had written her those letters about reality not existing except when she was round, it would have broken her heart if he had taken fright as Timmy did.

So the scene she had planned with May took an entirely different turn from what she intended, as planned scenes usually do. May just sat there, cold and white and detached and Joan floundered and sobbed through her explanations. She knew it was none of her business, but she had done it for the best, and of course, she wasn't mature enough for the responsibilities she had taken on, and she hoped May would forgive her, but May was a hundred times the man Timmy was.

'That's what I'm beginning to think myself,' May said curtly as though from a great distance, and Joan would have done almost anything to make it up between them again but she knew she couldn't. Somewhere beneath May, as beneath her father, there was that slight streak of ice beyond which the most devoted interference could not live.

Timmy, according to Chris, who had it from Tony Dowse, took to his bed with an incurable disease and was nursed devotedly by Eily Geraghty. But Timmy knew that the doctor and Eily were in a conspiracy to conceal from him what was really wrong, so he applied for a life insurance policy, saw the doctor and went straight back to bed. When the policy was returned to him, completed, he got up, went into town and had a roaring evening with his group. 'An imaginative man' as Tony had always said, almost with admiration.

It seemed to take little out of May. She was different from Kitty in that. Within a month she was walking out with a handsome young journalist who drove a sports car, and pleading with him to get him interested in the winding roads of Ireland, but all he would say was that 'the surfaces were very bad'.

Fortunately for their own peace of mind, men rarely realize that the intellectual charms of a woman usually derive from the previous man.


7


It seemed to bring Joan closer to Chris. He wasn't scandalized as she had feared he would be. Instead, he told her a new and franker version of his life story, which contained some astonishing revelations about his brother, Bob. As usual, it was Chris who had been left with the job of clearing things up with the woman's husband. Joan admired his reserve in not having told her before. Apparently every family, even the best brought-up, had things to conceal; and respectability, far from being the dreary and monotonous virtue it was supposed to be, was athletic, perilous, and exhausting. You don't get bathrooms for nothing. Joan at last succeeded in getting Mick to put in one for them, and the first night Chris came briskly up the hill, hitting his thigh with his folded paper, she nearly suffocated with pleasure at the thought that now she could say to him: 'Wouldn't you like to go upstairs?' Besides, she had rented a summer cottage in Crosshaven for a whole month.

Of course, there were drawbacks. The neighbours hadn't minded about the electric light or even the living room, but the bathroom was an innovation and unpleasant remarks were made about it. Now, when she went to Mass in the mornings she no longer knew who among the congregation did not mind the bathroom and who did, so she tended to give them all the same thin smile. As a result, people were inclined to say that the Twomeys were growing out of their knowledge.

At the same time her worries with the children continued. On her previous holiday Kitty had dodged going to Mass. Joan had discovered it by accident, and it worried her a lot.

Then one morning, soon after Kitty had gone back, May got a letter from her that made her smile.

'I suppose we'd better tell Daddy about this,' she said questioningly. 'Did you know Kitty was going to have a baby?'

'A what, May?' cried Joan.

'A baby,' May replied almost enviously. 'It's this fellow Rahilly she's knocking round with. I thought she had more sense.'

'Show me!' said Joan, realizing that the bathroom was all in vain. Better, indeed, if there had never been a bathroom. Kitty was pregnant, and the father was a student of engineering, who though a boy of very fine character and intelligence, had no job and was entirely dependent on his parents. Deduct a bathroom from a baby and there was an awful lot of plain discredit left. Chris' mother would have the advantage of her at last. It was even doubtful if May's fellow could marry her, but it was no use saying that to May. She would only begin to argue about a woman's right to have a baby if she wanted it. And already Joan had a shrewd suspicion that May was beginning to feel left out of things.

Her father was no better. Weak as ever, he wanted to put the blame everywhere except where it belonged.

'Ah, I can't be angry with the girl, Joanie,' he said crossly. 'It was my own fault for letting her go to a strange town by herself. This would never have happened if she was in her own home. Sure, what is she only a child?'

'But what are you going to do about, Daddy?' she asked.

'What can you do? You can't let her have a child up there, alone. Let her come home and have it.'

'Is it for the whole road to laugh at us?' she asked incredulously.

'Oh, them!' he said contemptuously. 'Do you think they didn't laugh at your mother when I was in gaol, and she hadn't enough to keep the house going? When did they ever do anything but laugh, for all the good the laughing did them?'

'But, Daddy, what about May?'

'What about her?'

'You don't think or imagine the Mahoneys will let Jim

marry her with a scandal like that in the house?'

'If Jim Mahoney is the sort to let his people decide whether he's going to marry or not, she's better off without him,' said her father. 'Anyway, what do you expect me to do? You'd think I was the father, the way you go on!'

'I thought you'd go to Dublin and talk to him.'

'How can I go to Dublin, with work ahead of me that I have to finish or pay a fine?' he shouted.

'Oh, all right, then,' cried Joan, who had heard about that fine too often to believe in it now. 'I suppose I'll have to go myself. Somebody will have to go.'

That evening she told Chris about it in a cinema teashop overlooking Patrick Street. She was surprised how little she did have to tell him, because he seemed to see difficulties and complications that she hadn't guessed at.

'This isn't a job for you at all, Joan,' he said with a worried air. 'This is a job for a man.'

'I know that, Chris,' she said, 'but Daddy won't go, and even if he did you know what he's like.'

'Pretty hopeless, I'd say,' Chris said with a nervous giggle, and talked tangentially for ten minutes about things in the office. 'Would you like me to go?' he asked suddenly.

She almost laughed at the idea of the refined and modest Chris trying to arrange Kitty's marriage for her, but at the same time she was touched.

'No, thanks, Chris,' she said. 'I'm sure you'd handle this fellow better than I could, but you'd never be able to handle Kitty. To tell you the God's truth, I don't know that I can handle her myself,' she added sadly.

'You'll have to see his father and mother, of course,' Chris said modestly. 'It's going to be very unpleasant. They may even try to buy you off. If they do, refuse to discuss it. If you do discuss it, you're lost. You have to keep threatening them with exposure. That's a purely legal thing, I needn't say. Your father would have to sue for the loss of his daughter's services. Kitty's services wouldn't be of any financial importance, but you have to stick with them. You won't want a law case any more than they will, but you have to pretend it's the one thing you're looking forward to. It's a game of bluff, really. You have to pretend you're in a stronger position than you are.'

Then, hearing himself talk, he went into a loud lonely laugh and cheered up at once.

'You'd think I was a real Don Juan, wouldn't you?' he asked.

'I was wondering how you knew all about it,' said Joan timidly.

'Oh, family business,' he said.

'Not Bob?'

'Unfortunately, yes, Bob,' he replied, almost in a whisper. 'We don't like talking about it. You have to take the line that you don't care about proceedings. They settled for a hundred and fifty. Otherwise, Bob would have had to marry her.'

'My God!' Joan said.

She was really appalled at the things you brought on yourself merely by having a sense of duty. Here was Chris, pious, innocent, and interested mainly in classical music, and he had to try and outwit the outraged parents and avert a shotgun wedding while she went to Dublin to compel some scoundrel to marry her flighty sister.

Next afternoon she set off for Dublin by the afternoon train, and was met at Kingsbridge by Kitty in a wide summer hat, looking swollen-faced, sullen and resentful. Joan felt pretty bitter herself. The evening light was flooding the river, and columns and towers and spires stood up in it, but she couldn't even enjoy it. While they sat in the front seat of the bus Kitty asked politely but without enthusiasm for her father, May and the neighbours. Each of them knew a struggle was on.

'How long are you going to stay, Joan?' Kitty asked innocently.

'I suppose that depends on you,' replied Joan.

'How does it depend on me?' asked Kitty.

'I thought I was coming here to arrange about your wedding,' Joan said.

'I know,' Kitty said with quiet fury. 'The way you arranged

the wedding between Dick Gordon and me, and Timmy McGovern and May.'

'I suppose you think I should have let Timmy McGovern run away with May?' asked Joan.

'I don't see what the hell business it was of yours,' said Kitty.

'You wouldn't be long seeing what business it was if you had to get married with that scandal in the family,' said Joan. 'I suppose you'll tell me now that your Mr Rahilly is married already?'

He wasn't, but, as far as Joan could see, that was about the only thing that wasn't wrong with him. She shared a room with Kitty and another girl in Pembroke Road, and, in spite of the fact that she was worried out of her wits, she found herself staring in fascination at the sunlit rank of tall, red-brick houses opposite, or glancing out of the bathroom window at the mountains over Rathfarnham, and thinking how much nicer the world was than she had ever imagined.

She met Con Rahilly next evening in a teashop in Grafton Street. He came in with a heap of books under his arm – an overgrown schoolboy.

'Really, Miss Twomey,' he said with an anguished air, the lines over his eyes disappearing into his cropped hair, 'I'm terribly sorry for giving you all this trouble. I really am! I know you don't believe me, but it happens to be true.' Later, she learned that he had this self-pitying trick of imagining what you felt about him and expressing it.

'Well, it's no use worrying about what's already happened,' Joan said practically. 'It's just a question of what we're going to do about it.'

'I know,' he said despairingly. 'I never think of anything else. I keep racking my brains, but I don't seem to be able to think of anything.'

'I hope you've thought of marrying Kitty?' said Joan.

'You're hoping a hell of a lot,' Kitty said gruffly, but Joan knew she was ready to cry and that young Rahilly was the same.

'I don't see what the difficulty is,' she said brightly.

'That's because you haven't had the pleasure of meeting

my mother,' he explained with the same mixture of misery and cheek. 'It's going to be a shock to her.'

'I suppose you think it hasn't been a shock to my father?' asked Joan, and he shuddered. Clearly, he didn't like people speaking roughly to him.

'Con doesn't mean that at all,' Kitty said hotly, and Joan saw that she was in a bad way about him.

'Then would you let him explain what he does mean?' asked Joan. 'My goodness, I can't see what all this hugger mugger is about.'

'I mean I have nothing to marry on,' he said with anguish. 'If I marry Kitty now, my mother will throw me out.'

'And what about your father?'

'She'll probably throw him out as well. She's been threatening it long enough. She really is a woman of remarkable character,' he added with rueful admiration, and again Joan didn't know whether or not he was mocking her. 'It's not that I don't want to marry Kitty, he added eagerly. 'She knows that. It's just that if I do, I'll have to do it quietly.'

'That would be a very peculiar sort of marriage,' said Joan.

'Oh, I know, I know,' he said wearily, clasping his hands and looking down the restaurant as though he had recognized an old enemy.

'I'm afraid my father wouldn't agree to that at all,' Joan said with growing decisiveness. 'After all, who's to support Kitty until you've finished college and got a job?'

Young Rahilly gave another shrug and looked piteously at Kitty, but even Kitty didn't seem to be able to help with this one. Instead, she lit another cigarette and pushed the packet towards him. It was a little gesture of love, but he only shook his head with a crucified air as if wondering how she could think a cigarette would make up to him for a broken heart. Joan began to like him even less.

'I suppose you think Father will support her while she hides away in a furnished room like a criminal?' she asked angrily. 'And all to spare your mother the shock! Really, Mr Rahilly, I think you're as bad as Kitty.'

'It's easy for you to talk,' Kitty said brassily. 'You don't know his mother.'

'Well, she can't eat him, Kitty,' Joan cried at the end of her patience.

'I wonder,' he said with perfect gravity. 'I've sometimes thought it might be a case of suppressed cannibalism.'

'Well, she isn't going to eat me,' said Joan.

'Look, Joan, you keep away from Con's mother,' said Kitty. 'This is my business, and I'll handle it my own way. I'll keep my job up to the last month or so, and after that I'll find something. I won't be a burden on you at all. You talk as if Con was the only one responsible, but I had something to say to it too.'

And Joan knew at once that Rahilly would accept it from her. Whatever his mother had done to him, she had deprived him of all initiative, and he would go on like that, petulantly waiting for some other woman to make up his mind for him. This time, Joan was going to do the making up.

'Oh, all right, Kitty,' she said. 'I thought I could settle this thing quietly but I see I can't. I'll just wire for Father and let him deal with it.'

'In that case I can give up all hope of getting a degree,' Rahilly said with resignation. Then he glanced at her with a certain sort of boyish frankness. 'To tell you the truth, I don't really mind,' he added ruefully. 'I don't think I have the brains for an engineer. I suppose I can be a clerk if anyone will take me on. I'm not the type for a labourer – even a labourer,' again anticipating the slight that Joan hadn't altogether intended. After that, she had no doubt though. She had never seen a more spineless specimen.

Next morning, before Kitty left for the office, Rahilly called at their lodgings. When they went into the sitting room he was looking out the window. Kitty went up to him eagerly. Joan realized that all Kitty wanted was to take him away somewhere and nurse him, which was probably what he wanted too.

'What happened, Con?' she asked.

'Oh, what I expected,' he said jumpily. 'Into the night. Cut off with a shilling. I can't help admiring the woman.'

'But what will you do now?' Joan asked, shocked in spite of herself.

'Get married as soon as I can,' he replied with a shrug. 'No point in getting thrown out for wanting to get married and then not doing it, is there?'

'Oh, but this is silly,' she cried. 'No mother in her senses is going to behave like that to her only son. There must be some misunderstanding. I'll go and see her.'

'Do,' he said. 'You might like her. Several people do, I'm told.'

It was only that afternoon on the bus out to Rahillys' that his words came back to her, and she wondered precisely what he had meant. She decided that he couldn't mean what he'd seemed to mean. It was just that, like all weak people, he had no control of his tongue.

The door was opened by a pale, dark-haired woman who moved with a certain actressy dignity. She gave Joan a pale smile that seemed to be directed at someone on the strand behind her. The parlour was a small room with a high window that overlooked the strand. Mrs Rahilly's chair was at one side of the window from which she could view the passers-by. In the first few minutes, Joan realized from the furniture that there was money somewhere – not a lot, perhaps, but sufficient. Joan rattled on, raising her voice and speaking with affected brightness. She was in a dilemma. To treat the behaviour of the 'children', as she called them, too gravely would imply such a reflection on Kitty as would justify any mother in having nothing to do with her. To treat it too lightly would imply that she herself was no better and justify a mother even more. It was essential to create an impression of respectability – a little impulsive, but definitely stable. But Mrs Rahilly seemed to care very little for the stability of the Twomey character, and Joan's gay tone came back to her with a hollow echo.

'Well, what do you expect me to do, Miss Twomey?' Mrs Rahilly asked at last with a sad smile, and Joan felt at once that it would be most improper to expect anything from such a figure of tragedy.

'Well, they have to get married,' she said reasonably.

63

'That's what my son seems to think.'

'And doesn't it seem a pity if he can't take his degree, when he worked so hard?'

'It is not only my son who had to work hard,' said Mrs Rahilly, making Joan feel she had again said the wrong thing.

'No, of course not,' she replied too eagerly. 'Everybody had to work. But that's what I mean – everyone's work going for nothing.'

'That is something my son should have thought of first, Miss Twomey,' Mrs Rahilly said with the same sad smile. 'Of course, if your family is in a position to support them and the child until Con qualifies, I have nothing to say to it. But if you mean that I should provide a home for them here' – she rose with an actressy gesture of dismissal – 'I've worked hard too. My health would not permit it.'

Now that she had Joan on her feet again she became quite friendly, almost motherly. As she reached for the door handle she rested on it and added: 'I'd better be frank with you, Miss Twomey. I don't wish to criticize my own son, but I'm afraid he would not make a good husband for your sister. His father was always a weak man. He drank, and, of course, like all drunkards, he did not keep his hand where it belonged. I had to pay back what he stole. But that is neither here nor there. My son is weaker still. I did not expect to rear him, Miss Twomey. It is his digestion. He has every delicacy in his own home, but he cannot keep it down. What business has a boy like that with a wife and family?' Then she raised her head with a calm and tragic air and added: 'If she were my sister, I'd send her to the poorhouse first.'

Joan left almost in tears with frustration. At the same time she observed a small man in a blue serge suit and a bowler hat get up from a bench. She noticed that he had a fresh-coloured kindly face and a small grey moustache. She had no doubt that she was looking at Con's father, the man who had not been able to keep his hand where it belonged. She felt dirty all over. Bitch! Bitch! Dirty bitch! she said again and again to herself.

## 8

That night she went back to Cork, without having effected much except to fix the date of the wedding. She was as sure as she could be of anything that Con Rahilly would not turn up, so she arranged for them to marry on the same day as May. Then, if he didn't turn up the scandal wouldn't be quite so bad. To Chris she admitted that she didn't feel too secure of herself even then. It seemed impossible that she should ever steer two such irresponsibles as Kitty and May to the altar without one or the other running off with a lover, giving birth to a baby, or something equally inappropriate.

No wonder she was hard on Kitty when her notice was up and she came back to Cork to prepare for the wedding. Joan warned her father not to encourage her in any way, and, except for stolen confidences with May, who was as shameless as herself, Kitty was treated as an abandoned woman who had brought disgrace on them all – or would if she weren't stopped.

Meanwhile, her attitude to Chris changed in an extraordinary way. They spent August in a little seaside cottage in Crosshaven. Her father of course didn't come. He'd tried it once, and after forty-eight hours he was like a raging demon, complaining that there was nothing in that bloody place but the water. Kitty and May were staying there, with May's boy, a tall, athletic fellow given to practical jokes that irritated Joan. One night, when the other three had gone to a dance, Joan and Chris were sitting in a nook on the cliffs. Something about the beauty of the harbour in twilight made her despondent.

'I don't know how it is,' she said irritably. 'You work and work, and do your best for everybody, and meantime, your own life slips by.'

'Oh, I know, I know,' Chris said, taking her hand. 'It seems futile, of course, but if you're born with that sort of character you have to go through with it. You don't do it for other people's satisfaction, you know. You do it for your own as well.'

'And a hell of a lot of good it is for you,' she replied impatiently. 'Ah, Chris, nobody's born with that sort of character. You weren't born just to be censorious and bossy and quarrel over halfpence. You could get just as much out of life as the others, and more.'

'That's true, of course,' he said thoughtfully. 'Up to a point, I mean. It's funny, but everything in life is only up to a point. And families do force you into a certain mould, even if it doesn't suit you. Like me, for instance. I suppose I'm really only interested in music. But then Bob turns into a bit of a playboy, and as a result Jim gets religion in the wrong way, and I have to be the Old Reliable and look after the pair of them as well as Mother. It's silly really, I suppose. I sometimes think only children have an awful lot to be thankful for.'

'One of these days I'm going to be an only child,' Joan said.

They went back to the cottage, hand in hand. Chris went to bed and lay awake reading. Suddenly the bedroom door opened and Joan stormed in in her nightdress. He had never seen her like this before. She was angry, amused and very, very beautiful.

'For God's sake, push in there, Chris Dwyer!' she said shrilly. 'I have to have someone to talk to, or I'll go out of my blooming mind.'

Chris, who was always modest, blew out the candle. As a romantic lover, Chris was no great shakes, but he knew desperation when he saw it, and he put his arm about her and patted her gently as one would pat a child.

And then, to Joan's great astonishment, he stopped patting her, and said a number of things that astonished her and made her want to weep, so that she was not quite up to it when he treated her as Dick Gordon had never done. Then he yawned and asked if it wasn't wonderful and said they should go to Italy at once. He had always wanted to go to Italy and something had always stopped him, but this time he was determined about it. When they heard the voices of the others from the cliff, Joan jumped out of bed and rushed into the hall. Suddenly, at the door she stopped and shouted back at him in laughter and delight –

'Now, Chris Dwyer, you've got me into trouble, and you'd better marry me quick!'

9

In that haze, it seemed even more impossible for Joan to do what she had set out to do, but she did it. To her great surprise, Con Rahilly arrived in time for the wedding – when driven to it, those dependent mother's boys sometimes showed extraordinary manliness. His father had shaken him silently by the hand and slipped him a five pound note, borrowed specially for the occasion, and Con said he was going to get it framed. Mrs Rahilly had refused to leave her room or even say goodbye. 'You can't beat the true Irish mother,' Con said with his abstracted air. He had already rented a furnished room in Leeson Street, and the father of a college friend had made a small job for him, selling women's underwear – of all things! Chris, with whom he stayed, could make nothing of him and thought he wasn't quite right in the head, but Joan's father, for some reason, took a fantastic liking to him, laughed at his grisly jokes, told him there would always be a room in his house for him, offered to back a loan for him, and then told Joan that Kitty had picked the best man of them all. When she asked what he meant, he said Con was the only man that he'd trust with a rifle – a typical obscure joke from an old revolutionary.

It was a lonely house when the double wedding was over and the guests had gone. Now that her task was completed and her responsibilities almost at an end, Joan felt empty inside. It was as though her mind could not settle on the present and ranged back over the years to the time when she had been a little girl. She sat over the fire in the front room with her father, talking into the early hours of the morning. Though neither of them mentioned it, it was her mother's death they were both thinking of – the sitting there at the same hour, listening to that ghastly breathing overhead. This, too, was a sort of death, and the new life that was waiting for her was something that she shrank from.

'I suppose Chris and I will be getting married too, as soon as we can,' she said lightly. 'I hope you won't mind?'

'Mind?' he asked. 'Why should I mind?'

'Because I'm afraid we'll have to go and live in Dublin.'

'Why in Dublin?' he asked.

'Oh, well,' she said, dabbing her eyes, 'Chris is mad on classical music, and you can't hear a single thing in this blooming place. There are concerts and all sorts in Dublin.'

'And what about Chris' mother?' he asked. 'Is she going with you?'

'Indeed, she is not,' said Joan. 'She can stay with Bob if she wants someone to look after her. She won't find him as easy to get on with as Chris, but that's her look-out. What about you, though? Wouldn't you like to live with May?'

'I would not,' he said flatly.

'Chris said to tell you you could always come and live with us,' she said, realizing for the first time how big it was of Chris.

'Ah, Chris has enough responsibilities without me,' her father said. 'I'll be all right, you'll see. I'll get some old woman in to cook my supper and I'll be fine.'

And she knew he would do his best to die where he had lived, among the little memorials of the woman he had loved, and for one wild minute she felt she wanted to do the same. She put her head in her hands and began to sob quietly. Her father got up and re-filled her glass. Then he stood, looking down at her.

'What's wrong, child?' he asked quizzically.

'I don't want to go to Dublin,' she sobbed. 'I don't want to leave Cork. I want to stay here and look after you.'

'If you don't want to you don't have to,' he said gently.

'I do.'

'Why?'

'I'm – I'm having a baby – oh, Jesus!'

At first she thought he was going to hit her, and then she saw he was almost on the point of laughing.

'Here!' he said, thrusting the glass on her. 'Take a pussful of this! What's wrong with having a baby?'

'I'd be disgraced if I stayed on here.'

He poured himself a drink.

'Is it Chris?'

'Yes.'

'And ye're getting married?'

'Yes.'

'What the hell disgrace is there? Isn't it your own business?'

Snivelling into her glass, she saw him back in his own chair, grinning at her as he had grinned when she had come to him for the 'loan' of a shilling.

'It isn't. I'm a liar and a hypocrite. I bullied you and the girls and ye have every reason to despise me.'

'Do you think I despise you?'

'You have good reason to. And Dick Gordon was so good, and I was rotten to him, and I was rotten to May and rotten to Kitty, and they'll never forgive me.'

'Come here to me!' he said, and she got up like a sleep-walker and crossed the room to him. 'Come on! You can sit on my knee. It's a long time since you did. Now, I want you to listen to me. You know I was fond of your mother, and what sort of life do you think I gave her? I had the best wife the Lord God ever gave a man in this world, and I treated her as I wouldn't treat a dog. I wake up in the middle of the night and think about it and cry, and a hell of a lot of good that is to her or me! But even if I was as decent a man as I wanted to be, what sort of life do you think I'd have given her? A damn poor life, but all I had.'

Then his voice took on the curious formality she had noticed once before.

'If your mother is anywhere, she's here tonight, and what she has to say, I'm saying for her. We're proud of you, and we're delighted you're getting married. There's nothing we'd hate more than to see you without kids of your own. You're a great girl, and we're glad you're getting a fine steady fellow like Chris. And thank Chris from both of us for offering me a home, but I'll stick with the one that she made for me.

'Now, it's a long time since I put you to bed, and probably it's the last time, but it's time little girls were asleep. Come along! Sleepy bye!'

*More Stories* (1954)

# THE SORCERER'S APPRENTICE

### I

Their friends said that, whenever Jimmy Foley named the day, Una slipped a disc. For five years now they had been keeping company, and three times Una had slipped a disc, or its equivalent. Jimmy blamed Una, who was an only child, and, according to him, spoiled to death by her father. Una blamed Jimmy's mother, an old lady of great sweetness, who deferred so much to Jimmy that she couldn't even stay in the same room with him and hear him contradicted.

The third time she slipped a disc she went to Dublin to recover. Joan Sheehy was an old school friend, a tall, dark, intense girl, who was very happily married to a Dublin solicitor. They lived with their two children in an old-fashioned house on the strand. As usual, Joan and Una had no opportunity for intimate discussion till Una went to bed. Then Joan came in in her dressing gown; first she sat in the armchair, then on the bed, and finally threw off the dressing gown and slipped into the double bed beside Una. That way they could talk better.

They were interrupted by slow and heavy footsteps descending the stairs and Joan sat up with a long-suffering air.

'Bother that fellow!' she said. 'He's worse to me than a baby.'

Slowly the door opened and Mick Sheehy, a tall man with a dark moustache, stumbled in. He was clutching a pillow as if it were a baby, his pyjamas were dangling about his crotch, and his eyes were closed. Joan jumped up and made room for him.

'Lie there and keep quiet!' she said fiercely. 'I'm not done talking to Una yet.'

'What are ye talking about?' he asked, wedging his shoulder comfortably into Una's hip. 'Anything interesting?'

'Only about herself and Jimmy.'

'Oh, that!' he said with a noisy yawn and composed himself to sleep again between the pair of them, his hands crossed piously on his stomach. Una, who was a well-read girl, wondered what Joan would say if any Irish writer reported a scene like that.

'I don't mind what you say, Una,' Joan said, pushing her husband rudely against Una. 'I think it's high time you stopped making excuses and settled down. My God, girl, you must be thirty, and if you go on like this you won't get married at all.'

'But what's going to happen if I marry someone like Jimmy that I don't agree with?' Una asked indignantly.

'What has agreeing got to do with it?' Joan asked. 'Do you think for an instant I agree with this? Wouldn't you fight with him?'

'Me?' said Una, looking at him as he lay between them, making funny faces and snoring. 'God, I'd murder him!'

'I want to murder him too,' said Joan in her intense way, 'but I love him just the same. Men are like that, Una. You're too damn critical – honest to God, you are. There was Ned Buckley,' she went on, ticking the names off on her fingers. 'You said *he* had no religion. Mick Doyle had too much religion. He went to Mass every morning and never talked about anything only the lives of the saints.'

'Oh, God, Joan, Mick was awful,' Una said in horror. 'Do you know I nearly lost my religion over him.'

'Never mind your religion,' Joan went on remorselessly. 'We know about that. Then there was Paddy Healy, who had a lovely voice only he drank too much. I forget the rest.

Damn it, Una, you had a fair choice. What the hell is wrong with Jimmy?'

'You have no idea, girl,' Una said despondently. 'Jimmy wouldn't let you have an opinion of your own. He thinks you shouldn't even open your mouth about anything except what's in his silly old paper. It's easy to see you never had anything to do with a journalist.'

'And journalists have nothing to do with it either,' said Joan. 'Do you think any man wants you to have an opinion of your own?'

'But this is different, Joan,' Una said positively.

'They're all different, girl,' said Joan.

'But Jimmy is different, Joan,' said Una. 'I'm sure it's his mother. She has him ruined.'

'And you're the very one who told me that I was ruining Tommy!' said Joan. 'What's the good of talking? They're all ruined! There's something wrong with every man if you look at him long enough. Not that you'd need to look at this lump,' she added, giving a friendly kick to the sleeping form between them, which grunted with pleasure and threw a hand over her stomach. It clawed at her impatiently till, with a sigh, she pulled her nightdress up, and at once it relaxed and its owner began to snore again.

'Ah, it's not like that at all, Joan,' Una said thoughtfully. 'Daddy says I attract the wrong sort of man.'

'And, in the name of the Almighty God,' Joan said piously, 'when did your father ever see the right sort of man for you? Look, I don't want to interfere between the pair of ye, but surely you're grown-up enough to realize that your father doesn't want you to marry at all? Damn it, Una, every fellow that got as much as a squeeze off you, your father got jealous of him. Do you think I didn't see it? Every boy you ever brought to the house was treated as a tolerable sort of leper. Either his mother came from Blarney Lane or his grand-uncle was in the asylum. And you know, Una, I have to be frank. Sometimes I think you and your old fellow are lick alike. If only you could get rid of your mother, you'd be settled for life. I hate saying it, but, honest to God, you are turning into a proper old maid.'

72

'Ah, no, I'm not, I'm not,' Una said, trying to look as though she knew things that were lost on her friend. All the same she was scared. The last thing in the world she wanted to be was an old maid, and she was beginning to realize that old maids were not wallflowers at all, but girls who had more charm than was good for them.

'You see, Joan, what's wrong with me is indecision,' she said with an air of great enlightenment. 'Somehow or other, I can't make up my mind.'

'And you know what happens girls who can't make up their minds?' asked Joan.

'I do, I do,' Una said glumly. 'They don't marry at all.'

'Oh, no,' said Joan. 'Nothing as comfortable as that. Girls who can't make up their own minds soon get their minds made up for them. And mark my words, that's what's going to happen to you, Una . . . Sheehy,' she added with a further friendly kick. 'Back to bed, boy! Back to bed!'

2

As Una thought afterwards, Joan could have been prophetic, because the following evening, Denis O'Brien came to supper. Denis was in his middle forties, married and separated, poor and plain. He had a plump, bright, beaming face, a small, dark moustache, a high, bald forehead, a quiet voice and the most insinuating manners. The nicest thing about him was his eyes, which were very gentle, but the least bit mad. He was a lonely man who got little in the way of nourishment except what he provided for himself, which was mainly bacon and eggs, but he was always welcome at the Sheehys. He did not leave till very late, but Una noticed that while Mick drank steadily, Denis only supped at his glass of beer. She liked that little touch of asceticism in him.

'Isn't he nice?' Joan asked in her enthusiastic way when he left. 'Isn't he a real pet?'

'He's a pity anyway,' said Una, who didn't know whether he was a pet or not.

'Ah, what a pity he is!' Joan exclaimed. 'A flat of his own

and every doll in the office falling over him.'

'Now, that's only hearsay, Joan,' Mick said, staring at his wife over his glasses. 'We know nothing about his private life, and we shouldn't repeat things we hear ... I quite agree with you, Una. He is a pity.'

A couple of evenings later Una heard a knock and found him standing on the doorstep against the glowing strand, hatless, his greying hair very long behind his bald brow, and his trousers, which needed pressing, flapping about his heels. His clothes were cheap, but he wore them with an air of well-bred carelessness that made them seem better than they were.

'Oh, come in, Denis,' she said. 'I'm delighted to see him. I'm all alone and the kids are asleep.'

It wasn't only that she was bored. She was glad to see him, and afterwards she felt that she might have been a little less flirtatious, but he invited that sort of behaviour. He had the sort of insinuating manner that is a compound of father and elder brother; apparently he kissed girls on sight and without intending much harm, held their hands, patted their shoulders and invited their confidences.

In no time at all, Una was holding forth to him about her troubles with Jimmy, and Denis was advising her in the manner of an old family friend. Naturally, he was advising her to marry Jimmy. Everybody seemed to be doing that. In his excitement he got up and stood before the fireplace, the light from the strand catching his round sunburned face and kind, anxious eyes. She could see why the girls in the office would fall for him – a man who took them as seriously as that. He talked in a solemn, unctuous, almost clerical tone, with flashes of what might almost be religious mysticism. Being a very pious girl, Una could not see what mysticism had to do with marriage. What she wanted from marriage was security, the hope that in ten years time she wouldn't regret her bargain.

'But, Una,' he said, burying his right fist in his left palm, 'there's no such thing as security in marriage. You can be friends with a man for twenty years, and when you marry him, you find out things about him you never guessed at.

Everybody keeps a bit of himself to himself, even if it's only something to die with. Sooner or later, you have to take a chance, and it's better to take it before you get too set in your ways. That's hell, when you have to smash yourself up again, just to adjust.'

'Haven't you ever regretted taking a chance, Denis?' she asked pertly.

'No, dear, I haven't,' he replied without taking offence. 'My wife represented what I could grasp at that age, and I couldn't predict – not infallibly that is,' he added carefully, as though infallibility were his rule on all other occasions – 'how either of us would develop. What I mean is that when we separated we weren't the same people who got married. That's where the Church goes wrong. People become different, and it's no use trying to be wise before the event.'

'It's not much use being wise after it,' she retorted.

'No, dear, it isn't,' he retorted imperturbably, as though nothing she said could interrupt the flow of his gab. 'That's true. You have to use your common sense in deducing the line of development you're both going to follow. You've got to ask yourself if a girl or a fellow who's been sleeping around before you married them is going to change just because of living with you. But you can abuse your common sense just as you can abuse your feelings, you know.' By now, he was very excited and striding to the door and back, giving her brooding glances. 'You can put too much responsibility on your common sense as you can put too much responsibility on a boy or girl with an unstable family, and all that happens is that it collapses under it, exactly as a boy or girl will collapse if you ask too much of them. Think of all the women you know who made fools of themselves in their thirties.'

'And what about all the men who make fools of themselves in their forties?' she asked, and that stopped the flow all right. She noticed that when you did stop the flow, he was so pleased that he went off into a roar of laughter that seemed almost as uncontrollable as the sermonizing. There were tears in his eyes as he turned to her and said, 'Doesn't

75

Jimmy ever knock you about, Una? That's what I'd do if you were my girl.'

To Una's great surprise, Joan Sheehy didn't seem at all pleased that Denis agreed with her about Una's marrying. On the contrary, she became as irritable as hell.

'And do you mean to tell me you talked to *Denis* about *Jimmy*?' she asked.

'Oh, only generally, of course,' said Una.

'God help you if you go round talking like that about him when ye're married,' said Joan. 'Sheehy would take a gun to me.'

All the same, Una went to the pictures with Denis the following evening and returned to his flat for coffee. She was curious to know where he lived. It was in one of the city squares in a third-floor apartment of two draughty rooms with high windows, the kitchen cut out of the bedroom, and, in a return room upstairs a bathroom that seemed to be connected directly with a cave of the winds. Even from downstairs you could hear the gale roaring up into the lavatory basin. The sitting room wasn't too bad. It had a big print of Rembrandt's 'Golden Helmet' over the mantelpiece and bookshelves along one wall. Una could see that a lot of them were religious books, a thing she hardly expected.

All the same it was pleasant to turn off the light and sit by the window and talk about all the fellows she had. Denis was a good listener, and everything she said moved him to comment and generalization.

'It's no good telling me what you think of Jimmy now, Una,' he said at last. 'You and Jimmy are at a dead end. You've taken it as far as it will go. You'll think differently when you're married because then you'll change again.'

'As much as all that?' she asked in mock alarm.

'You'll be surprised,' he said. 'And mind,' he added menacingly, pointing at her, 'it won't be all for the better. It may even be for the worse.'

'And all after one night?' she exclaimed in the same tone.

'Not necessarily after one night,' he said, rolling over her in his usual infallible way. 'Maybe not till after a good many nights – and days. You make too much of the nights you know,' he said, laughing uproariously again as the meaning of her little joke broke in upon his monologue. 'Damn it all, you can sleep through the nights, girl. It's the blooming days that get you down.'

'Denis, do you think I'm an old maid?' she asked.

'No, dear, I don't,' he replied, refusing to be put off his new tack. 'Girls like you, with lots of energy, if you're not married by the time you're thirty, start exaggerating things. Your minds have gone off in one direction and your bodies in another. You see, Una, you talk too much about sex. You've got sex in the head instead of where it belongs. Where it belongs, it's not all that important. When you get it in the head it makes everything go cockeyed. That's why you're so afraid of committing yourself. That's why you and Jimmy fight the way you do. You see, your mind and body have to work together, in harmony, the way they did when you were a kid. But when one of the principal bodily functions gets into the head, then they can't work together.'

Una found him so entertaining that she stayed late and almost ran home. When she reached the strand, Mick had already gone to bed, but Joan was waiting up for her in her dressing gown. She seemed in an unusual state of tension, even for her.

'Will I get you a glass of hot milk, Una?' she asked nervously.

'No, love,' Una replied with a sly grin. 'Was there something you wanted to say to me?'

'As a matter of fact, there was,' Joan said tragically, collapsing into a chair. 'Una, do you think you're being fair to Denis?'

'Aren't I?' Una asked in mock surprise, though she knew what was coming.

'You know that Mick and myself are very fond of him?'

'And I know he thinks the world of you,' Una said firmly.

'And don't you think you're not being fair? Honest now, Una! Aren't you amusing yourself with him?'

'You mean, you think he's not amusing himself with me?' Una asked in a gentle parody of her friend's tone.

' 'Tisn't alike, Una,' Joan said nervously, clasping and un-clasping her long beautiful hands. 'You're young. You have a fellow you'll probably marry eventually. Denis has nobody.' Joan shook her head as though she were imitating some bad actress on the movies, which she wasn't – Joan had been that way from childhood. 'Una, can you even under-stand what it means, having nobody – nobody at all in the world? When he's sick or lonely, this is the only place he can come. He's not a young man any longer; when he sees his kids it has to be in Mick's office; he has only a little job in the Corporation, and he'll never do any better because he's too proud and honest. He won't take bribes and he won't lick boots. And even then he has to pay more than half he earns to that bloody bitch! God forgive me, there are some women I'd like to strangle, and that's one. All I'm saying, Una, is if anyone is going to get hurt, it's going to be him, not you. And, God damn it, the man has been hurt enough!'

Una was suddenly deeply moved. It was clear that Joan's lecture was the result of some discussion between Mick and his wife. Mick gave a false impression of sluggishness, but it was clear that he liked Denis. Joan didn't merely like him; she loved him, and Una didn't in the least resent the fact that she was as jealous as hell.

'All right, love,' she said. 'I'll sleep on it.'

'And you don't mind my talking to you?'

'I wouldn't change an iota of you for all the women that were ever born,' said Una, giving her a kiss, and then Joan began to sniffle and Una had the job of consoling her for what she thought of, no doubt, as an exceedingly sinful at-tachment. God help us all! Una thought.

3

The more Una thought of it, the more she felt that Joan was right. She had been flirting with Denis, regardless of the consequences to him, though she had to admit that she was humanly flattered by the suggestion that it was she rather than Denis who had been doing the flirting.

The following evening she met him coming out from work and they went to sit in Stephen's Green. She was at her brightest and most eloquent. She admitted that she was becoming too attracted by him, thought she took more blame for this than she felt she deserved. At the same time she could not resist pointing out to him how irresponsible he was, and what little concern he showed for the kids. Up to this he had listened politely, but suddenly it was as if he had pulled down the shutters on her. 'Let the kids out of it, Una, like a good girl,' he said.

She knew that had been a bad mistake, but at least, her conscience was clear and that night she rang up Jimmy and told him she had been having a violent flirtation with the father of two children. Una never could keep a good thing to herself.

'Some people have all the luck,' Jimmy said darkly.

'Why? What's wrong with the flappers?' she asked.

'Not biting this weather,' he replied.

'Maybe I'd better come back,' she said.

'Maybe you'd better,' said Jimmy, and she laughed and said good night. If only Jimmy were always that way there was no one who suited her half as well.

But next morning, she woke in a real agony of mind, thinking not of Jimmy but of Denis. She dressed before the window, looking out at the long back gardens of the old houses, and feeling older than they. She was sure she had not been deliberately hypocritical with Denis, but the very thought of what she had said to him about the children, about whom she didn't give a damn, and the cold way he had cut her off, made her squirm. 'God!' she thought desperately. 'I *am* becoming an old maid!' At the same time she wished that she were not so damnably critical of herself: self-knowledge was all right in its own way, but, if you took it too far, it made you feel like a worm. She rang up Denis and arranged to meet him again after work.

The explanation, which somehow turned into an apology, was all right, but the consequences were simply awful. At midnight, through no apparent fault of her own, she found herself in bed with him in a single bed in the back room with the kitchen attached. She was lying in a most extraordinary position that made her want to giggle. God, she felt, could never have intended anything as absurd as this. She was angry with Joan who had failed to warn her of her real danger, because what a dozen men with twice his attraction had failed to do, this round-faced, ageing man had done with no great difficulty, and now she was no longer in danger of being an old maid. In fact, the sooner she could find some- body to marry her, the better.

What made her still angrier was that Denis seemed to be deeply attached to religious emblems, and there was a crucifix over the bed and a copy of the *Imitation* on the shelf beside it. It reminded her of a friend of her father's who, having lost his religion, played 'Nearer My God to Thee' on the clarinet.

At one o'clock Denis was fast asleep and snoring, and somehow the snoring struck her as far more compromising than anything that had happened before. She rose and dressed hastily, and then stood for a long time, peering down at the round, red, innocent face with the gaping mouth and drooping dark moustache. Then she glanced at herself in the mirror on the dressing table and frowned. Her face, except for a few abrasions, seemed just the same. 'His mistress,' she whispered in a horrified tone, and the face in the mirror looked back at her and echoed: 'His mistress.' She tiptoed hastily out of the room, took off her shoes to descend the long, dark stairs, closed the great front door almost sound- lessly behind her, and was startled by the echo of her own footsteps from the other side of the square. They sounded like those of a secondary personality that had taken her place and was now returning furtively from its midnight adultery.

'Adultery!' she added aloud in the same horrified tone, just to make sure that this was what her mind had suggested, and as she reached the canal bridge, she began to run as though she could outstrip the adultery that was stealing up on her. All she wanted was the quiet of her own little back room,

where she could meditate on the strangeness of her behaviour, away from Denis' snores and kicks. She was
alarmed and disillusioned; alarmed because a pious girl like
herself had suddenly behaved in this irresponsible and irremediable way; disillusioned, because, so far as she could see,
it had produced absolutely no effect on her character. If *this*
was what was supposed to change people, she thought, they
must be a damn sight more susceptible than she was.

But next morning, she woke appalled by her own danger.
It was all very well for Joan to worry about Denis, but it
wasn't Denis who had to do the worrying now. He wasn't the
one who was liable to have the baby. 'Baby' for some reason
sounded in her mind like 'mistress' and 'adultery'; things
that didn't happen to decent girls. Merely because she had
begun to behave in this queer way, she decided that the time
had come to marry Jimmy, so she rang him up to tell him
she was returning. Even to hear his nice Sunday's Well
accent was a relief, so she hurried into town and spent a lot of
money on a really beautiful pullover for him. In a wave of
self-mockery, she decided that if men only knew what pull-
overs meant, they wouldn't wear them at all; but the sheer
extravagance of it, and the crowds in the sunlight of
Stephen's Green reassured her and helped to banish the
memory of the night, and the stealthy echoing steps in the
dark and silent square proclaiming to all who listened 'Adultery! Adultery!'

4

She cooked Denis' dinner that evening in his flat, though
how anyone could cook in that cubbyhole off the bedroom
was beyond her. But she was a good cook, and she wanted to
show off to him. He seemed touched by the sight of her,
making a muck of his kitchen, and shambled behind her,
begging her not to use three pots when one would do. It
looked like the kitchen of a man who used only one pot.

But she could see his attitude to her had changed. Now, he
was all for her staying on in Dublin as long as possible.

'The sooner I get back to Cork and marry Jimmy, the better for all parties,' she said ruefully.

'You still want to marry Jimmy?'

'I thought that was what you were advising me to do,' she said in mock alarm.

'Things were different then,' he said.

'They were,' she agreed. 'They weren't quite so urgent.'

'You know, Una,' he said, walking restlessly about the room, 'I think I might be able to get a divorce. I don't say I could. I might.'

'But I thought your wife was a Catholic, Denis.'

'Annie is whatever it suits her to be. I never raised the matter with her because, to tell you the truth, I didn't expect I'd want to marry again.'

'Well, even if she's not, I am,' said Una. It wasn't even as if she wanted to marry Denis. Emotionally, she had been taken at a disadvantage, but her judgement was still clear. The sight of all those religious books had reminded her again of the man playing 'Nearer My God to Thee' on the clarinet. 'Even if you did get a divorce, I couldn't possibly marry you.'

'Not in this country. I understand that,' Denis said, not understanding her at all. 'But after all, I don't see why I should have to live here for the rest of my life. I could go to England. Other people have had to do it.'

'England!' Una thought despairingly. He was making it sound worse and worse. It would be bad enough to live with a man you didn't believe you were married to, but as well as that, to give up her family and friends, and never again be able to walk up the Western Road in the evening light! The very idea of it was punishment enough for any sin she had committed.

'You don't know my father, Denis,' she said. 'Mind you, he's broad-minded enough in his own way. I think if I was to tell him what happened between us, he'd only ask me was I able to look after myself, but if I was to marry a divorced man, out the door I'd go. Straight! And after all, you can't blame him. Damn it, that's what he believes.'

After that, she refused to repeat her performance of the previous evening. The rational side of her was in control

82

again, and, as she said, it was one thing to make a fool of yourself when you felt free, but a different thing entirely to do it in cold blood when you realized how dependent you were on another man.

All the same, when she embraced Denis for the last time at Kingsbridge Station, Joan's face suddenly went black with rage and even Mick looked a bit embarrassed. It was only too plain that whatever there was between them was no mere holiday flirtation. Una managed to keep from weeping until the train pulled out and then began to sob uncontrollably. In a nice rational mood you could make love-making seem unimportant enough, but it changed your character all right. Suddenly, seeing the look of consternation on the face of a young officer who was sitting opposite her, she began to giggle through her sobs.

'It's all right,' she said. 'It isn't a death. Only a fellow.'

'Oh, is that all?' he said in relief. 'In that case you'd better have tea with me.'

'I'd love to,' she sniffled. 'Just give me time for one more bawl. God, I am an idiot!'

It was pleasant and restful to slip back into the routine of home and Jimmy, though even the pullover did not entirely wipe out her feeling of guilt towards him. It was only then that she really began to notice the change in herself. She felt big and motherly and mature. For the first time she realized how many of their quarrels had originated in her own unsettled state, and how much better a man he was than she had imagined. At the same time she realized that he was not an easy man to understand because he had so little understanding of himself. He was resentful about any criticism of orthodoxy because he wasn't really happy with it. There was an objective, critical side to Jimmy that he rarely exposed, and didn't expose at all except to a passive listener.

Jimmy himself noticed the change and said that the holiday seemed to have done her good.

'Joan always has that effect on me,' she replied eagerly.

'Was it Joan or that fellow with the five children – what's his name?'

'Ah, that's something I'll have to confess to you one of

these days,' she said with a laugh. 'There's more to that than you think, boy.'

It was half joke and wholly earnest, because in fact Denis was never far from her mind. Their queer little love affair was like a dark background of woods that threw every figure that moved against it into startling relief. It was the secrecy that gave it such power. There was no one she could tell, and because of this it lent to everything a quality of dramatic irony. Jimmy's mother would be knitting and describing some wonderful sermon, or Una would be walking down a hill with her father, and bang! there it would all be again, and again she would be alone with the echoing footsteps in the silent square, now romantic and faraway. Sometimes she wondered if Jimmy had any such dark secret from her, and, deciding he hadn't, wished for his own sake that he had.

But one night they had a thundering row after Jimmy's mother had gone to bed. Like all their rows it was about nothing – a current political scandal about a distillery – and Una said that political scandals always seemed to be about a distillery or a bacon factory, thus reviving an earlier row, and Jimmy said pompously that she used the word 'scandal' with a rare lack of discrimination. Una, who had forgotten how violent their quarrels could be, was appalled as she heard herself shouting at him. She even refused to let him see her home, and said that anyone who accosted her would probably be a pleasant relief.

By the time she reached home she saw that the old pattern had re-asserted itself exactly as before, and this time it wasn't her fault. Whatever she might have done, at least she had straightened herself out about certain things, but Jimmy was as big a mess as ever. He took the wrong side in an argument and stuck by it because in life he had taken the wrong side and couldn't break free.

Immediately, this made her again feel prudent and mature. She looked at her own angry face in the mirror over the fireplace and said authoritatively: 'Una, girl, someone in this blooming group has to act grown-up.' So she rang Jimmy up and apologized and proposed that they should go to Glengarriffe for the weekend. He was still hurt, and still sounded like a small boy of twelve, but though he accepted her apology ungraciously, he agreed to go with her.

Glengarriffe had always been a great haunt of theirs, and by the time they began to drive between lake and mountain Jimmy was already in high spirits. Whenever he let himself go, he was the best of company; considerate, sly and full of crude schoolboy jokes. After supper at the hotel, they walked down the sea front and watched the moon rise over Cab Dhu. They knew all the boatmen and chatted with them about the latest visitors, and leaned on the sea-wall, watching the moon's reflection in the bay like a great silver tree of quivering leaves.

When Jimmy said goodnight to her in her bedroom she grabbed him tight.

'Jimmy,' she asked, 'aren't you going to stay?'

'Are you sure you want me to?' he asked with a sombre smile, and she knew the same idea had been in his own mind.

'That's right,' she said reproachfully. 'Put all the responsibility on the girl! The least you might have done is to let me swoon respectably.'

She turned her back and pulled her frock over her head. When she saw him standing there still, tall, embarrassed and silent, she gave him a playful push on to the bed. She felt in command of the situation again. Denis had been right about that at least. She and Jimmy had come to a dead end, and, by hook or crook, they must break out of it. And with Jimmy it was all so much easier. He wasn't only someone who attracted her, but someone she loved; someone she had known since her girlhood, whom she trusted and understood.

He fell asleep in her arms, but Una remained awake till morning in a daze of happiness and fulfilment. She had seen her duty and done it, and to hell with everybody! Before the maids began their work she waked him and sat cross-legged on the bed, watching him pull on his trousers and socks. It was only when he raised the blind that she noticed his unusual gravity. It was as though the sky must look very dark over the mountains.

'What's it like outside, Jimmy?' she asked.

'I wasn't looking,' he said without glancing at her. 'It seems all right. I was just thinking we'd probably better get married at once.'

'Oh, do you think so?' she asked. She felt rather let-down. This was not how a lover should sound after a first night with a girl he'd been courting for years. But maybe all Irishmen were like that. To do anything at all with them, you had to seduce them, and then they could hardly wait to make respectable men of themselves again. And yet Jimmy had never looked more attractive. He leaned against the window-frame in his white shirt sleeves, and the morning light caught his big-boned obstinate face and brought out the deep vertical lines between his eyes.

'We don't want to have to rush it,' he said. 'Your father wouldn't like that at all. Neither would my mother, I dare say.'

'I dare say they wouldn't,' Una said coolly. 'To tell you the truth, I wasn't thinking of them.'

'Unfortunately, I have to think of them.'

'Jimmy,' she cried in consternation, 'you're not upset about it, are you?'

'Aren't you?' he asked in his Sunday's Well accent, giving her a dark look.

'Me?' she said with a laugh. 'I'm enchanted, of course. I thought I'd never see the day.'

'Maybe upset is the wrong word,' he said pompously, and then nodded towards the bed. 'But we don't want any more of *this*.' The contempt in his tone as he said 'this' angered her. It reduced it all to a child's messy game.

'We haven't had such a lot of it,' she said sharply. 'Do you mean it's too furtive?'

'Oh, yes,' he said almost with a shudder. 'And *wrong*!'

'Wrong?' she repeated angrily. 'I thought we were supposed to be engaged.'

'I don't see what that has to do with it.'

'If you want to know, I don't think it's half as wrong as quarrelling over old distilleries,' she snapped. 'At any rate, it's human.'

'That only makes it worse,' he said coldly. 'We stuck it so

long, we could have stuck it a little longer. After all, we're not just out together for a good time.'

He sounded as though he were explaining the policy of his paper, and at any other time it would have made her really furious. Now, she felt despairingly that he was probably right. Their squabbles and misunderstandings had been part of the normal behaviour of two responsible grown-ups who took marriage seriously.

'Honestly, Jimmy,' she said, 'there are times when I think I'm not right in the head. This is all my fault.'

'Oh, no, it isn't,' he said, showing what she called his 'Sunday's Well' character. 'I'm entirely to blame.' She knew he didn't mean a word of it, but she liked it just the same.

'You are not, Jimmy,' she said flatly. 'I made you come here deliberately, with that intention. I only wish you'd told me to go to Hell.'

'Oh, intentions!' he said wearily. 'Do you think I don't have intentions, too? No, it's not that. It's just that things have changed between us, and I don't seem to be able to talk to you as I used to do.'

'But that's exactly what I felt about you, Jimmy,' she said. 'That's why I felt we had to do something desperate.'

'Yes,' he added bitterly, 'and it's all the fault of the damn fellow in Dublin. He's the one who made you change.'

The suddenness and bitterness of the attack took her by surprise. Then she got out of bed and put her arms on his shoulders.

'You really think that?' she asked.

'I know it, girl,' he said with tears of rage in his eyes.

'Well, you're wrong,' she said earnestly. 'I swear you're wrong. I'm just the same as I always was, and Denis did nothing to me. You do believe that, don't you? You have to believe that. If you don't, we'd better chuck it.' Then, as the falsehood touched the chord of hysteria in her, she began to sob and pull her hair. 'Oh, I'm just a bloody fool. I do my best – honest to God I do my best – but everything I do goes wrong, God, it's beastly!'

'It isn't beastly, Una,' he said. 'I know you acted for the

best. So did I. It's just that it's not right for us. We're not the sort.'

And again she saw it through his eyes, something beautiful that had been irretrievably spoiled by a few hours of boredom and dissatisfaction and could never be the same again because innocence had gone out of it.

When Jimmy left her she threw herself on the bed and really bawled. Now, she didn't know where to turn to or what to do. She had tried everything, and everything had been wrong. And yet she knew she wasn't worse than other girls. She had sense enough to realize that, as girls went, she was rather better than most. She had acted with the best of intentions out of what she had thought a sense of responsibility. In fact, when it came to good intentions, she was almost tripping over them. And yet she had done worse than any flighty irresponsible girl would have done. She had let herself be seduced by Denis, and seduced Jimmy in her turn. And what was worse, she had lied to Jimmy, lied to him in the most flagrant way.

She wasn't really apologizing for that. Now that Jimmy was out of the room she was very cross with him, but she was crosser still with Denis. She could almost imagine him laughing at her folly. So now she thought she could get along on her own, did she? She thought there was nothing left for her to learn? Like the sorcerer's apprentice she had learned how to produce magic but not how to control it!

It made her so angry that she actually began talking to him as though he were there.

'All right, you old bastard,' she muttered vindictively. 'You started it, with all your old talk. "Everything would be fine once we made the breakthrough." Well, I made the breakthrough, and where the hell am I? I'm worse off than I was before. What did I do wrong? As you think you're so smart, maybe you'll tell me that?'

And suddenly, almost as though he had opened his mouth and replied to her, she knew what she had done wrong, and the very idea of it made her feel sick. She dressed and went downstairs to the telephone. It was on the wall beside the back door, near the kitchen. The back door was open and there were hens strutting by in the early morning light. She had minutes to wait for her call, and she stamped nervously up and down the yard, afraid that at any moment Jimmy would appear, as good-looking as ever, and ask her to go for a swim. In that state she felt she couldn't even talk to him. Even the memory of the night they had spent together made her feel dirty all over. 'Prostitution,' said that queer voice in her head, and she shuddered and wished the phone bell would ring.

Suddenly it sounded and she grabbed at it. A meek, sleepy voice answered her. As it expanded into awareness she could almost see that awful bedroom with the kitchen attached and her heart overflowed. In her excitement she began to stutter.

'Denis,' she said, 'about that divorce business you were mentioning—'

'Yes, dear,' he replied snugly.

'You didn't do anything about it, I suppose?'

'As a matter of fact, I did, dear,' he said, coming gradually awake. 'Why?'

'Oh, nothing,' she said lightly. 'Only I've been thinking about it myself. That it might be the best way, I mean.'

'It's the only way, dear,' he said in his most infallible tone, and Una almost chuckled at how little he knew. 'And I'm pretty sure now it's going to be possible. Gum, it *is* early, isn't it? You haven't been lying awake thinking of it, have you?'

'Not altogether,' she said dryly.

'Where are you speaking from, Una?' he asked with concern. 'Not from home, surely?'

At this she chuckled. It wouldn't do at all to tell him that she was speaking from a hotel where she'd been spending the night with another man. He mightn't understand.

'I'll see you soon and tell you all about it,' she said, and when she had hung up, she went briskly down the sea-road in the morning sunlight, singing and not caring much where she went. She would get a cup of tea and a slice of home-made bread in a country cottage, and thank God, that was about all she wanted. All the same she knew perfectly well that she would tell Denis where she had rung from, and why, and knew that though he might be furious for a couple of hours, it would really make no difference. So far as he was concerned, innocence had not gone out of it.

Being a pious girl she thanked God for having discovered in time what was wrong with her. In her simple way she had thought she was learning the business of love, and she was, but in a way that no one had told her of. Now she realized that even Denis didn't know the half of it. Every man and woman is a trade in himself, and however bad a bargain she might have in Denis, Denis was the only trade she knew.

*More Stories* (1954)

# THE OLD FAITH

The Pattern at Kilmulpeter turned into a great day. Mass was said in the ruins of the cathedral and the old bishop, Dr Gallogly, preached. Father Devine, who was a bit of an anti-quarian, had looked up the details of St Mulpeter's life for him. There were a lot of them, mostly contradictory, and all very, very queer. It seemed that like most of the saints of that remote period, St Mulpeter had put to sea on a flagstone and floated ashore in Cornwall. There, the seven harpers of the King had been put to death through the curses of the Druids and the machinations of the King's unfaithful wife. St Mulpeter miraculously restored them to life and, through the great mercy of God, they were permitted to sing a song about the Queen's misbehaviour, which resulted in St Mulpeter turning her into a pillar-stone and converting the King to the one true faith.

The Bishop had been Professor of Dogmatic Theology in the seminary; a job that had suited him excellently for he was a man who dogmatized about everything. He was a tall, powerfully-built, handsome old man with a face that was both broad and long, and high cheek-bones that gave the lower half of his face an air of unnatural immobility but drew attention to the fine blue, anxious eyes. He had a quiet manner and a low voice, but with a touch of the piledriver about him.

For a dogmatic theologian he showed great restraint on reading Devine's summary of the saint's life. He raised his brows a few times, and then read it through again with an air of resignation.

'I suppose that's what you'd call allegorical, father,' he said anxiously.

'So long as you don't call it historical,' said Devine, who had a tongue he couldn't control.

The Bishop rarely showed signs of emotion, and he seemed quite unaffected by the scene in the ruined cathedral, though it impressed Devine – the crowds of country people kneeling in the wet grass among the tottering crosses and headstones, the wild countryside framed in the mullioned windows, and the big deeply-moulded clouds sailing over-head. The Bishop disposed neatly of St Mulpeter by saying that we couldn't all go to sea on flagstones, which required great faith in anyone who attempted it, but the family Ros-ary was just as good.

After Mass, Father Devine showed the Bishop and some of the other clergy round the ruins. Suddenly, a couple of men who had been hiding in the remains of a twelfth century chapel took to their heels. One of them stood on a low wall, looking down on the little group of clergymen with the ex-pression of a terrified rabbit. The Bishop raised his um-brella and pointed it accusingly at him.

'Father Devine,' he said in a commanding tone, 'see what that fellow has.'

'I have nothing, Your Eminence,' wailed the man on the wall.

'You have a bottle behind your back,' said the Bishop sternly. 'What have you in that?'

'Nothing, Your Eminence, only a drop of water from the Holy Well.'

'Give it here to me till I see,' said the Bishop, and when

Father Devine passed him the bottle he removed the cork and sniffed.

'I'd like to see the Holy Well that came out of,' he said ironically. 'Is it any use my preaching to ye about poteen?'

'Ah, 'tis a wild, windy quarter, Your Eminence,' said the man, beginning to scratch himself, 'and I have the rheumatics something terrible.'

'I'd sooner the rheumatics than the cirrhosis,' grunted the Bishop. 'Bring it with you, father,' he added to Devine, and strode on with his umbrella against his back.

The same night a few of them had dinner with him at the Palace – Father Whelan, an old parish priest, who was a cross between a saint and a half-wit; Father Fogarty, who was a bit of a firebrand, Devine and Canon Lanigan. The Bishop and the Canon never got on because the Canon's supporters were giving it out that the Bishop was doddering and needed a coadjutor. Besides, the Canon gave himself too many airs. He was tall and thin, with a long nose and a punchinello chin, and he let on to be an authority on Church history as well as on food and wine. The last item was enough to damn him in the Bishop's eyes, because he maintained almost *ex cathedra* that the best food and wine in the world were to be found on the restaurant car from Holyhead to Euston.

When Lanigan made a fool of himself by recommending Chateauneuf-du-Pape, the Bishop turned to Father Devine.

'Talking about drink, father,' he said with his anxious glare, 'what happened to the bottle of poteen you took off that fellow?'

'I suppose it's in the hall,' Father Devine said vaguely. 'I can assure you I wasn't indulging in it.'

'You could indulge in worse,' said the Bishop with a dirty look at the Canon. 'Many a good man was raised on it. Nellie,' he called, turning his head a few inches, 'bring in that bottle of poteen, if you can find it . . . You can have it in your tea,' he added to the Canon. 'Or is it coffee you want?'

'Oh, tea, tea,' sighed the Canon, offering it up. He knew only too well what the Bishop's coffee was like. According to the Bishop, it was the best bottled coffee in the world.

When the housekeeper brought in the poteen, the Bishop took out the cork and sniffed at the bottle again with an anxious air.

'I should have found out who made it,' he said. 'When they can't get the rye, they make it out of anything.'

'You seem to be quite an expert, my Lord,' said Devine with his waspish air.

'Why wouldn't I?' asked the Bishop. 'Didn't I make it myself? My poor father – God rest him! – had a still of his own. In milk he used to give it to me, for colds. Or like a liniment, rubbed on the chest. Not that I tasted it now in sixty, sixty-five years.'

He poured a stiff glass for each of them, and drank his own in a gulp without any change of expression. Then he looked anxiously at the others to see what they thought of it. Lanigan put on an air of consternation, but the Bishop knew that was only showing off. Father Fogarty drank it reverently, as though it were altar wine, but he was a nationalist and felt that anything that came from the people had to be treated accordingly. Father Devine disgraced himself; spluttered, choked, and then went petulantly off to the bathroom.

Meanwhile, the Bishop had decided that it was good poteen and treated them to another round, which they seemed to feel it might be disrespectful to refuse. Father Devine did refuse, and with a crucified air that the Bishop did not like at all. The Bishop, who knew everything and had one of the most venomously gossipy tongues in the diocese, was convinced that he was a model of Christian charity and had spoken seriously to Father Devine about his own sharpness.

'Was it on an island you made this stuff?' the Canon asked blandly.

'No,' replied the Bishop, who didn't know what irony was. 'A mountain.'

'A rather desolate one, I fancy,' Lanigan said dreamily.

'It had to be if you didn't want the police on top of you,' said the Bishop. 'They'd have fifty men out at a time, scouring the mountains.'

'And bagpipes!' said the Canon, bursting into an old woman's cackle at the memory of the hilly road from Beaune to Dijon with the vineyards at each side. 'It seems to go with bagpipes.'

'There were no bagpipes,' the Bishop said shortly. 'As a matter of fact,' he added nostalgically, 'it was very nice up there on a summer's night. They'd hide the still in a hollow, and then sit round and tell stories. Very queer stories, some of them, like that life of St Mulpeter Father Devine wrote out for me.'

'Ah, the people were half-savage in those days,' the Canon said.

'They were not,' the Bishop replied mildly, but from his tone Father Devine knew he was very vexed. 'They were more refined altogether.'

'Would you say so, my Lord?' asked Father Fogarty, who, as a good nationalist was convinced the people were rushing to perdition and that the only hope for them was to send them all back to live in whitewashed cabins.

'Ah, a nicer class of people in every way,' Father Whelan said mournfully. 'You wouldn't find the same nature at all in them nowadays.'

'They had a lot of queer customs all the same, father,' said the Bishop, who always spoke with peculiar affection to Whelan. 'I remember they used to put the first mug of poteen in hiding under a rock. Would that be something to do with the fairies?' he asked Devine.

'Well, at any rate, you can't deny that the people today are more enlightened,' the Canon said warmly.

'I deny it *in toto*,' retorted the Bishop. 'There's no comparison. The people were more intelligent altogether, better balanced and better spoken. What would you say, Father Whelan?'

'Oh, in every way, my Lord,' moaned Father Whelan, taking out his pipe.

'And the superstitions, my Lord?' the Canon hissed superciliously. 'The ghosts and fairies and spells?'

'They might have good reason,' said the Bishop with a flash of his blue eyes.

'By Gor, you're right, my Lord,' said Fogarty, in a loud voice, and then, realizing the attention he had attracted, he blushed and stopped short.

' "There are more things in heaven and earth, Horatio, than are dreamt of in our philosophy," ' added the Bishop complacently.

'Omar Khayyam,' whispered Father Whelan to Father Fogarty. 'He's a fellow you'd want to read. He said some very good things.'

'That's a useful quotation,' said the Canon, seeing he was getting the worst of it. 'I must remember that next time I'm preaching against fortune tellers.'

'I wouldn't bother,' the Bishop said curtly. 'There's no analogy. There was a parish priest in our place one time, a man called Muldoon. Father Whelan might remember him.'

'Con?' defined Father Whelan. 'I do, well. His nephew, Peter, was on the Chinese Mission.'

'A well-meaning man but a bit coarse, I thought,' said the Bishop.

'That was his mother's side of the family,' explained Whelan. 'His mother was one of the Clasheen Dempseys and they were always a rough lot.'

'Was she so?' the Bishop asked with a great air of enlightenment. 'I never knew that. It would explain a lot. He was always preaching against superstition, you might remember, and he had his knife in one poor old fellow up the Glen called Johnnie Ryan.'

'Johnnie the Fairies,' said Father Whelan. 'I knew him too.'

'I knew him well,' said the Bishop. 'A gentle poor man but a bit soft in the head. He was their Living Man.'

'Their what?' cried Father Devine in astonishment.

'Their Living Man,' said the Bishop.

'Whose Living Man?' asked Divine with a baffled air.

'The fairies,' explained the Bishop. 'They had to have a Living Man to go with them, or else they had no power. That was the way I heard it anyway. I remember him well playing the Fairy Music on his whistle. They taught it to him.'

'You wouldn't remember how it went?' Father Fogarty asked eagerly. Devine could see the scheme forming in his head, for the convent school orchestra to play it. He could even imagine it on the programme – 'The Fairy Music, by kind permission of his Lordship the Bishop of Moyle.'

'I was never much good at remembering music,' said the Bishop. 'Anyway, I was only a child. Of course, there might be something in it. You'd often see queer lights on the mountain over our house. They said it was a fairy funeral. They had some story about a man from our place who interrupted a funeral like that one night. The fairies left down the coffin and ran away. The man opened the coffin and there was a girl inside. A fine-looking girl, too, I believe. When he breathed on her she woke up. They said she was from the Tuam direction – a changeling or something. I never checked the truth of it.'

'From Galway, I believe, my Lord,' Father Whelan said respectfully.

'Was it Galway?' asked the Bishop.

'I dare say with enough poteen in, a man could even believe that,' said the Canon indignantly.

'Still, Canon, strange things do happen,' said Father Fogarty.

'Why, then, indeed, they do,' agreed Father Whelan with a sigh.

'Was this something that happened to yourself, father?' the Bishop asked kindly, seeing the young man straining at the leash.

'It was, my Lord,' said Fogarty. ' 'Twas when I was a kid, going to school. I got fever very bad and the doctor gave me up. The mother – God rest her – was in a terrible state. Then my aunt came to stay with us. She was a real old country-woman. I remember them to this day arguing in the kitchen, about what they ought to do. "Don't be a fool, woman!" said my aunt. "You know there's ways." '

'Well, well, well,' Father Whelan said, shaking his head.

'Then my aunt came up with a scissors,' Father Fogarty

continued excitedly. 'First, she cut off a bit of the end of my shirt, and then a bit of hair from behind my ear, and then a bit of fingernail, and she threw them in the fire. All the time she was muttering to herself like an old witch.'

'My! my! my!' exclaimed Father Whelan.

'And you got better?' said the Bishop with a quelling glance at the Canon.

'I got better, all right, but that wasn't the strangest part of it.' Fogarty leaned across the table, scowling, and dropped his eager, boyish voice to a whisper. 'Inside a year, her two sons, two of the finest young fellows you ever laid eyes on, died.' Then he sat back, took out a cigar and scowled again. 'Now, wasn't that extraordinary?' he asked. 'I say, wasn't it extraordinary?'

'Ah, whatever was waiting to get you,' Father Whelan said philosophically, emptying his pipe on to his plate. 'I suppose it had to get something. A similar thing happened an old aunt of my own. The cock used to sleep in the house, on a perch over the door – you know, the old-fashioned way. One night, the old woman had occasion, and when she went to the door, the cock crowed three times and dropped dead at her feet. Whatever was waiting for her, of course,' he added with a sigh. 'The cock gave them away, and they took their revenge on him.'

'Well! Well! Well!' the Canon exploded. 'I'm astonished at you, Father Whelan, absolutely astonished! How can you even repeat such old wives' tales?'

'I don't see what you have to be astonished about, Canon,' said the Bishop. 'It was no worse than what happened to Father Muldoon.'

'That was a bad business,' muttered Father Whelan, shaking his head.

'What happened him?' asked Devine.

'I told you he was always denouncing old Johnnie,' said the Bishop. 'One day they had words and he struck the old man. It wasn't fair. The old man was too feeble. Within a month Muldoon got a breaking out on his knee.'

'Poor fellow, he lost the leg after,' Father Whelan said, stuffing his pipe again.

'I suppose next you'll say that was the fairies' revenge?' said the Canon, throwing discretion to the winds. It was too much for him, a man who knew Church history, had lived in France and was a connoisseur of wine.

'That was what Father Muldoon thought,' said the Bishop smugly.

'More fool he!' retorted the Canon.

'That's as may be, Canon,' said the Bishop. 'Anyway, the doctors couldn't do much for him. He went back up the Glen again to ask Johnnie's advice. "I had nothing to do with it, father," said Johnnie, "but you can tell the doctor from me that he might as well take the leg off you while he's at it." "Why so?" says Muldoon. "Because it was the Queen of the Fairies that fired the shot at you, father, and the Queen's wound never heals." No more it did,' added the Bishop. 'As you say, father, he ended his days on a peg leg.'

'He did, God rest him, he did,' muttered Father Whelan mournfully, and there was a long pause. It was clear that the Canon was routed, and soon after they all got up to go. Father Fogarty had left his car outside the Seminary, and the Bishop, in a benevolent mood, offered to guide them across the field by the footpath.

'No, I'll do that,' Devine said irritably. In his cranky way he was fond of the Bishop and he didn't want him perambulating through the fields at that hour.

'Ah, I need the little walk,' said the Bishop.

He, the Canon and Father Fogarty went first down the palace steps. Father Devine followed with Father Whelan, who went down sideways with the skirts of his coat held up.

'That was a very good drop of poteen,' the Bishop was saying. 'For some reason, bad poteen strikes at the extremities. I used to see the people at home, talking as clearly as yourself or myself, and then dropping off the chairs, paralysed. You'd have to take them home on a door. The head might be quite clear, but the legs would be like gateposts.'

'Father Devine,' Father Whelan whispered girlishly, stopping in his tracks.

'Yes, father, what is it?' Devine asked gently.

'What his Lordship said,' whispered Father Whelan guilt-ily. 'That's the way I feel. Like gateposts.'

And before the young priest could catch him, he put out one of the gateposts which failed to alight properly on its base: the other leaned slowly towards it, and he collapsed in an ungraceful parody of a ballet dancer's curtsey.

'Oh, my, my, my!' he exclaimed guiltily. Even in his liquor he was melancholy and gentle.

The other three turned round slowly, very slowly, to study him. To Devine they looked like sleep-walkers.

'Hah!' the Bishop said with quiet satisfaction. 'It wasn't as good as I thought. We'd want to mind ourselves.'

And off the three of them went, arm-in-arm, as though they recognized no responsibility to their fallen colleague. Paddy, the Bishop's 'boy', who had been anticipating trouble, immediately appeared, and he and Devine carried the old man back to the hallway. 'Father Whelan isn't feeling well,' he explained unnecessarily to the housekeeper. Then, the two of them took the hall bench and set out after the others. They were in time to see the collapse of the Canon, but in spite of it, the other two went on. Devine shouted a warning, but they ignored him. Father Fogarty had begun to chuckle hysterically. It occurred to Devine that he was already be-ginning to rehearse his story of 'the night I got drunk with the Bishop'.

Devine and Paddy left the Canon and pursued the other two. They had gone wildly astray, turning in a semi-circle round the field, till they were at the foot of the hill and before a high fence round the plantation. The Bishop never hesitated but began to climb the wall.

'I must be gone wrong, father,' he said anxiously. 'This never happened to me before. We'll go over the wall and up the wood.'

'I can't,' shouted Fogarty in a paroxysm of chuckles.

'Nonsense, father!' the Bishop said sternly, holding on to a bush and looking down at him from the top of the wall. 'Why can't you?'

'The fairies have me,' roared Fogarty.

'Pull yourself together, father,' the Bishop said sternly.

'You don't want to be making an exhibition of yourself.'

Next moment Fogarty was lying flat at the foot of the wall, laughing his head off. Devine shouted again to the Bishop, but the Bishop only turned his back contemptuously and slid down at the other side of the wall. They found him there under a tree in the starlight, quite powerless but full of wisdom, resignation and peace. When they lifted him on to the bench he reclined there, his hands crossed meekly on his breast, like an effigy on a tomb-chest.

'The most remarkable example of historical regression I've ever seen,' Devine told young Fogarty when he woke up later with a terrible head. 'I must write a paper on it for the Archaeological Society. I didn't mind your retreat into the Early Bronze Age so much, but I was afraid you'd forget yourselves and go neolithic on me all of a sudden.'

'Ah, how bad the neolithic fellows were!' groaned Fogarty. 'I'm damn full sure they never felt as bad as I do.'

'The neolithic fellows?' Devine said in mock surprise. 'And have the Bishop proposing to build Lanigan into the wall of the new cathedral? My dear fellow, believe me, you can take this historical regression business too far.'

*More Stories* (1954)

# VANITY

There are a lot of things bishops have to put up with beside old age, loneliness and domestic discomfort, and the worst of these is coadjutors. To be God Almighty – the just and moral Governor of your own private universe – for years, and then have an assistant God Almighty tagged on to you is enough to break the spirit in most men. The Bishop of Moyle, the Most Reverend Dr Gallogly, called his coadjutor the Stump, the Spy or the Boy, according to the way he felt about him. Mostly it was the Boy. The Boy had nasty supercilious ways that the Bishop detested. He let on to know a lot about

French history, gave himself out as an authority on food and wine, jeered at Dr Gallogly's coffee – the best bottled coffee on the market – and mocked at his statement that the best food and wine in the world were served on the train from Holyhead to Euston. As a one time Professor of Dogmatic Theology, the Bishop was vulnerable to that sort of criticism.

Worst of all, the coadjutor had the illusion that at eighty-six the Bishop was past his prime while the Bishop himself knew that he had never been younger or livelier. Just to prove it, he would suddenly order round his car, drive a couple of hundred miles to Dublin and interview three Ministers. The Bishop was such a nice, friendly, inquisitive old man that the Ministers fell over themselves, telling him things he wanted to know, and then, of course, everybody in Moyle learned about them except Lanigan. Lanigan let on to be amused at this because it showed up the Bishop's senile fatuity, but, being an inquisitive man himself, the Bishop knew Lanigan was furious, and only pretended indifference out of vanity. Vanity – the besetting sin of people in religion, according to the Bishop – was Lanigan's weak spot, and the Bishop continued to play on it.

Whenever the notion of going to Dublin struck the Bishop he always made inquiries about people from Moyle whom he might call on there. He knew they liked that. Everyone is impressed by a Bishop, and it gave people like that an advantage over their city friends, and later they came home and said what a wonderful old man he was – so modest! – so considerate! – another thorn in the coadjutor's side.

One morning before setting out he made inquiries and discovered that one of his curates was in a nursing home for an operation.

'Father O'Brien?' he exclaimed, hitting his brow. 'What's he being operated on for? Surely, he's only – what is he, father?'

'Forty-five, my Lord.'

'Forty-five? And having an operation like that? Sure, there's no sense to it. Remind me to go and see Father O'Brien, Paddy,' he added to his chauffeur.

Even the Bishop's best friend would not have pretended that this was all kindness, though the Bishop had plenty of that. It was mainly delight and wonder at himself for having reached the age of eighty-six without a pain or an ache while a whole generation of priests was growing up who couldn't get to forty-five without an operation. 'Motor cars!' he said to himself. 'It's all the blooming motor cars!'

And every step he climbed up to the first floor of the nursing home the Bishop vacillated between good nature and complacency: good nature because he was genuinely glad to be able to do a good turn for a lonesome young priest, far from his family and friends, and a furious complacency because it wasn't the young fellow of forty-five who was coming to visit the sick old man of eighty-six. The two emotions mingled in the triumphant smile with which he opened the curate's door and trumpeted joyously: 'Father O'Brien, what does this mean? Do you want me to suspend you?' That would get back, too.

The Bishop was no fool, but he was so pleased with himself that he talked with more freedom than usual about the Moyle clergy and their families, particularly the families. 'If you want to know about a man, father, find out about his family,' he pronounced oracularly. 'Now, there's Dr Lanigan. To understand Dr Lanigan, you would have to know his brother, Mick, the way I did. Now, Mick was a clever sort of man, and a conscientious one in his own way, but he died when he was only sixty of some sort of children's disease that was never known to kill anyone else, and for years before he died he was suffering from religious scruples. Scruples! You see, father, that whole family was a bit neurotic.'

The Bishop returned to his hotel, saying to Paddy, his 'man', 'That'll show them, Paddy,' and Paddy grinned with perfect comprehension. Nobody resents a coadjutor more than a bishop's man. The lounge of the hotel was crowded and several people were waiting for the lift. By this time the Bishop's complacency had assumed monstrous proportions. 'Ah, I can't be bothered waiting for that old machine,' he said testily, loud enough to be overheard, and went up the stairs 'like a hare' according to Paddy, though this was a slight exaggeration.

He negotiated the main flight of stairs successfully, but when he came to one of six steps leading from one level to another, he tripped. He had only six steps to fall, but he knew they might as well be twenty. He was dished. He didn't move; he knew it wasn't safe. 'Pride goeth before a fall,' he thought ruefully. 'I should have waited for that blooming old lift.'

But when an old waiter appeared he did not lose his composure.

'I think I'm hurt,' he said placidly. 'Don't tell anyone. Get something to lift me in on and call Dr Jameson.'

It was agony being transferred to the stretcher and laid on the bed, but pain was the least of the Bishop's troubles, and the tears in his eyes were as much humiliation as anything else. He was only beginning to realize the full extent of the disaster that had overtaken him. After an irreproachable life of eighty-six years he was suddenly, because of what he thought of now as 'a mad vagary', no longer his own master, and as much the property of stretcher-bearers, doctors and nurses as any poor curate. Lanigan had his chance at last. No longer would they think of him in his own diocese as a marvellous old man. The shock of it was almost enough to make him lose his reason. But his voice remained steady and unemotional, the voice of a theologian.

'Am I bad?' he asked the doctor, who was a brisk, moon-faced young man.

'It looks as if you've broken your shoulder and your leg,' said the doctor. 'We'll have to get you to hospital to see if there's anything else.'

'Am I going to die?' the Bishop asked almost hopefully. If he were going to die there would be no further problem.

'I doubt it,' said the doctor, who was privately convinced that the Bishop wouldn't leave hospital outside a box. 'You must be pretty tough.'

'Ah, I'm tough enough,' the Bishop replied complacently. 'Couldn't you do whatever you have to do here?'

'I couldn't, my Lord.'

'Why couldn't you?' the Bishop asked angrily. He hated to

be contradicted in that positive way – it is one of the drawbacks of having been Almighty God.

'Because I've got to have an X-ray taken at once.'

'Then why can't you get it taken here? They must have portable ones. I don't like hospitals.'

'Why? What's wrong with hospitals?'

'They're too public,' the Bishop said flatly. 'When a man has a bit of authority, the way I have, he can't be making a spectacle of himself. He has too many people round him, trying to make out he's not fit to look after himself. They treat you as if you were a child.'

'But an accident can happen to anybody,' said the doctor.

'An accident can happen to a young man,' the Bishop said. 'If the same thing happens to an elderly person, people go on as though you did it out of spite. Boland, the manager here, is an old friend. He'll keep quiet about it. If I went into a hospital 'twould be all round Moyle tomorrow.'

'It'll be all round Moyle anyhow.'

'Not if I can help it,' the Bishop said, clamping his long thin lips.

'But people will have to know.'

'Why will they have to know?' the Bishop asked with sudden fierceness. It was bad enough to endure helplessness and agonizing pain without being contradicted into the bargain. 'What business is it of theirs? Or I could go into hospital under a false name.'

'You couldn't do anything of the sort,' said the doctor. 'You'd have to tell the nuns.'

'I would *not* tell the nuns,' said the Bishop with renewed irascibility. 'You don't know nuns the way I know them. I wouldn't tell a nun anything.'

'They'd have to know you were a clergyman.'

'Ah, a clergyman in this country can have no privacy,' the Bishop said, becoming weaker and more fretful. 'The first thing they'd want to know is what diocese I was from, and then they'd have a nun or a nurse checking up on me. I'm in a most unfortunate position. What sort is the Reverend Mother in that place?'

'Ah, she's a nice homely sort.'

'Never mind how homely she is. Where is she from?'

'I never asked her.'

The Bishop was so upset by this that it took him a full minute to collect his thoughts. He was astonished that a professional man wouldn't inquire about a thing like that, and wondered if the young doctor was quite as good as he was supposed to be.

'Send her over here to talk to me,' he said. 'I see I'll have to make my own arrangements.'

'Do you know, my Lord, you're a very obstinate old man,' said the doctor with a grin.

'That's what has me where I am,' the Bishop replied ambiguously. He never minded being told he was obstinate or even pig-headed because it showed he was making the right impression.

Ten minutes later the doctor returned with Reverend Mother and left her alone with the Bishop. She was an elderly, soft-mannered, gigglesome woman who almost smothered the Bishop with solicitude. Knowing it was only her stock-in-trade, he let her moan on, and then rested his good hand lightly on hers. From the gentleness of his face, you might have thought he had become reconciled to his fate, but that was only the Bishop's stock-in-trade as well – his manner for hysterical females.

'The doctor is a bright young man, Mother,' he said earnestly, 'but I don't find him easy to talk to. Laymen can never understand the difficulties of people in religion. The reason is that every calling has its own graces and its own temptations. Now, the great temptation of religious people is vanity.'

'I wonder, my Lord,' she said coyly.

'You needn't,' the Bishop said firmly. 'That's what makes it so hard for people in religion to be growing old. You're a young woman yet,' he continued with brazen flattery, 'so you mightn't know. Tell me, where are you from?'

'Mayo, my Lord,' she said. 'Mayo, God help us!'

'Are you from Mayo?' the Bishop asked with a sinking heart. He did not trust nuns, and he did not trust Mayo people. 'But as I was saying, your turn will come. You'll see the young people pushing you out to make way for themselves, watching and criticizing, waiting for you to make a slip.'

'Ah, you needn't tell me, my Lord,' she said in a wail. 'I saw it already.'

'Ah, you're an observant young woman,' the Bishop said ingenuously. 'Now, Mother, this is something I wouldn't like to admit to a lay person, but I know you'll understand. I have a coadjutor and we don't get on – I know this won't go any further. He thinks I'm not able to look after myself. If it got round that I had an accident, he'd be saying I wasn't fit to make decisions on my own. Now, you must have had cases like that before.'

'My Lord,' she said in mock-girlish alarm, 'I don't think you know what you're asking.'

'In fact, if I'm not mistaken, 'tisn't so long since you had a certain member of the Government in your place.'

'Well, of course, we always have special patients.'

'They called it pneumonia, I believe,' the Bishop said gravely. 'However, it was greatly appreciated in government circles.'

'Ah, 'tisn't alike, my Lord,' she said anxiously. 'A Minister is one thing but a Bishop – how could I?'

'There is nothing an intelligent woman can't do if she puts her mind to it, Mother,' he said.

'No, nor anything an inquisitive woman can't find out if she puts her mind to it, my Lord,' she replied wryly.

That evening, the Bishop was comfortably settled in a room corridors away from the rest of the building with two old nuns to guard him. The old nuns had long ceased to be active: Sister Dympna was crippled with the rheumatics and Sister Martha was slightly gone in the head, but they rejoiced in their new responsibility, exulted in the fact that at last somebody reliable was needed, and revenged themselves on those who had slighted them by silence and cunning.

The Bishop was in great pain, but even this did not take from his feeling of triumph. The curate was upstairs, probably lying awake and marvelling at the Bishop's sturdy health while unknown to him, the Bishop was lying awake, helpless as himself but knowing something he didn't know. The essence of authority consists in keeping your secrets.

But after a few days even the Bishop became aware of the fury of curiosity his secret roused. Reverend Mother was the only nun permitted to visit him and nurses were not allowed in his room at all. But the trouble with the Bishop's gallant old watch-dogs was that they had lost their teeth. They were easy game for the younger nuns and nurses, because Sister Dympna's bad legs and Sister Martha's bad head meant that once they left the room there was no guarantee that they would ever get back. On the third day the door opened suddenly and a middle-aged scraggy nurse came in and looked at him in apparent astonishment.

'I'm sorry,' she said. 'I must be in the wrong room. Are you Mr Murphy?'

Now, if there was one thing the Bishop could not stand it was inquisitiveness. He was an inquisitive man himself, so he understood the vice in all its manifestations.

'No, I'm Mr Dempsey,' he said. 'Who are you?'

'My name is Fitzpatrick,' she said smoothly, and he knew as if God had revealed it to him that it wasn't. 'You wouldn't be one of the Dempseys from Limerick?'

'No. My family came from Kanturk,' he said curtly.

'We had a nurse one time from Kanturk,' she said, screwing up her eyes. 'Lucey, her name was. You wouldn't know her?'

'She must be from another part of Kanturk,' said the Bishop.

'I dare say,' she said, realizing she had met her match. 'What happened you anyway?'

For a moment the Bishop was so mad that he nearly asked her if she knew who she was talking to. Then he recollected that she probably didn't.

'A fall I got off my bicycle,' he said, glaring at her.

'At your age!' she said with a sweet smile. 'I'm astonished at you.'

She left him in a state of blind rage. Never, never, since the time he was a boy had anybody spoken to him in that coarse familiar way. Then he broke into a chuckle. As a young priest he had noticed how conversation changed when he entered a room, and wondered how people really behaved when there wasn't a priest around. Now, in his old age, he had discovered. 'The religious life is too sheltered,' he thought. 'Too much play-acting about it. "Father, what do you think of this?" and "Father, what would you say to that?" No wonder the Jesuits were supposed to have spies to report on what people said. No wonder at all they had the reputation of being so clever. He waited impatiently for the nurse to come back.

Instead, there came a young and good-looking nurse who didn't even pretend to have strayed in by accident. She gave him a guilty look and then shrugged and smiled, but all the time her small, keen, beautiful eyes wandered about the room, searching for a clue.

'They say you were in America,' she burst out without preliminaries.

'What makes them think that, girl?' the Bishop asked good-humouredly.

'How would I know?' she replied with another shrug. 'I suppose because you don't seem to have a family.'

'Well, I'll tell you the truth,' said the Bishop slyly. 'I haven't. I was never what you'd call a marrying man.'

'Why would you?' she asked. 'I suppose you can get them without.'

The Bishop was so stunned that he almost gave himself away again. He stared at the nurse, but her charming little face still remained vague and sweet and innocent.

'Isn't that a shocking thing for a girl like you to say?' he asked.

'What's shocking about it?' she asked lightly. 'I suppose you didn't do without them. I'd know a queer a mile off.'

This left the Bishop very thoughtful indeed. Even in a long life there were apparently many things that had escaped his eye. He shook his head over it. 'Too sheltered,' he muttered again to himself. 'Too blooming sheltered. We don't know the half that's going on. We might as well have blinkers.'

What really surprised him was that he was becoming quite

attached to his own anonymity, and grew quite hopeful when he heard a woman's step outside his door. He felt a match for any of them now. When the first nurse came back and told him a dirty story, he guessed at once that it was to test some new theory of his identity and let on to be very amused by it, though he had never realized that women knew dirty stories. 'We live and learn,' he thought. 'I don't know do even the Jesuits know the whole thing.'

It took the Bishop the whole of ten days to recover from his fractures, but it was a great day for him when he left the hospital by the back door. The two old nuns knelt for his blessing, and wept because they would again be regarded as old and useless. The curate was still upstairs.

'I suppose you'll go straight to the hotel?' said the doctor.

'I'll do nothing of the sort,' said the Bishop, whose only plan was to put a couple of hundred miles between himself and the hospital before they found anything else wrong with him.

'You're a very lucky man,' said the doctor. 'I can tell you now I was sure you were for the long road. I have a patient of twenty-two that the same thing happened to, and he'll never walk again. I can't even keep you quiet.'

'Ah, poor fellow! poor fellow!' the Bishop said perfunctorily. 'I suppose he hadn't the stamina.'

The Bishop was like a boy. He had always been a great student, and never before had he noticed how beautiful was the road back to Moyle. Illness, he thought, was a great thing, because it made you see more of life. For the future he must meet more laymen, and not laymen like the old crawthumpers who were always round the palace, but broadminded people he could describe his adventures to.

It was something of a disappointment to him when he got home to find a large crowd waiting for him outside the gate of the palace. When the car stopped they began to cheer, and Jerry Cronin, on behalf of the County Council, stepped forward shyly to congratulate him on his recovery. Then they all dropped on their knees and the Bishop gave them his blessing.

'Tell me what's all this about, Jerry,' he said, propelling Cronin to the car. It didn't occur to the Bishop that in a small town the presence of two bishops is nearly as good as a boxing match.

'Ah, well, you know, people were very upset when they heard of the accident, my Lord,' said Jerry.

'And I suppose they knew all about it inside twenty-four hours?' the Bishop asked with a glare.

'Oh, sooner than that, my Lord, sooner than that,' said Jerry.

'Nuns, nuns, nuns!' said the Bishop petulantly. 'Take a fool's advice, Jerry, and never trust a nun. And whatever else you do, never trust anybody from Mayo.'

*More Stories* (1954)

# A BRIEF FOR OEDIPUS

To watch a law case between husband and wife is like watching a performance of Oedipus. You know that, whatever happens, the man has no chance, because every judge has a mother fixation and any lawyer would as soon take a brief for Oedipus.

It has been said that the nearest a man ever got to averting the Furies was the day Micky Joe Spillane defended a countryman called Lynam whose wife was suing for legal separation on the usual grounds of cruelty and adultery. Separation was all she could get, and, indeed, all she wanted; and even this she could not get without proving cruelty, which, in the present-day decline of manliness, is not as easy as it sounds.

Mrs Lynam at least had no trouble about that. The adultery was admitted, if not actually gloried in, and all that was needed to prove the cruelty was to put the Respondent in the box. He was a big, good-looking man with a stiff, morose manner – one of those Irish countrymen who are deceptively gentle, who are so generous that they will give you the shirt off their back, and will then knock you unconscious over some trifling remark about politics.

His wife was a trim, mousy little woman of about half his height and a quarter his weight, with an anxious face and a gentle, bedraggled, virginal air. She was pathetically anxious to make a good impression: she cocked her little head as she listened to her counsel's questions, as though they were in French, and replied to them in something like the same way, raising her colourless little voice and illustrating her answers with vague, half-completed gestures.

You could see that O'Meara, the judge, adored her. 'Come over here where we can hear you, ma'am,' he said, pointing to a seat beside him on the bench. Poor O'Meara was a bad case: he had blood pressure as well as a mother fixation.

Once or twice as she gave her evidence she glanced forgivingly at her husband who only stared back with a gloomy hatred that was awe-inspiring. Most men are embarrassed, hearing what they are supposed to have done to their wives, but Lynam paid attention to nobody, and just watched his wife as if he were wondering why the blazes he hadn't taken a hatchet and finished the job while he was at it.

'And what did he do then?' asked her counsel, Kenefick, having gone through the demolition of the house, chair by chair and cup by cup.

'He called me – do I have to repeat it, my lord?'

'Ah, not at all, ma'am, not at all,' he said encouragingly. 'Write it down.'

The clerk gave her pencil and paper. Mrs Lynam wrote as she talked, slowly and carefully, raising her eyes to the ceiling. Then she handed the paper to the clerk, who passed it to O'Meara. O'Meara glanced at it expressionlessly and passed it down to counsel. Tom Lynam, black with rage, whispered something to his solicitor, Quill, but Quill only shook his head. He had never liked the case from the first day, and if he had had his way, would have settled it out of court. He had allowed himself to be over-persuaded by his truculent client and by his counsel, Mickie Joe, who had got into a tantrum and said it was a scandalous case and should be fought in the public interest. Public interest, indeed! Quill felt it was his own fault for briefing an unstable man like Mickie Joe.

'And did he say anything else?' Kenefick murmured sympathetically.

'Only if I didn't get out of the house in five minutes, sir, that he'd do to me what the Jews did to Jesus.'

'What the Jews did to who?' O'Meara asked incredulously.

'Jesus, my lord,' she repeated, bowing reverently for the second time. 'Our Blessed Lord, my lord. Crucify me he meant.'

'Huh!' snorted O'Meara, his blood pressure going up. Adultery and cruelty were bad enough, but when you had blasphemy thrown in Ireland was certainly going to the dogs.

'Now tell my lord what happened then,' prompted Kenefick, scaling up the sympathy to the degree of emotion the judge seemed to require.

'So then I told him I could not go out of the house at that hour and the state I was in,' Mrs Lynam continued with growing animation. 'And with that, he dragged me off the sofa and twisted my wrist behind my back.' ('Wrist' and 'back' she illustrated by another feeble gesture that she did not complete.)

'And this was at a time when you were seriously ill?'

'I was at death's door, sir,' she said candidly. 'The whole day I wasn't able to get up off the sofa even to feed the children. That was what he had against me the whole time,' she said, shaking her little head vivaciously. 'Shamming, he said I was.'

'And then what happened?' Kenefick asked, yearning over her.

'He kicked me right out the front door, sir,' she replied, raising her hands as though to avert the crash. 'I fell on the path on my hands and knees. Tommy – that's our little boy – ran out and began to cry, and my husband said for him to get to bed quick or he'd do the same to him.'

'And your little boy is – how old?' Kenefick asked with a positive tremolo in his voice.

'Five, sir, the fourteenth of February.'

'And did your husband make any effort to see if you were injured by the fall?'

'Why, then, indeed, he did not, sir,' she replied with a smile that was like a rainbow – an optical illusion between two downpours. 'Only to give me another kick into the flower bed. Then he made use of a filthy expression and banged the door behind him.'

'And those were the marks that you showed next day to Dr O'Mahoney?'

'They were, sir. The very same. A week he made me stop in bed, with my back.'

After this, it was scarcely necessary to emphasize her husband's bad behaviour with Nora Magee, a woman of notorious bad character, for in fact, she had had a child by him, he had been seen minding it, and rumour in the town held that Nora had never had it so good.

'And did you have any conversation with your husband about this woman?' Kenefick asked gravely.

'A dozen times, sir,' she replied. 'I asked him a dozen times, practically on my bended knees, to give her up, for the children's sake if not for mine.'

'And what was his reply?'

'His reply, sir, was that the child was a Lynam, and he wouldn't give up one Lynam for all the Hanafeys that were ever pupped ... Hanafey is my maiden name,' she added. 'He meant the children took after me.'

At this Kenefick sat down, looking old and broken, and Mickie Joe got up. Now, the best day he ever was, Mickie Joe was no great shakes as a lawyer. He had begun life as a schoolmaster and given it up for the law. He really loved the art of oratory, and would sit with a childish expression of delight, listening to a good sermon or a good speech or a good summing up, but his own voice was like a train-whistle, and the only effect he had on an audience was to make it laugh. If it laughed too much, he would stop and scold it, which only brought more laughter.

He had a tendency to identify himself with his client, a thing no real lawyer will do. A client is a fact, and a true lawyer hates facts. He is an artist – a dramatist and actor –

whose job it is to make little dramas out of the sordid and trivial material his clients provide. The one thing he hates is to be reminded by the characters themselves of what the real story is. Mickie Joe had very little of the artist in him, and as a result, had a tendency to get rattled when his client got the worst of a case and start barging his opponent like an old market-woman.

Kenefick had obviously told Mrs Lynam not to be afraid of him and she wasn't. She clutched the arms of her chair, raised herself in it as if in anxiety to give the best that was in her and answered patiently and quietly. Yes, sir, she had been educated in a convent. Yes, indeed, she was a very old friend of Sister Dominic. *And* of Father O'Regan, the parish priest. Yes, she had asked their advice before beginning proceedings because it was a thing she would not take on herself. Yes, she was a member of the Women's Sodality and the Children of Mary as well as the St Vincent de Paul. Kenefick looked up doubtfully at Mickie Joe, wondering where the hell he was going from that, unless it was to prove that Mrs Lynam was a saint as well as a martyr.

Kenefick saw soon enough and it startled him even more.

'And when you went to the Women's Sodality, who got your husband's supper?' Mickie Joe asked in a wailing voice.

'Ah, well, sometimes he got it for himself.'

'And the children's supper as well?'

'He might get that, too, of an odd time.'

'And when you were at Mass, I dare say he got his own breakfast?'

'Unless he waited till I got in.'

'But you always got it for him when you came in?'

'Always, except when I wasn't able.'

'And I take it, Mrs Lynam, you weren't always able?'

'Well, no, I wasn't,' she admitted candidly. 'Not always.'

She still didn't take him seriously or realize her danger, but she was the only one who didn't. Breakfast, after all, is a serious matter.

'You were able to go to Mass, but you were not able to get your husband's breakfast?' asked Mickie Joe. 'Is that what you're telling my lord?'

'I often went to Mass when I wasn't able either,' she replied with a noble pathos that would have silenced anyone else but Mickie Joe. He was still hot on the trail of the missing breakfast.

'You went to Mass when you weren't able, but you didn't get your husband's breakfast when you weren't able?' he asked in his shrill monotonous voice. 'Is that what you mean?'

'I think I should explain that,' she said, looking nervously at the judge. 'I'm rather delicate, of course. I have a pain in my back. I hurted it years ago in a fall I got on the ice. Doctor O'Mahoney treated me.'

This was a really dangerous admission which any other counsel would have been after like a greyhound, but Mickie Joe didn't even seem to realize that it had been made. By this time he was getting furious.

'And you suffer from headaches, too, I suppose?' he went on.

'I do, sir,' she replied, with one small hand sketching a gesture at her stomach. 'Bilious.'

But O'Meara was tired of Mickie Joe. He liked his breakfast as well as the next, but for a judge with a mother fixation to listen to the poor victim being badgered like that was too much.

'Really, Mr Spillane,' he asked in a distant voice, 'do we have to go into the lady's bilious headaches?'

But for once Mickie Joe did not give way. He looked reprovingly at O'Meara over his pince-nez and his voice went off into an unearthly wail.

'My lord, if the Petitioner is presented to the court as something out of a medical museum, I can hardly say much more.'

'Oh, go on, Mr Spillane, go on!' O'Meara said. All the same he blushed. It was beginning to dawn even on him that you couldn't always treat Mickie Joe as a figure of fun. He did not quite know why. It never occurred to him that the one man who can stand up to a mother fixation in fair fight is a woman hater.

And, in a curious way, Mickie Joe's passion was beginning

to affect the general view. It wasn't only that you couldn't any longer afford to bully or patronize him. A picture was beginning to emerge of a woman who was not only useless but was at the same time bold, ruthless and designing.

The court had begun to fill as it usually does when a case grows interesting, and Lynam himself seemed to pluck up courage. Instead of glowering at his wife, he looked back defiantly at the court as though to see whether anyone now believed the lies that had been told. A tall, bald man at the back gave him an encouraging wave and Lynam returned the salute austerely.

'Did you and your husband go out together much, Mrs Lynam?' Mickie Joe asked, changing his tack abruptly.

'Well, you can't do much with two children, can you, sir?' she asked with soft reproach.

'That depends, ma'am,' he said with a wintry smile. 'Don't other people do it?'

'I dare say they have servants,' she said nervously.

'You don't mean that people in the humbler walks of life have no friends, do you, ma'am?' he asked.

'Or neighbours, of course,' she added, filling out her original reply.

'I'm glad you thought of the neighbours,' he said. 'I was coming to them.'

'But you can't always be asking them for favours, can you?' she said.

'When you quarrelled with your husband, ma'am, didn't *you* go to the neighbours?'

'Sure, when I was crippled with the kicks he gave me!'

'But you couldn't ask them to mind the children when he wanted to go out and enjoy himself?'

'Ah, 'tisn't alike,' she said, showing irritation for the first time.

'No, ma'am, it isn't,' he agreed. 'How old did you say the little girl was?'

'Ten.'

'And you mean to say a girl of ten couldn't look after her brother for a couple of hours?'

'Well, I can explain that,' she said hastily. 'You see, they don't get on – you know the way it is between girls and boys – and you wouldn't like to leave her alone with him.'

'Do you mean she'd beat him?'

'Well, she mightn't *beat* him exactly,' Mrs Lynam replied nervously, 'but she might be tormenting him.'

'Mrs Lynam,' he asked severely, 'isn't it true that those children of yours are utterly ruined?'

'Ruined?' she cried indignantly, starting up with an outraged glance. 'Certainly not. I never heard such a thing!'

'On your oath, ma'am, wasn't that what your husband meant when he said they weren't Lynams at all?'

'How could he?' she asked. 'There isn't a word of truth in it.'

But Lynam looked at Mickie Joe with such an expression of astonishment that everyone knew there was. Mickie Joe knew it too, and for the first time a prim, watery smile of satisfaction played on his thin, old-maidish mouth.

'Did many of your husband's friends visit you?'

'Some of them, yes,' Mrs Lynam replied anxiously, trying to grasp the drift of the question. She was afraid of him now, all right.

'He had a lot of friends when he married you?'

Kenefick rose with an air of deep distress to say his learned friend was straying from the point, but even O'Meara realized that straying was the one thing Mickie Joe was not doing.

'Answer the question, ma'am.'

'He had – of a kind.'

'Of the wrong kind, you mean?'

'Well, not my kind.' It was not exactly a tactful answer.

'He was what you'd call a popular man?'

'Well, he was an athletic sort of man. I don't know you would call him popular exactly.'

'And at the time of this unfortunate break-up, how many of them were still coming to the house?'

Mrs Lynam's eye sought out the tall bald man at the back of the court and confirmed an impression that he might have a story to tell.

'Well, I'm sure I couldn't say,' she replied doubtfully. 'Mr

Malone was at the house two or three nights a week.' You could almost hear the note of grievance in her voice.

'And what happened the rest?'

'I'm sure *I* couldn't say, sir.'

'They just stopped coming, and you never once asked your husband "What's wrong with Joe or Pat or Willie?"'

'No. What business was it of mine?'

'I'm asking the questions, Mrs Lynam. You never gave them reason?'

'Never,' she replied earnestly.

'Never let them see that they weren't your – kind, as you call it?'

'Certainly not,' she replied self-righteously. 'I hope I always behaved like a lady.'

'And I dare say,' Mickie Joe drawled with the first really pleasant smile he had shown that day, 'when this last remaining friend – this Last Rose of Summer left blooming alone – came to bring your husband out, it sometimes happened that they couldn't go?'

'Well, I explained about my back,' she said, sketching another gesture behind her.

'You did, ma'am, fully,' Mickie Joe agreed with a wicked chuckle. 'We're better acquainted with your back now than we are with any other part of you.'

The bald man at the back was having the time of his life. It was his day as much as Mickie Joe's. He smiled and nodded amiably at the judge, the clerk and even the pressman. The Last Rose of Summer – a shy, neighbourly man – was clearly delighted that at last someone was getting down to business. Lynam, who had been staring in surprise at Mickie Joe, whispered something to his solicitor, but Quill only shook his head and frowned. As producer of the show, Quill was beginning to be impressed by the performance of his great new star, and, like any other theatre man, had no time to spare for the author's views.

'Tell me, ma'am,' Mickie Joe asked keenly, 'when did you last have relations with your husband?'

'When did I what, sir?' she asked in a baby voice, putting her finger to her mouth.

'When did you last go to bed with him with a view to matrimony?' Mickie Joe translated boisterously.

'Oh, I forgot to mention that,' she said hastily. 'He has a room of his own, of course.'

'Oh, has he?' Mickie Joe asked with a new light in his eye. 'But that wasn't the question I asked you. I asked how long it was since you had relations with him.'

'Well, with my back . . .' she began pathetically, and suddenly Mickie Joe interrupted her with a positive squeal of rage.

'Ah, give your back a rest, ma'am!' he cried, growing purple. 'Give your back a rest! It isn't your back we're discussing now. How long is it, I say.'

'Oh, I suppose a couple of years,' she replied doubtfully, and he pounced on her.

'Two years?'

'Two or three.'

'Or four?'

'I don't think 'twas as long as that,' she said wonderingly. 'What difference does it make?'

'Only the difference between a human being and a monster, ma'am,' he said. 'So in those impassioned scenes in which you begged your husband, "almost on your bended knees", to come back to you, you didn't want him to come back? And when he was at Mrs Magee's, looking after his child, he was in the only decent home he ever had?'

Mickie Joe, of course, had made his usual mistake and lost all restraint. At once, Kenefick was on his feet, protesting, and O'Meara rebuked Mickie Joe, who stood there humbly with his head down, thanked O'Meara for the rebuke, and went on just the same.

'Would it be true to say that you don't think much of marriage, ma'am?'

'Oh, I wouldn't say that,' she replied almost patronizingly. 'The Church of course takes a rather high view of it.'

'I was asking about you, ma'am, not the Church,' Mickie Joe said icily. 'The Church is quite capable of speaking for itself. But weren't you always grousing to Sister Dominic about married life?'

'I went to her for advice,' Mrs Lynam said anxiously, clearly wondering whether Mickie Joe was guessing or Sister Dominic gossiping.

'And to Father O'Regan when you were trying to turn him against your unfortunate decent husband?'

'I never tried to turn Father O'Regan against him,' she cried. 'Never! All I asked Father O'Regan to do was to talk to him and tell him to be more natural.'

'Natural?' repeated Mickie Joe bitterly. 'Four years sleeping in a room by himself? Is that what you call natural?'

'Natural, reasonable – call it what you like. Ah, now, Mr Spillane,' she went on angrily, ' 'tis all very well for you to be talking. That sort of thing may do all right for young people that don't know better, but for people of our age, 'tis disgusting. Positively disgusting!'

She had said too much. Even she knew that, though she didn't know how much damage she had done herself. A judge with a mother fixation may overlook the prospect of having to get his own breakfast but not that of four years in the spare room. There is a limit to human endurance. Even the policemen at the back of the court who had wives of cast iron were looking disapprovingly at the gentle, insinuating little woman who had revealed herself as a grey, grim, discontented monster with notions above her station.

When the court adjourned Mickie Joe had not done with her though he could well have left his case there. She was probably the only one who didn't yet know that she had lost, but even she was badly shaken. She grabbed her handbag and waddled quickly out. To everyone's astonishment, Tom Lynam hurried after her. Kenefick made an alarmed face at Mickie Joe who went after Lynam as fast as he could. Neither he nor Quill wanted to see their client finish off the job in the hall.

But when they got out Lynam was talking to her in a low voice. She was half turned away from him as though interrupted in flight. At last he came over to Mickie Joe and Quill.

'She wants to settle this,' he muttered apologetically, blushing and stammering.

'I'm damn full sure she does,' said Quill. 'Tell her there's nothing to settle.'

'I know that, Mr Quill,' said Lynam gloomily. 'I know you and Mr Spillane did your best for me. But I wouldn't like her to have to answer any more questions. She thinks I made them up. Sure, I never told Mr Spillane half the things he said.'

'You mean you're going to go back and live with that woman?' Mickie Joe asked with cold anger.

'That's what she wants, sir,' said Lynam.

'And do you know that in forty-eight hours she'll be making your life a hell again?'

'She says she'll try to do better the next time,' Lynam said, staring at him.

'Is it a woman that five minutes ago was perjuring herself black in the face only to destroy you?' Mickie Joe asked savagely. 'How could you believe daylight from a woman like that? And next time she gets you here you won't be so lucky.'

'She says she won't go to court again,' Lynam said, scowling.

'And when she does, she needn't be afraid of me,' Mickie Joe said shrilly. 'You can find someone else to represent you. A man is only wasting his time trying to save people like you. It is like trying to keep a lunatic from suicide.'

'Nor I wouldn't have you again,' Lynam shouted, flaring up. 'Nor I wouldn't have had you today if I knew what you were going to do. I don't know who your spies were but they were no friends of mine, and for the future I'll see you keep your tongue off my wife.'

He was flushed and incoherent, and Quill realized again that he was an ugly customer to cross. But Mickie Joe was good enough for him.

'Fitter for you to make her keep her tongue off yourself,' he hissed. 'You would if you were man enough.'

'Mickie! Mickie!' said Quill, pulling his arm.

'What's that you said? I'll show you whether I'm man enough or not.'

'Come on, man, come on!' Quill said in alarm.

But all that evening Mickie Joe was in a terrible humour. He knew now that he would never see justice done to a husband in a court of law. You might as well hold a brief for Oedipus against the Fates.

*More Stories* (1954)

# FATHER AND SON

There were times when Dan felt Mildred's English superficiality as a sort of judgement. Flurry (short for Florence, a great name among men of the MacCarthy family) was their child. Bawn and Tim were Dan's children by his first wife. Mildred had made an excellent stepmother. Girls, even small ones, soon get to know whether they have the right accent and the right frock, and, as Mildred knew everything about accents and frocks, Bawn and she got on fine. Boys are different. Boys don't care about frocks. Tim was older than Bawn: he stole, he told lies, and, to show his contempt for Mildred, hacked his way through the house in his heaviest boots, speaking in a common Cockney accent. Mildred had been very patient with him, explaining everything, affecting nothing and boxing his ears when he cheeked her. But it hadn't worked. One day he kicked her savagely. Mildred, a woman of great spirit and resource, had kicked him back, but Dan, mad with rage, had decided he must go to boarding school. Mildred, who had been to a boarding school herself, thought that this was really taking things too far.

'Oh, Danny, you do make an awful fuss about things,' she sighed in her weary, well-bred way. 'Anyway, it's nothing to the kick I gave him. He'll be sore for weeks, the poor little bugger.'

In spite of her words Dan knew she was as conventional as they came; it went with the accent and the frocks, and it suited him fine, but, he knew that though they got on better than most husbands and wives, she still had the guilty feeling that he was Min's husband, not hers, Tim's father, not Flurry's.

During the holidays, Min wrote to say that she would like to see the kids again before they grew out of her knowledge and asked Dan to find her a room for the weekend in some pub nearby. As he read the letter he was full of foreboding. It was as though he were being haunted by the ghost of his first marriage.

'Something wrong?' Mildred asked when the childre... had left the dining room.

'Only Min wanting to come for the weekend,' he said expressionlessly.

'Well, there's nothing wrong with that, is there?'

'Only that it may prove a little awkward. She wants us to get her a room.'

'Why on earth doesn't she stay here? There's heaps of room ... Or do you think she might be embarrassed?' she asked, seeing his face.

'I wasn't thinking of her,' he replied coldly.

'Then why don't I take Flurry to Helen's for the weekend and let you have the house to yourselves?' she asked reasonably.

'Can you ever think sensibly for five minutes?' he asked angrily.

'Really, ducky,' she sighed in that maddening, superficial way of hers, 'you do make a crisis out of everything.'

'Let's put it the other way round,' he said sternly. 'Suppose you'd been married instead of me, and your first attempt came here to see the kids, would you have liked my going off with Flurry and leaving you here with him?'

This reversal of parts was a favourite device of Dan's, guaranteed, according to him, to produce a really objective estimate of any situation, though it never seemed to work with Mildred. Her long, bony, aristocratic face took on its usual smooth smile.

'Really, Dan, one of these days you'll end up like a fly, walking upside down on the ceiling.'

'Never mind about me,' he said curtly. 'Isn't it true?'

'Then in that case I can go to Helen's with an easy mind,'

she said blandly. 'What have I said wrong now, ducky?' she asked when she saw his scowl.

'Never mind,' he said. 'You wouldn't understand.'

And she wouldn't. It was no use telling Mildred that nothing in the world was so over as a marriage that was over. It was not until she was leaving with Flurry for Helen's that she really realized how depressed he was.

'Maybe I shouldn't go,' she said.

'It's a bit late to change your mind now,' he said, rubbing it in.

'Danny, don't let Min upset you!' she begged. 'I'm a silly bitch, but you knew that when you married me. And I'm not going to get more sensible with age.'

He made a suitable gloomy reply, and later set off down the road to meet Min's train. He knew it was all going to be desperately unpleasant.

In fact, it proved the opposite. Min came out of the little suburban train, holding out her arms to him as though she had only been away for a holiday. She was older and fatter, and he thought she had a shade too much make-up on, but she was as lively and natural as ever. Within five minutes they were sitting in the bar opposite the station, chattering away like the old cronies they were. They had so much to talk about; there were so many of the old neighbours who had died or married or had families. When they got out of the bus and Min saw the big house, with Bawn peering anxiously out the front door for them, she pretended to change her mind.

'Is this Mildred's house?' she asked. 'My God, I feel like the new maid!'

Bawn came running up the path and Min gave her a great hug.

'Child of grace!' she cried. 'Where did you get the looks from? Not from your father?'

Tim appeared, a bit red and a fraction of a second off the beat, and Dan could have murdered him. He had a heavy, sullen, angry face, though he did warm up a little when he saw Min.

'Oh, Tim,' she cried, 'you've grown such a great big man!'

Dan and she got the supper together. She was all lit up, and it wasn't only the effect of the children and himself. It was plain inquisitiveness as well. She poked her nose shamelessly into cupboards and rooms, commenting loudly on the taste and utility of everything. Dan suddenly felt curiously guilty at having put her to sleep in the spare room. He could hardly have put her anywhere else, because there wasn't room for another bed in Bawn's little den, but with all of them together, it seemed uncouth, as if he were emphasizing a gap that was already only too plain.

It wasn't that she attracted him any more but that he could not erect artificial barriers between himself and someone who at any moment could let drop a remark that brought back all their past life together. Her remarks about the neighbours had already reminded him of Tim's infant crush on the tall girl next door who used to advise him about the garden. Those two nice sisters and their kindly old mother – how could he have forgotten them so completely?

The telephone rang and Dan answered it. It was a long distance call, and he was sure it must be Mildred, reassuring herself about him. Instead, it turned out to be a man, who apparently wanted to reassure himself about Min, and he found himself raging against Mildred – and the man. Then he grinned, amused at his own touchiness.

Min returned from the hall, red and laughing, obviously delighted at having been rung up and embarrassed at having to explain it.

'Just a friend giving me a tip for the big race tomorrow,' she said modestly.

'Oh, still keen on the horses!' said Dan. The horses had been one of the things they disagreed on. He was a prudent and censorious man, and Min had far too much wildness in her for his taste.

He felt a bit of a fool when he went to her room to show her how the electric fire worked. She did one of her sly school-girl acts, joining her hands behind her back and raising herself on her toes. She felt none of his awkwardness and was getting great fun out of his embarrassment. At last, she made him laugh too and he threw a cushion at her.

'Ah, don't stop, Dan,' she said. 'Mildred's made a proper toff out of you.'

She went to the kitchen and made another pot of tea, and they sat over the electric fire till late into the night, discussing the children.

'Of course, Bawn is lovely,' she said thoughtfully. 'Anybody would get on with Bawn.'

'Ah, Tim is all right too,' Dan said defensively. 'It's just that he's so moody. That's why I sent him to school. Not that it seems to have done him much good.'

'I fancy there are times when Tim hates the whole damn lot of us,' Min said. 'He's more sensitive than Bawn, really.'

'Don't let me disillusion you,' he said and kissed her goodnight.

'Goodnight, love,' she said, and gave him a warm embrace in which there was no mockery. After it he found himself very wakeful. He was all churned up inside, going over his own conduct and Min's and getting so heated over it that he felt like going downstairs and having it all out with her again. Then he wondered if she wasn't feeling the same. For a few moments he even fancied he heard her crying.

Crying in a sleeping house had always been a peculiar horror to him. He imagined he heard it even when there was nothing to hear but the wind. It was like no one you knew crying about anything you could understand. It was more like the whole world crying in its sleep. A couple of times this weakness had got him into extraordinary situations, even to holding the hand of a drunken old woman in a boarding house while she complained of her daughter-in-law. Faces you saw in the street or about the house rarely told you anything; it was only faces that you scarcely saw at all that told the truth.

Now, in his cautious way he got up and stood on the landing for several minutes listening. Either the crying had ceased or he had been imagining it. All the same, he tiptoed down the stairs and listend at Min's door till he heard her breathing evenly.

Next morning, when he returned from a brief visit to the

office, Bawn beckoned him into the kitchen.

'Daddy, I wish you'd talk to Tim about the way he's carrying on,' she said.

'Why? What's Tim up to now?' he asked with no great interest. As a small child Bawn had made quite an art of getting Tim into trouble and she hadn't altogether got over it yet.

'He won't even make an effort to be nice to Mummy,' she said angrily. 'I'll fling something at him if he goes on. He just sits there with his book and his disapproving air as if Mummy were the Penitent Thief or the Prodigal Son or something.'

'It's probably only strangeness, you know,' Dan said defensively.

'You can call it that,' snapped Bawn. 'I call it plain snobbery. Mum isn't good enough for him now. And the trouble is, she cares more about that fellow's big toe than about my whole body.'

Dan reflected for a moment on the remarkable understanding that girls showed of their mothers, and wondered whether this wasn't the reason that their mothers usually appreciated them so little.

'If I catch him at it, I'll knock the snobbery out of him,' said Dan. 'Where is Mummy?'

'In your room, dolling herself up,' Bawn replied guiltily. 'You can't even see your face in that old bathroom mirror.'

Dan gave a snort of amusement. It was plain that whatever grief Tim had caused them, Min and Bawn had been having a heavenly time, trying on Mildred's dresses. However differently they might feel about her personality, they were at one when it came to her frocks.

'By the way, did Mummy tell you her friend had bought a new house?' Bawn asked, trying hastily to divert him.

'Which friend?' asked Dan cautiously.

'The lady who rang her up last night.'

'Oh, the *elderly* lady,' said Dan, amused at Min's access of modesty and relieved that there were limits even to Bawn's understanding of her. 'Yes, I believe she goes in for house property.'

But he also realized that Bawn had not been making it up about Tim. At lunch he was sulky, silent, superior, scowling at them all from under heavy brows.

When Min asked him when they got up at school he corrected her bluntly.

'We rise at seven,' he said. 'We retire at nine thirty,' he added.

'And when do you go to bed?' asked Dan.

'At nine thirty,' he said. 'I told you.'

Bawn handled it magnificently in a way that, Dan knew, would have really endeared her to Mildred. A high-spirited, working-class, Irish girl in a snobbish English school, she had a hard time of it, but she made it sound so funny that Dan and Min both laughed outright. The attention they paid her seemed to irritate Tim.

'It's entirely your own fault if they treat you like that,' he said in his deep authoritative voice.

'How is it Bawn's fault, Tim?' Dan asked, trying to keep the rancour out of his tone.

'She behaves exactly like the Stuarts,' said Tim. 'She treats other girls as the Stuarts treated their parliaments.'

'I'd sooner be Charles II than your old Cromwell anyway,' Bawn said.

'I was not defending Cromwell,' said Tim.

'And how do you manage, Tim?' asked Dan.

'I model my conduct on Queen Elizabeth,' Tim said solemnly.

'And if Queen Elizabeth had the girls in our school to handle, she mighn't be such a model either,' spluttered Bawn.

That evening they all went to the pictures and had tea in the kitchen when they got home. Having had one restless night Dan went straight to bed. This was a bad mistake, as he discovered when he tried to sleep. He put the light on again and began to read. Then he thought he heard a noise downstairs and opened the bedroom door. This time there could be no mistake about it. He could distinctly hear the weeping. He went straight downstairs to Min's room. He would have done the same if Mildred had been there. All he wanted was to take that stupid, pig-headed woman in his arms and comfort her for the wrong she had done to himself and the children.

'Asleep, Min?' he asked, opening her door.

Her breathing was enough to tell him he had guessed wrongly. Then real panic swept over him. He closed Min's door quietly and rushed back to Tim's room. He switched on the light.

'What's going on in this house?' he asked in a jovial voice.

Tim started up with a brave show of astonishment, but his red eyes betrayed him.

'Hullo, Dad,' he said. 'What time is it?'

'Too early for me,' Dan said, sitting on the side of his bed. 'I suppose you didn't hear any noise?'

'No, Dad,' said Tim. 'Did you?'

'My imagination, I suppose,' said Dan.

'It might be the pictures,' said Tim. 'Pictures keep me awake too.'

'No, I don't think it's the pictures,' said Dan. 'I think it's having Mother in the house, don't you?'

'What's that, Dad?' Tim asked, sitting up and feeling for his hand.

'Don't you find it upsetting, after all these years?'

'I suppose I do,' said Tim, and Dan saw the flash of fresh tears.

And suddenly Dan realized that he must tell the child everything, good and bad. Dan was a cautious, secretive man. He knew perfectly well that more harm was done by well-intentioned people who tried to explain themselves than was ever done by those who kept their mouths shut. But he knew as well that Tim and he were in the same trouble and that Tim could not handle it alone. This was something that even Mildred wouldn't understand. It was something that could happen only between father and son. He hadn't even told Mildred the full story of his married life, and now he went through it to the end, not seeking words, nor evading them when they came – trying to be fair to Min but not trying too hard. After all, it wasn't fairness the boy wanted but some understanding of the human reality behind, even if it hurt.

Tim was in a state of enchantment. He sat up in bed, his hands about his knees, his eyes fixed on Dan's as though he might miss some shade of meaning. It reminded Dan of the way he had sat years before, listening to *Treasure Island*. Then he had tried to project himself into a world where boys were strong and brave. Now he was trying to project himself into a world in which grown-ups were hurt and powerless, striking out wildly at people they loved.

'So that's how it is,' Dan concluded gently. 'I was fond of your mother once, and I'm still fond of her, but we've been apart too long. She has new friends, like the man who rang her up the first night she came. I have new friends. The real reason I wasn't sleeping was that I'd behaved like a pig. I didn't go to her room to say goodnight as I should have done.'

'Why didn't you, Dad?' asked Tim, and Dan knew he wasn't being merely critical. He was trying to get Dan to explain to him his own behaviour.

'I suppose I was modelling my conduct on Queen Elizabeth,' said Dan with a grin and Tim smiled sadly. Probably that bit of rudeness had been on his conscience too.

'For all I knew,' said Dan, 'she was lying awake, brooding on it. I knew it might be years before I could make up for it. I knew one of us might die even before I got the chance. That's how the damn thing happens, Tim. You pass a room, and wonder if it's worth your while dropping in, and day after day for the rest of your life, you pass it again and feel you'd give anything on God's earth for the chance of one word with somebody who isn't there to hear it. Nobody knows how cruel he is until it's too late. So I just went down to see if Mother was asleep.'

'And was she?' asked Tim.

'Don't worry,' said Dan. 'I'll make up for it tomorrow. Good night, old man.'

'Goodnight, Dad,' said Tim. And then, in a sniffle, 'Don't worry about Mummy. She knows you like her all right.'

Dan noticed the slight emphasis on the 'you'. Half an hour

later he heard Tim's door open and shut. This was something he hadn't calculated on, but he decided it was better to leave it that way. If it was Min's turn for a sleepless night she might as well resign herself to it.

The weekend was a great success, and the children were to spend part of the Christmas holidays with Min. They all saw her off and the children's eyes were red. When they sat together in the front room it was as though the bottom of the world had dropped out for them. Then Tim suddenly started up and charged into the hall.

'There's Mildred,' he said, as though he had been waiting for her and from the hallway Dan heard his voice. 'Hullo, Mildred, welcome home! Hullo, Flurry, old scout! You sit down and I'll get the tea, Mildred.'

'Don't attempt it,' Bawn cried, storming out after him. 'You'll only make a mess of the kitchen again.'

'Please, Bawn, put Flurry to bed for me,' said Mildred. 'Poor Flurry is exhausted.'

'I am not,' screamed Flurry. 'I want to play.'

Dan saw that Mildred only wanted to get him alone. She was all lit up about something, and though he was glad to see her, he suspected her of making fun of him.

'What is it?' he asked.

'Don't you know?' she whispered. 'Didn't you hear? What on earth have you done to Tim? Do you know he kissed me?'

*More Stories* (1954)

# PRIVATE PROPERTY

My mother was never really happy about my being in the secret revolutionary army, and Father hated it. Father was a natural conservative who hated change on principle, and he had a shrewd idea of the sort of family whose lack of balance would cause them to be mixed up in it. Having relatives in the lunatic asylum would naturally be a predisposing factor. Another would be having come from some backward place like Carlow. Father disliked my great friend, Mick Ryan for no other reason than that.

Now, I was a well-balanced young fellow. I will say that for myself. I didn't drink; I smoked very little; I was regular at work and contributed my fair share to the housekeeping. So I didn't fly off the handle as another might have done, and I did my best to explain to Father that this was all only passion and prejudice on his part, that nothing would ever improve if it depended on people like him, and that it didn't really matter who a man was or where he came from. It had no effect on Father. He didn't want things improved. He wanted them to last out his lifetime the way they were.

He tried to keep me in check by making me be home at ten, but I felt that as a revolutionist as well as a wage earner, I had to stick out for half past. It was the old story. He wouldn't give me a key and go to bed like a sensible man. One lock wasn't enough for him. The world was too uncertain with thieves and murderers forever on the prowl. He had three separate bolts on the front door and had to bolt them himself before he could sleep. There was no use arguing with a man like that.

We of the secret army met in a Gaelic League hall in a back street and discussed dispatches from Dublin telling us to be armed and ready for the great day. I didn't see how we were to arm ourselves at all, the way things were going. Our Quartermaster – a stocky little stone mason called Johnny Forrestal – was a bitter old pill who had been a revolutionary from the age of fifteen and had been in five gaols and on three hunger strikes. He was above suspicion, and almost above criticism by kids like ourselves, but he had no luck. As soon as ever we scraped together a few pounds from the men's subscriptions and bought a couple of rifles the police nosed them out. It was making us all depressed, and the Adjutant, Tom Harrison, was really savage. He said Johnny was too old, but I knew it wasn't Johnny's age that came against him; it was his vanity.

Johnny simply couldn't walk down a street in that stocky

portentous way of his without advertising that he was a man who had fought in two wars and was only waiting his chance to fight in a third. He had toadies who gave him all the admiration he needed, and I suspected that he spilled everything to them.

But if Johnny was tough, Harrison was tougher. He was a grocer's curate from down the country and looked like a seminarist in mufti. He was a man who never hesitated to speak his mind, and as this was a privilege Johnny liked to reserve for himself, there was always bad blood between them.

'I tell you again there's a spy in the camp,' Harrison shouted one night we were discussing the latest catastrophe.

'Maybe you'd tell us who he is,' Johnny said with a face on him like one of his own tombstones.

'If I knew he wouldn't be there long,' said Harrison.

'You'd shoot him, I suppose?' Johnny asked with a sneer.

'I would shoot him.'

'He got no information out of me anyway,' Johnny said in a surly tone. 'I could keep my mouth shut before some people here were born.'

This was Johnny at his old game of turning the discussion into a vote of confidence, and he'd done it too often for my liking.

'I'm afraid I agree with Tom, Johnny,' I said.

'Then why don't you do the job yourself?' asked Johnny, leaving it to be understood what would happen if I did.

'I don't want to make a personal matter of it, Johnny,' I said, keeping my temper.

'And I *do* want to make a personal matter of it,' said Harrison, losing his. 'Damn it, we're only wasting our own time till we learn to keep our equipment safe. I say Larry is the man for the job.'

So that was how, at the age of seventeen, I came to be Brigade Quartermaster, and, though it may sound like self-praise, they never had a better. Mick Ryan was a tower of strength to me. He was a tall, handsome, reckless devil who worked on the railway, and the pair of us made a grand team because he made me do things that ordinarily I'd have been too shy to do, while I stopped him doing things he would have done when his imagination ran away with him. In the evenings we went into pubs on the quays, talking to sailors and giving assumed names. When we began, we had only one Smith and Wesson pistol belonging to Mick's brother who was in the British Army, and even for this we had only Thompson gun ammunition, but within six months we were getting in guns from Hamburg and Lisbon and packing them away in a dump we had built on the hill behind the church. Mick and I had dug it out ourselves and propped it with railway sleepers. We even put an old bed in it so that we could sleep there. Not that I ever stayed out all night, but Mick was a bit of a rambler.

By this time the police were beginning to realize that it wasn't old Johnny Forrestal they had to deal with and they panicked. Dwyer, the superintendent, called the detectives together and warned them that there would be sackings if something wasn't done. They did their best but it wasn't very good. You could see that someone had tipped them off about me and Mick because our houses were watched by detectives with bikes, and we made a new game out of giving them the slip.

To tell the truth, I was a bit flattered by all this attention. It was the first time that anyone had taken me seriously. At first, Father couldn't believe it, and after that he was stunned. He stood for hours behind the curtains in the front room, watching the detectives, and sometimes getting mad with the detective and sometimes with me. He discovered that the detective's wife kept hens, so he dropped poisoned bread in her garden. At the same time he tried to make me stay in at night, but no Brigade Quartermaster with an ounce of self-respect could let himself be locked in at ten. Father locked me out, but behind his back Mother left the window open. Then he fastened the window catch himself but I got over the back wall. After that he contented himself with muttering prophecies to himself about what was in store for me.

'Aha, they think they're cleverer than their fathers, but

they'll be taught. Mark my words! The rope will teach them. *Then* they'll see how clever they were.'

I made a point of it that no one should know the whereabouts of the dump except Mick, myself and Harrison. Mick was opposed even to Harrison's knowing, but, seeing that both of us were liable to be picked up any day, I thought this was carrying secrecy too far.

Besides, I knew that Mick was prejudiced against Harrison for reasons that had nothing to do with the organization. In his own way Mick was as bad as Father. It was one of the main drawbacks of the movement – private quarrels – and I was forever begging Mick to keep out of them and think only of the principle. But Mick hadn't a principle in his head; he liked or hated people, and that was all there was to it.

Now the reason he hated Harrison was this. Harrison was married to the sister of Mick's friend, Joe Ward, another member of the organization and as decent a poor devil as ever drew breath, only for his misfortune. He had married a flighty woman who bore him four kids but omitted to make a proper home for them because the horses took up all her spare time and money. Between illness and debt poor Joe was half-distracted. Mick, being a single man and very open-handed, was always helping him, but Harrison – at least according to Mick – would do nothing for him. This cut poor Joe to the heart because he was an emotional man, always laughing or crying; he dearly loved his sister, and, when she married Harrison, he had given them a magnificent clock as a wedding present – something he could badly afford.

Now, I didn't doubt that for a moment, but I could see Harrison's point of view as well. That was always my trouble; being a reasonable man I could see everyone's point of view. After all, Harrison was a married man, too, with a kid of his own, and he wasn't earning so much in the grocery and bar that he could afford to be generous on Mick's scale. Besides, I had the feeling that helping Joe was really an acute case of casting your bread upon the waters. Personally, I would have been damn full sure it wouldn't come back.

But for the sake of the organization I tried to keep the peace between Mick and Harrison. I praised them both to one another, and any little admission I could wring out of one I passed on to the other. It was all for the cause. I was a conscientious officer, even if I was only seventeen, and in those days I was innocent enough to believe that this was all that was needed to keep Ireland united.

That was where the ferry-boat left me. It began innocently enough the day Joe Ward discovered that his wife had been to a money-lender and borrowed seven pounds. To poor Joe, weighed down with troubles, this seemed like the end of the world. He was never what you'd call a well-balanced man, and for a while he was probably a bit off his head. Instead of going to his sister, who might have raised a few shillings for him unknown to Harrison, or to Mick, who would have borrowed the money himself to help him, he went to the pub where Harrison worked. He stood at the door with his hands out and the tears streaming down his long clown's face and said dramatically: 'Look at me, Tom Harrison! Look at me! Happier men floated out Lough Mahon.'

Now, in spite of what happened afterwards, I want to be quite fair about this. Though Mick called Harrison a mean bastard, my own impression of him was that he wasn't a bad chap at all, really, and that, given time to get used to the idea, he might have done something substantial for Joe. I understood his position. I might have taken the cautious line myself, for after all, where was this thing going to end?

'Begor, Joe,' he said, 'if I had it you'd be welcome, but the way it is with me, I haven't.'

'I'm sorry for your troubles, poor man,' said Joe with withering scorn and stalked out on him. Of course, Harrison was leaping. After all, he had only been playing for time, and while it's bad enough to be asked for money, it's a hard thing to be insulted when you don't fall over yourself giving it. I sympathized with Harrison. As I say, the only excuse I could see for Joe was that he wasn't in his right mind at the time. I saw his point of view, too, of course. That's the worst of being a fair-minded man; you can't buy any friends with half-hearted sympathy.

Well, next evening, when I was pushing my bicycle back up Summerhill from work, who did I see but Harrison,

136

coming towards me, looking very serious. He barely saluted me.

'Nothing wrong, is there, Tom?' I asked.

'Plenty, I'm afraid,' he said stiffly, and made to go on.

'Nothing to do with the organization, Tom?' I asked, turning the bike and walking back down the hill with him. Of course, it was the organization that was on my mind.

'Oh, nothing,' he said in the same tone. 'A purely private matter.' You could take it to mean I should mind my own business, but I didn't think he intended it that way. I could see he was very upset. 'Larceny!' he said then. 'Burglary! My house broken into and looted while I was at work. Oh, nothing to do with the organization!'

'For God's sake!' I said. 'Was much taken?'

'Oh, only a clock!' he snapped, and then, in case I might think he hadn't enough cause to be in a state about it: 'A valuable clock.'

The word struck a familiar chord, but for a while I couldn't place it. Then I remembered where I'd heard of that clock before.

'That wouldn't be the clock Joe Ward gave you, Tom?' I asked.

'It would,' he said, stopping to give me a suspicious glance. 'It is. How do you know about it?'

'Oh, only that Mick Ryan mentioned it to me once,' I said in confusion.

'Whoever gave it, the clock is my property now,' said Harrison, moving on.

'And what are you going to do about it?' I asked.

'I'm going to put the police on him,' Harrison said defiantly, and I knew by his truculent tone that he was a bit ashamed of himself. To us, of course, the police were never anything but enemy spies. It gave me a nasty turn. Besides, I was tired and beginning to feel that to keep our fellows together would take more than compliments.

'On who, Tom?' I asked.

'Who do you think? On Ward, of course. It's about time that fellow was taught a lesson.'

I had not been thinking of anyone in particular, and the

137

name gave me a start. Then I could feel myself getting red with embarrassment.

'Oh, was it Joe took it?' I said.

'Walked into the house and took it from under my wife's eyes,' Harrison said indignantly.

'And you're going to put the enemy police on him?' I asked.

'Who else is there, man?' he retorted hotly.

'Well, I was thinking that maybe the organization might do something,' I said.

'And while I was waiting for the organization to do it my clock would be sold.'

'Oh, I'm not criticizing you,' I said. 'I was only thinking of the effect it would have on young fellows in the organization – an officer going to the enemy about another member.'

'But damn it, man, if someone broke into your house to-night and stole valuable property wouldn't you do the same?' he asked.

'If I had any property, and the man was a common thief, I dare say I would,' I admitted.

'There's nothing uncommon about Joe Ward only his impudence,' said Harrison. 'Now it's all very well to talk, Larry,' he went on in a more reasonable tone, 'and you and I agree about most things, but whatever government you have, you must protect private property. Even an army of occupation has to do that.'

'Oh, I'm not denying it, Tom,' I said, making the best I could of an argument that was a bit abstract for me. 'Only I don't think you're being fair to poor Joe. I don't really, Tom. My own impression is that the man can't have been right in the head.'

'He was sufficiently right in his head to come to my house while I was out at work,' said Harrison.

So we went on together, past the church at the foot of the hill and over the New Bridge, with me still arguing for the sake of appearances. It was the organization I was thinking of, and the scandal and disagreements that were bound to follow, with some of the lads backing Harrison and others backing Joe Ward, but nothing was farther from Harrison's mind. He hadn't a principle in his head any more than Father or Mick. All he could think of was his blooming old clock. I knew if he didn't do something about it he wouldn't sleep, only lie awake, noticing the silence in the house, and mourning for his clock as if it was someone that had died on him. I felt gloomy and desperate. It was a spring evening, coming on to dusk, and the metal bridges and the back streets full of old warehouses gave me the creeps. There seemed to be no hope for idealism, the way things were.

I remained outside on the quay while Harrison went into the barracks. It was a big, red-brick building with a few lights burning. I wondered if I should be there at all and what I'd say about it to the lads at our next meeting. I decided that there was nothing wrong in waiting since the man was so upset. It was the same thing as with Mick. He'd get in a bake, and do something he shouldn't, and then regret it after. It all came of a want of principle.

Nothing happened for a long time, and I began to wonder whether Dwyer, the superintendent, hadn't taken the chance of locking Harrison up. There was a light in his office, which I recognized because I had plans of the whole building in the dump. I saw a figure come to the window and look up and down the river and decided that I'd better get a move on quick. I jumped on the bicycle and started to ride away. Then I glanced back and saw two detectives get into a car and follow me. I got cold all over because I knew I had no way of escape. But then the car passed me out and I realized that they had not been following me at all. I decided to follow them instead. I had a good notion of where they were going, and I knew Harrison would be inside till they came back.

They stopped outside a tenement house on another quay. There were no curtains in the windows and no lights but candles. A couple of women were leaning out of the windows and they began to pretend the police had come to call on them. The detectives paid no attention and walked straight in the hallway as though they knew where they were going.

When they came out three minutes later, each of them was carrying a clock. Joe Ward followed them out in his shirt sleeves, a thin, consumptive man with glasses and a mad air. He stood on the steps of the house and addressed the detectives and the crowd that had gathered. Like all emotional men, he laughed as if he was crying, and cried as if he was laughing, and only that I knew him so well I'd have laughed at him myself.

'There's the great Irish patriot for you!' he bawled, waving one arm wildly. 'There's the great Republican chief, General Tom Harrison, putting the Free State police on his own poor misfortunate brother-in-law, and all over an old clock! A clock I gave him for his wedding when 'tis a dose of poison I should have given him! There's the great patriot, a fellow that wouldn't lend you a bob if the children died of hunger at his feet. God help Ireland and God help the poor! Give me back my own clock anyway, ye robbers of hell! Give me back the clock I bought with my own couple of ha'pence!'

They ignored him and drove off. This time they got well away from me and I only arrived back at the barracks in time to see Harrison coming out. He had his own clock under his arm, wrapped up, and you could see the comfort it gave him. He wasn't the same man at all. That is the only way I can describe him. He was bubbling with good nature towards myself and the whole world, and nothing would do him only to unwrap the clock for me to admire it. It was a good clock all right.

'Ah, it may teach that fellow some sense,' he said, but there wasn't a hint of indignation left in him, nothing but his own basic good humour. 'He should know better than to think he can get away with things like that.'

With the picture of Joe fresh in my mind, I didn't feel like discussing it. I had the impression that poor Joe would get away with damn little in this world or the next. In a curious way I began to understand Mick Ryan's attitude to Harrison. It was against my principles but I couldn't help it.

'Who did you see inside?' I asked.

'You'd never believe,' said Harrison with a chuckle.

'Not Dwyer, surely?' I asked. I could hardly believe that Dwyer would concern himself about a thing like a stolen clock.

'Oh, one of the detectives recognized me, of course,' said Harrison. 'Dwyer came down himself and brought me up to his office to wait. He took it more seriously than I did, as a matter of fact, but I suppose he has to; it's his job. He told them to bring in every clock in the place. They brought two.'

'I saw them at it,' I said.

'Did you follow them?' he asked eagerly. 'What happened?'

'Joe came out and made a bit of a scene. There was a crowd.'

'Tell me, Larry, was he mad?'

It was all too palsy-walsy for me.

'He was upset. You'd hardly blame him.'

'I do not blame him, Larry,' Harrison said gravely. 'I'm genuinely sorry for that unfortunate wretch. We all told him what that woman was like, but he wouldn't believe us. God knows, if there was anything I could do for him, I'd do it.'

The benevolence that clock produced in Harrison was simply astonishing. He was so full of good nature that he never even noticed that I didn't share it with him.

'Tell us about Dwyer,' I said to get away from it.

'Oh, he stood me a drink, man,' said Harrison, beginning to chuckle again. 'You should have come in with me. You'd have enjoyed it.'

'I saw him in the window.'

'Oh, he saw you as well. There are no flies on Dwyer.'

'Did he ask any questions?'

'Questions? He never stopped.'

'About what?'

'About you and Ryan and the dump. Oh, naturally pretending to have a great admiration for us all, particularly you. He said he was like that himself when he was younger. Like hell he was . . . Stand in here for a minute.'

He whispered the last words, glancing hastily over his shoulder to see if we were being followed, and then pulled me into a dark archway. He was very excited.

'Do you know that he offered me money to tell him where the dump was?' he whispered angrily. 'Big money! He said the organization was riddled with spies; that every gun Johnny Forrestal bought was reported to him twice over inside twenty-four hours. They meet him after midnight at some hideout of his in town.'

I believed him, unfortunately, and my feeling of gloom deepened. Of course, I had always suspected that there was a spy, but it was a different thing to be sure of it. For the future I knew that I should trust nobody. All the same I wasn't feeling so kindly towards Harrison as to look for sympathy from him.

'I was afraid of that,' I said. 'I guessed Johnny talked too much. Dwyer isn't getting the information now though.'

'That's what I told him,' said Harrison. 'He said he was getting plenty, but that's only bluff. Otherwise, why would he offer to bribe me? ... But imagine it! Fellows you'd be drinking with one minute stealing down there the next to swear your life away. What sort of conscience can they have?'

'If they have a conscience,' I said despondently. In the badly lit street, supperless, cold, and tired, I was beginning to wonder if there was any opportunity for idealism, and if Father wasn't right after all.

'Dwyer laughed at me when I said that,' said Harrison ruefully as he walked on. ' "Nonsense, man," he said. "I could put a call through on that telephone this minute and bring in two men you know well that are giving information about you, and you'd damn soon see they're not so different from yourself. Poor devils! Maybe they got into a spot of trouble over a woman and they wanted the money." '

'They couldn't do without women, I suppose,' I said. Naturally, at seventeen they were about the last thing I wanted.

And then, three weeks later, the dump was raided and everything in it seized, including Mick Ryan with all the Brigade papers on him. It was a pure fluke that I wasn't there myself. Mick, who was a resourceful chap, got rid of the papers by distributing cigarettes wholesale to the detectives and lighting them with letters he pulled from his pockets. Only for that, I'd have been in gaol with him. From the barracks he slipped me out a note that just read: 'Shoot Harrison'. Mick was a dramatic sort of fellow on occasions.

Of course, I didn't shoot Harrison. To begin with, I hadn't any absolute proof, though I didn't need it. I was sick at the loss of my priceless dump, all the lovely rifles and automatics smuggled in from all over Europe, and all sold over an old clock. If I were to have Harrison shot it would mean that I would have to start again from the beginning, and I didn't have the heart. I just dropped out of the organization altogether.

Father was very cocked-up about Mick's arrest because it confirmed his old prejudice against Carlow people, and the first night the detective failed to show up near the house he positively purred. He gave me five shillings for myself and told me that in future I could stay out until eleven. 'Or so,' he added. He didn't want to seem severe, and he had been a bit wild himself at my age.

It was the first time he had been civil to me for a year and a half, and I got so sentimental that I broke down and told him the whole story. To my astonishment he flew into a wild rage and wanted to know why I didn't chuck a bomb into Harrison's house. That very night he took a pot of white paint and a brush and painted the front wall of Harrison's house with the words 'Spies and Informers Beware'. God, you can never tell with Conservatives!

I took the five bob, but I was home by half past ten. I had decided to go to the School of Commerce in the evenings. I was beginning to see that there was no future in revolutions – not in Ireland, anyway. It may be different elsewhere.

*Domestic Relations* (1957)

# FISH FOR FRIDAY

Ned McCarthy, the teacher in a village called Abbeyduff, was wakened one morning by his sister-in-law. She was standing over him with a cynical smile and saying in a harsh voice:

'Wake up! 'Tis started.'

'What's started, Sue?' Ned asked wildly, jumping up in bed with an anguished air.

'Why?' she asked dryly. 'Are you after forgetting already? There's no immediate hurry, but you'd better get the doctor.'

'Oh, the doctor!' sighed Ned, remembering all at once why he was sleeping alone in the little back room and why that unpleasant female was in the house. She only came when Kitty was having a baby, and she went round like a Redemptorist missioner on an annual retreat.

He dressed in a hurry, said a few words of encouragement to Kitty, talked to the kids while swallowing a cup of tea, and got out the car. He was a well-built man in his early forties with fair hair and pale grey eyes, nervous and excitable under his placid manner. He had plenty to be excited about. The house, for instance. It was a fine house, an old shooting lodge, set back at a distance of two fields from the main road, with a lawn leading to the river and steep gardens climbing the wooded hill behind. It was an ideal house, in fact, the sort he had always dreamed of, where Kitty could keep a few hens and he could garden and get in a bit of shooting. But scarcely had he settled in than he realized it was a mistake. The loneliness of the long evenings when dusk settled on the valley was something he had never even imagined.

He had lamented it to Kitty, and it was she who had suggested the car, but even this had drawbacks because it needed as much attention as a baby. When Ned was alone in it he chatted to it encouragingly; when it stopped he kicked it viciously, and the villagers swore he had actually been seen stoning it. This and the fact that he sometimes talked to himself when he hadn't the car to talk to had given rise to the legend that he had a slate loose.

He drove down the lane and across the footbridge to the main road. Then he stopped before the public-house at the corner which his friend, Tom Hurley, owned.

'Anything you want in town, Tom?' he shouted.

'What's that, Ned?' said a voice from within, and Tom himself, a small, round, russet-faced man came out with his wrinkled grin.

'I have to go to town. Is there anything you want?'

'No, no, Ned, I think not, thanks,' Tom said in his hasty way, all the words trying to come out together. 'All we wanted was fish for the dinner, and the Jordans are bringing that.'

'I'd sooner them than me,' Ned said, making a face.

'Och, isn't it the devil, Ned?' Tom said with a look of real anguish. 'The damn smell hangs round the shop the whole day. But what the hell else can you do on a Friday? Is it a spin you're going for?'

'No, for the doctor,' said Ned.

'Och, I see,' said Tom, beginning to beam. His expression exaggerated almost to caricature whatever emotion his inter-locutor might be expected to feel. 'Ah, please God, it'll go off all right. There's no hurry, is there? Come in and have a drop.'

'No, thanks, Tom,' Ned said with resignation. 'I'd better not start so early.'

'Ah, hell to your soul, you will,' fussed Tom. 'It won't take you two minutes. Hard enough it was for me to keep you sober the time the first fellow arrived.'

Ned got out of the car and followed Tom inside.

'That's right, Tom,' he said in surprise. 'I'd forgotten about that. Who was it was here?'

'Och, God, you had half the countryside in,' Tom said, shaking his head. 'It was a terrible night, a terrible night. You had Jack Martin, the teacher, and Owen Hennessey, and that publican friend of yours from town – what's that his name is? – Cronin. That's right, Larry Cronin. Ye must have dropped just where ye stood, glasses and all. The milkman found ye next morning littering the floor, and ye never even locked the doors after ye. Ye could have had my licence taken from me.'

'Do you know, I'd forgotten about that completely,' said Ned with a pleased smile. 'My memory isn't what it was. I suppose we're getting old.'

'Och, well, 'tis never the same after the first,' said Tom, and he poured a large drink for Ned and a few spoonfuls for himself. 'God, isn't it astonishing what the first one does for you, Ned?' he added in his eager way, bending across the counter. 'You feel you're getting a new lease of life. And by the time the second comes you're beginning to wonder will the damn thing ever stop. God forgive me for talking,' he said, lowering his voice. 'Herself would have my life if she heard me.'

'Still, there's a lot of truth in it, Tom,' said Ned, relieved to feel that the gloom in his mind was nothing unusual. 'It's not the same thing at all. And I suppose that even that is only an illusion. Like when you fall in love and think you're getting first prize in the lottery, while all the time it's only Nature's little way of putting you on the spot.'

'Ah, well, they say it all comes back when you're a grandfather,' said Tom with a chuckle.

'But who wants to be a grandfather?' asked Ned, already feeling sorry for himself with his home upset, that unpleasant woman bossing the house and more money to be found somewhere.

He drove off but his mood had darkened. It was a grand bit of road between his house and the town, with the river below him on the left, and the hills at either side with the first faint wash of green on them like an unfinished water-colour. Walking or driving, it was a real pleasure to him because of the prospect of civilization at the other end. The town was only a little run-down port, but it had shops and pubs and villas with electric light, and a water supply that did not give out in May, and there were all sorts of interesting people to be met there. But the prospect didn't cheer him now. He realized that the rapture of being a father doesn't go on repeating itself and it gave him no pleasure at all to look forward to being a grandfather. He felt decrepit enough the way he was.

At the same time he was haunted by some memory of days when he was not decrepit but careless and gay. He had been a Volunteer and roamed the hills for months with a column, wondering where he would spend the night. Then it had all seemed uncomfortable and dangerous enough, but at least he had felt free. Maybe, like an illusion of re-birth at finding himself a father, it was only an illusion of freedom, but it was terrible to think he wouldn't be able to feel it any more. It was associated in his mind with high hills and wide views, but now his life had descended into a valley like the one he was driving along. He had descended into it by the quiet path of duty – a steady man, a sucker for responsibilities, treasurer of the Hurling Club, treasurer of the Republican Party, secretary of three other organizations. He talked to the car as he did whenever something was too much on his mind.

'It's all Nature, old girl,' he said despondently. 'It gives you a set of illusions, but all the time it's only bending you to its own purposes as if you were a cow or a tree. You'd be better off with no illusions at all. No illusions about anything! That way, Nature wouldn't get you quite so soon.'

Being nervous, he did not like to drive through the town. He did it when he had to, but it made him flustered and fidgety so that he missed seeing who was on the streets, and a town was nothing without people. He usually parked his car outside Cronin's pub on the way in and walked the rest of the way. Larry Cronin was an old comrade of revolutionary days who had married into the pub.

He went in to tell Larry. This was quite unnecessary as Larry knew every car for miles around and was well aware of Ned's little weakness, but it was a habit and Ned was a man of more habits than he realized himself.

'I'm leaving the old bus for half an hour, Larry,' he called through the door in a plaintive tone that expressed regret for the inconvenience he was causing Larry and grief for the burden that was being put on himself.

'Ah, come in, man, come in!' cried Larry, a tall, engaging man with a handsome face and a sunny smile that was quite sincere if Larry liked you and damnably hypocritical if he didn't. His mouth was like a showcase with the array of false teeth in it. 'What has you out at this hour of the morning?'

'Oh, Nature, Nature,' Ned said with a laugh, digging his hands into his trouser pockets.

'How do you mean, Nature?' asked Larry, who did not understand the allusive ways of intellectuals but admired them none the less.

'Kitty, I mean. I'm going for the doctor.'

'Ah, the blessings of God on you!' Larry said jovially. 'Is this the third or the fourth? You lose count after a while, don't you? You might as well have a resiner as you're in. Ah, you will, you will, God blast you! 'Tis hard on the nerves. That was a great night we had the time the boy was born.'

'Wasn't it?' said Ned, beaming at the way people remembered it. 'I was only talking to Tom Hurley about it.'

'Ah, what the hell does Hurley know about it?' Larry asked contemptuously, pouring out a half tumbler of whiskey with the air of a lord. 'The bloody man went to bed at two. That fellow is too cautious to be good. But Jack Martin gave a great account of himself. Do you remember? The whole first act of *Tosca*, orchestra and all. "The southern sunlight" he called it. You didn't see Jack since he came back?'

'Was Jack away?' Ned asked in surprise. He felt easier now, being on the doctor's doorstep, and anyhow he knew the doctor would only be waiting.

'Ah, God he was,' said Larry, throwing his whole weight on the counter. 'In Paris, would you believe it? He's on the batter again, of course. Wait till you hear him on Paris! 'Tis only the mercy of God if Father Clery doesn't get to hear of it.'

'That's where you're wrong, Larry,' Ned said with a smile. 'Martin doesn't have to mind himself at all. Father Clery will do all that for him. If an inspector comes round while Martin

148

is on it, Father Clery will take him out to look at the anti-quities.'

'Begod, you might be right, Ned,' said Larry. 'But you or I couldn't do it. God Almighty, man, we'd be slaughtered alive. 'Tisn't worried you are about Kitty,' he asked gently.

'Ah, no, Larry,' said Ned. 'It's only that at times like this a man feels himself of no importance. A messenger boy would do as well. We're all dragged down to the same level.'

'And damn queer we'd be if we weren't,' said Larry with his lazy, sunny smile, the smile Ned remembered from the day Larry threw a Mills bomb into a lorry of soldiers. 'Unless you'd want to have the bloody baby yourself.'

'Ah, it's not only that, Larry,' Ned said gloomily. 'It's not that at all. But you can't help wondering what it's all about.'

'Why, then indeed, that's true for you,' said Larry, who, as a result of his own experience in the pub had developed a gloomy and philosophic view of human existence. After all, a man can't be looking at schizophrenia for ten hours a day without wondering if it's all strictly necessary. 'And 'tis at times like this you notice it – men coming and going like the leaves on the trees. Ah, God, 'tis a great mystery.'

But that wasn't what Ned was thinking about either. He was thinking of his own lost youth and what had happened to him.

'That's not what I mean, Larry,' he said, drawing neat figures on the counter with the bottom of his glass. 'What I mean is you can't help wondering what happened yourself. We knew one another when we were young, and look at us now, forty odd and our lives are over and we have nothing to show for them. It's as if when you married some good went out of you.'

'Small loss as the fool said when he lost Mass,' retorted Larry, who had found himself a comfortable berth in the pub and lost his thirst for adventure.

'That's the bait, of course,' Ned said with a grim smile. 'That's where Nature gets us every time. A small con-tribution, you'll never miss it, and before you know where you are, you're bankrupt.'

'Ah, how bad Nature is!' exclaimed Larry, not relaxing his grin. 'When your first was born you were walking mad round the town, looking for people to celebrate it with, and there you are now, looking for sympathy! God, man, isn't it a great thing to have someone to share your troubles with and give a slap on the ass to, even if she does let the crockery fly once in a while? What the hell about an old bit of china?'

'That's all very well, Larry, *if* that's all it costs,' said Ned darkly.

'And what the hell else does it cost?' asked Larry. 'Twenty-one meals a week and a couple of pounds of tea. Sure, 'tis for nothing!'

'And what about your freedom?' Ned asked. 'What about the old days on the column?'

'Ah, that was different, Ned,' Larry said with a sigh, and at once his smile went out and his eyes took on a dreamy, faraway look. 'But sure, everything was different then. I don't know what the hell is after coming over the country at all.'

'The same thing that's come over you and me,' Ned said with finality. 'Nature kidded us, the way it kidded us when we got married, and the way it kidded us when the first child was born. There's nothing worse than illusions for getting you into the rut. We had our freedom and we didn't value it. Now our lives are run for us by women the way they were when we were kids. This is Friday and what do I find? Hurley waiting for someone to bring home the fish. You waiting for the fish. I'll go home to a nice plate of fish, and I'll guarantee to you, Larry, not one man in that flying column is having meat for his dinner today. One few words in front of the altar and it's fish for Friday the rest of your life. And they call this a man's country!'

'Still, Ned, there's nothing nicer than a good bit of fish,' Larry said wistfully. 'If 'tis well done, mind you. *If* 'tis well done. And I grant you 'tisn't often you get it well done. God, I had some fried plaice in Kilkenny last week that had me turned inside out. I declare to God if I stopped that car once I stopped it six times, and by the time I got home I was after caving in like a sandpit.'

'And yet I can remember you in Tramore, letting on to be

a Protestant to get bacon and eggs on Friday,' Ned said accusingly.

'Oh, that's the God's truth,' Larry said joyously. 'I was a divil for meat, God forgive me. I used to go mad seeing the Protestants lowering it, and me there with nothing only a boiled egg. And the waitress, Ned – do you remember the waitress that wouldn't believe I was a Protestant till I said the *Our Father* the wrong way for her? She said I had too open a face for a Protestant. How well she'd know a thing like that about the *Our Father*, Ned!'

'A woman would know anything she had to know to make you eat fish,' Ned said, finishing his drink and turning away. 'And you may be reconciled to it, Larry,' he added with a mournful smile, 'but I'm not. I'll eat it because I'm damned with a sense of duty, and I don't want to get Kitty into trouble with the neighbours, but please God, I'll see one more revolution before I die, even if I have to swing for it.'

'Ah, well,' sighed Larry, 'youth is a great thing, sure enough ... Coming, Hanna, coming!' he boomed as a woman's voice yelled from the room upstairs. He gave Ned a nod and a wink to suggest that he enjoyed it, but Ned knew that that scared little rabbit of a wife of his would be wanting to know about the Protestant prayers, and would then go to Confession and ask the priest was it a reserved sin and should Larry be sent to the Bishop. And then he remembered Larry during the Dunkeen ambush when they had to run for it, pleading with that broad smile of his, 'Ah, Chris, Ned, let me have one more crack at them!' 'No life, no life,' Ned said aloud to himself as he sauntered down the hill past the church. And it was a great mistake taking a drink whenever he felt badly about the country because it always made the country seem worse.

Someone clapped him suddenly on the shoulder. It was Jack Martin, the vocational-school teacher, a small, plump, nervous man with a baby complexion, a neat greying moustache and big, blue, innocent eyes. Ned's face lit up. Of all his friends Martin was the one he warmed to most. He was a talented man and a good baritone. His wife had died a few years before and left him with the two children, but he had not married again and had been a devoted if over-anxious father. Yet two or three times a year, and always coming on to his wife's anniversary, he went on a tearing drunk that left some legend behind. There was the time he tried to teach Verdi to the tramp who played the penny whistle and the time his housekeeper hid his trousers and he got out of the window in his pyjamas and had to be brought home by the parish priest.

'MacCarthy, you scoundrel, you were hoping to give me the slip,' he said delightedly in his shrill nasal voice. 'Come in here one minute till I tell you something. God, you'll die!'

'If you wait there ten minutes, Jack, I'll be back to you,' said Ned. 'There's only one little job I have to do, and then I'll be able to give you my full attention.'

'All right, all right, but have one little drink before you go,' Martin said irritably. 'One drink and I'll release you on your own recognizances. You'll never guess where I was, Ned. I woke up there, as true as God!'

Martin was like that. Ned decided good-humouredly that five minutes' explanation in the bar was easier than ten minutes' argument in the street. It was quite clear that Martin was 'on it'. He was full of clock-work vitality, rushing to the counter for fresh drinks, fumbling over money, trying to carry glasses without spilling them, and talking thirteen to the dozen. Ned beamed at him. Drunk or sober, he liked the man.

'Ned, I'll give you three guesses where I was.'

'Let me see,' said Ned in mock meditation. 'I suppose 'twould never be Paris?' and then laughed boyishly at Martin's hurt air.

'You can't do anything in this town,' said Martin. 'Next, I suppose you'll be telling me what I did there.'

'No,' said Ned gravely. 'It's Father Clery who'll be telling about that – from the pulpit.'

'Ah, to hell with Father Clery!' said Martin. 'No, Ned, this is se-e-e-rious. This is vital. It only came to me in the last week. We're only wasting our time in this misfortunate country.'

'You're probably right,' Ned said urbanely. 'The question is, what else can you do with Time?'

'Ah, this isn't philosophy, man,' Martin said testily. 'This is se-e-e-rious, I tell you.'

'I know how serious it is all right,' Ned said complacently. 'Only five minutes ago I was asking Larry Cronin where our youth was gone.'

'Youth?' said Martin. 'But you can't call that youth, what we have in this country. Drinking bad porter in public-houses after closing time and listening to someone singing *The Rose of Tralee*. Sure, that's not life, man.'

'But isn't that the question?' asked Ned. 'What is Life?' Ned couldn't help promoting words like 'time' and 'life' to the dignity of capital letters.

'How the hell would I know?' asked Martin. 'I suppose you have to go out and look for the bloody thing. You're not going to find it round here. You have to go south, where they have sunlight and wine and good cooking and women with a bit of go.'

'And you don't think it would be the same thing there?' Ned asked quietly.

'Oh, God, dust and ashes! Dust and ashes!' wailed Martin. 'Don't go on with that! Don't we get enough of it every Sunday in the chapel?'

Now, Ned was very fond of Martin, and admired the vitality with which in his forties he still pursued a fancy, but he could not let him get away with the notion that Life was merely a matter of geography.

'But that's a way Life has,' he said oracularly. 'You think you're seeing it, and it turns out it was somewhere else all the time. Like women; the girl you lose is the one that could have made you happy. Or revolutions; you always fought the wrong battle. I dare say there are people in the south wishing they could be in some wild place like this. I admit it's rather difficult to imagine, but I suppose it could happen. No, Jack, we might as well resign ourselves to the fact that wherever Life was, it wasn't where we were looking for it.'

'For God's sake!' cried Martin. 'You're talking like an old man of ninety-five.'

'I'm forty-two,' Ned said with quiet emphasis, 'and I have no illusions left. You still have a few. Mind, I admire you for it. You were never a fighting man like Cronin or myself. Maybe that's what saved you. You kept your youthfulness longer. You escaped the big disillusionments. But Nature has her eye on you as well. You're light and airy now, but what way will you be next week? We pay for our illusions, Jack. They're only sent to drag us deeper into the mud.'

'Ah, 'tisn't that with me at all, Ned,' said Martin. 'It's my stomach. I can't keep it up.'

'No, Jack, it's not your stomach. It's the illusion. I saw other men with the same illusion and I know the way you'll end up. You'll be in and out of the chapel ten times a day for fear once wasn't enough, with your head down for fear you'd catch a friendly eye and be led astray, beating your breast, lighting candles and counting indulgences. And that, Jack, may be the last illusion of all.'

'I don't know what the hell is after coming over you,' Martin said in bewilderment. 'You're – you're being positively personal. And Father Clery knows perfectly well the sort of man I am. I have all Shaw's plays on my shelf, and I never tried to hide them from anybody.'

'I know that, Jack, I know that,' Ned said sadly, overcome by the force of his own oratory. 'And I'm not being personal, because it isn't a personal matter. It's only Nature working through you. It works through me as well only it gets me in a different way. My illusion was a different sort, and look at me now. I turn every damn thing into a duty, and in the end I'm good for nothing. I know the way I'll die too. I'll disintegrate into a husband, a father, a schoolteacher, a local librarian, and fifteen different sorts of committee men, and none of them with enough energy to survive. Unless, with God's help, I die on a barricade.'

'What barricade?' asked Martin, who found all this hard to follow.

'Any barricade,' Ned said with a wild sweep of his arms. 'I don't care what it's for so long as it means a fight. I don't want to die of disseminated conscientiousness. I don't want to be one of Nature's errand boys. I'm not even a good one. Here I am arguing with you in a pub instead of doing what I was sent to do.' He paused for a moment to think and then broke into his boyish laugh, because he realized that for the moment he had forgotten what it was. 'Whatever the hell it was,' he added. 'Well, that beats everything! That's what duty does for you!'

'Ah, that's only because it wasn't important,' said Martin.

'That's where you're wrong again, Jack,' said Ned, beginning to enjoy the situation thoroughly. 'Maybe it was of no importance to us but it was probably of great importance to Nature. What *was* the damn thing? My memory's gone to hell.'

He closed his eyes and lay back limply in his chair, though even through his self-induced trance he smiled at the absurdity of it.

'No good,' he said briskly, starting up. 'It's an extraordinary thing, the way it disappears as if the ground opened and swallowed it. And there's nothing you can do about it. It'll come back of its own accord, and there won't be any reason for that either. I was reading an article about a German doctor who says you forget because it's too unpleasant to think about.'

'It's not a haircut?' Martin asked helpfully, and Ned, a tidy man, shook his head.

'Or clothes?' Martin went on. 'Women are great on clothes.'

'No,' said Ned, frowning. 'I'm sure it wasn't anything for myself.'

'Or for the kids? Shoes or the like?'

'It could be, I suppose,' said Ned. 'Something flashed across my mind just then.'

'If it's not that it must be groceries.'

'I don't see how it could be. Williams deliver them every week, and they're nearly always the same.'

'In that case it's bound to be something to eat,' said Martin. 'They're always forgetting things – bread or butter or milk.'

'I suppose so, but I'm damned if I know what,' said Ned. 'Jim,' he said to the barman, 'I'm after forgetting the message I was sent on. What do you think of that?'

'Ah, I suppose 'twas fish, Mr Mac,' said the barman.

'Fish!' said Martin. 'The very thing.'

'Fish?' repeated Ned, stroking his forehead. 'I suppose it could be, now you mention it. I know I offered to bring it for Tom Hurley and I had a bit of an argument with Larry Cronin about it. He seems to like it.

'I can't stand the damn stuff,' said Martin, 'only the housekeeper has to have it for the kids.'

'Ah, 'tis fish all right, Mr Mac,' the barman said. 'In an hour's time you wouldn't forget it, not with the stink of it all round the town. I never could stand it myself since the last war and all the poor unfortunates getting drowned. You'd feel you were making a cannibal out of yourself.'

'Well, obviously, it has something to do with fish,' said Ned with a laugh. 'It may not exactly be fish, but it's something very like it. Anyway, if that's the case, there's no particular hurry. We'll have another of these, Jim.'

'Whether it is or not, she'll take it as kindly meant,' said Martin. 'The same as flowers. Women in this country don't seem to be able to distinguish between them.'

Two hours later, the two friends, more talkative than ever, drove up to Ned's house for lunch.

'Mustn't forget the fish,' Ned said with a knowing smile as he reached back for it. 'The spirit of the revolution, Jack – that's what it's come to.'

At that moment they both heard the wail of a new-born infant from the front bedroom. Ned grew very white.

'What's that, Ned?' asked Martin, and Ned gave a deep sigh.

'That's the fish, Jack, I'm afraid,' said Ned.

'Oh, God, I'm not going in so,' Martin said hastily, getting out of the car. 'Tom Hurley will give me a bit of bread and cheese.'

'Nonsense, man!' Ned said boldly, knowing perfectly well what his welcome would be if he went in alone. 'I'll get you something. That's not what's worrying me at all. What's worrying me is why I thought it could be fish. That's what I can't understand.'

*Domestic Relations* (1957)

# ANDROCLES AND THE ARMY

'Politics and religion!' Healy said when Cloone, the lion-tamer, announced that he was joining the army for the duration of the war. 'Even a lion-tamer you can't trust not to get patriotic on you. The next thing will be the Clown getting religion and wanting to join the Trappists.'

He argued, he pleaded, he threatened proceedings for breach of contract, but Cloone only retorted with arguments about the danger of the country. Threatened by the Germans, threatened by the English, threatened even by the Americans, she needed all her children. She did like hell, thought Healy, and his long red mournful nose shuddered and began to ascend like a helicopter.

'Look, Cloone, there's nothing wrong with the bloody country,' he said patiently. 'It's the show I'm thinking of. 'Twill only be the mercy of God if we can keep going at all. You know yourself there isn't another man in Ireland within a hundred miles of you, and if there was anyone outside it half as good, I couldn't get him in. Not with a war on.'

'Ah, damn it, I know, I know,' Cloone said in anguish. 'I like the show as well as you do, and I like my lions better than I like the show, but if I have to choose between my lions and my country, I have to choose my country. It's as hard on me as it is on you, but war is always like that. Look at the sugar rationing!'

Healy pleaded up to the very last minute. He knew that not only could he not get another lion-tamer, but that even if he could, the man would be nothing like as good as Cloone. He hated to admit it, because he was a professional, and

Cloone was nothing but an amateur, a Dublin stone mason who wasn't happy at home. But because he was a professional, Healy knew an artist when he saw one. What others could do by fear, Cloone could do by a simple dropping of his voice. Healy could not see what magic there was in that sudden change of pitch, but he could see the result all right, because an angry lion would suddenly uncoil his tightened springs of muscle and roll over to be stroked like a cat. And Cloone would play with it like a cat, his blue eyes soft with emotion, and mutter as though to himself, 'God, Ned, isn't he beautiful?' 'Beautiful my ass!' Healy would think, as his helicopter nose began to ascend, but he wouldn't say it. It was plain enough that the lion knew what Cloone meant, and there was no saying but that he might understand what Healy meant as well.

Anyone seeing Cloone with animals would be bound to think of St Francis of Assisi, but Healy knew that that was the only thing saintly about him. He had a wicked temper, and brooded for months on imaginary insults and injuries. He would begin to mutter about a half-crown that he said had been unjustly stopped from his pay six months before and go on nagging till Healy asked God for patience with him. 'Listen, Cloone,' he would say, 'I told you fifty times that there was nothing stopped. If you don't believe me, I'll give you the bloody half-crown to take your puss off me.' Then spasms of outraged pride would run through Cloone like electric shocks, and he would cry, 'It isn't the money, Ned. It's not the money. It's the principle.'

But Healy, who had been in show business from the time he was five, knew that artists had no principle; and it took a man like himself who hated animals but loved human beings to put up with it at all. Cloone knew that, too. He knew that Healy had some sort of hold over him and he didn't like it. 'I tame lions, but Healy tames me,' he said one night in a public-house with a sort of exasperated giggle that showed he was half ashamed of it.

But even Healy could not persuade him to stay on during the war. And it wasn't just because the show was only a ghost of itself, stripped by restrictions and regulations; it was pure unqualified, blood-thirsty patriotism – a thing Healy could not understand in a mature man. 'If you can ever say an artist is mature,' he added darkly.

It was a wrench for Cloone, because he really loved the few animals that had been left him, he liked Healy and the others, and he enjoyed the wandering life and the crowds of the small towns and fair greens. He had taken to the life as though he had never known any other. He left with a breaking heart to be shut up in a Nissen hut, dressed in uniform, stood to attention, stood at ease, presenting arms and forming twos and fours, as if he himself was only a mangy old circus lion. Besides, he was an awkward, excitable man who could never remember his right from his left, and he shouldered arms when he should have presented them and had to listen to the tongue-lashings of a sergeant without even replying. It often reduced him to mutinous tears, and he lay on his cot at night, exhausted, thinking of himself as a caged old animal with his spirit broken. Then he shed more tears because he felt he had never understood wild animals before.

All the same, his desperate sincerity stood to him. They had to make a corporal of him in the end, and in the way of other great artists, he was prouder of his two miserable stripes than of all his other attainments. Drinking in a pub with another man, he could not help glancing at his sleeve with a girlish smirk.

Then one day he opened a local paper and saw that Doyle's World-Famous Circus was visiting Asragh for one evening the following week. Filled with excitement, he went off to ask for a pass. Everyone in the battalion knew his trade, and there was no difficulty about the pass. The trouble was that the whole battalion felt it had a personal interest in the circus and wanted passes as well. On the afternoon of the show two lorry loads of troops left for town, and the Commandant, looking darkly at them, said, 'Well, boys, if the Germans come tonight, the country is lost.'

In the main street the soldiers scattered to the public-houses to wait for the circus, but Cloone hurried off joyously to the fair green. In his temperamental way he threw his arms round Healy and sobbed with pleasure till Healy grabbed him by the shoulders and inspected his uniform, the green gloves tucked in the shoulder strap and the natty little cane.

'God Almighty, John, you look a sight!' he said with affectionate malice.

'Ah, how bad I am!' Cloone said, giving him a punch. 'I'm all right, only for the hair,' he added self-consciously. 'I feel lost without the old wig.'

''Twould take more than a haircut to make a soldier of you,' said Healy.

'How well they had to give me the stripes!' said Cloone, looking admiringly at his sleeve.

'You're like a baby in a new sailor suit,' said Healy. 'Come in and have a drink.' They went into the caravan, and Healy poured half tumblers of neat whiskey for the pair of them. 'Ah, John, I thought you had more sense, boy,' he added as he handed one to Cloone.

'Oh, God, Ned, I know, I know,' said Cloone, wriggling miserably on the edge of the bed. 'I'm not suited to the life at all. But when you have it in the family! The father was in the Rising, and the two uncles were in the Volunteers, and I'm the same. Even now, when I'm in the Army I can never hear the Anthem without the heart rising in me.'

'I know. Like a pony when the band strikes up,' Healy said cruelly.

'Ah, 'tisn't alike, Ned,' Cloone said sadly. 'But believe me, the day I get my discharge, I'll be back. Tell me, who have you on the lions?'

'Who do you think?' Healy asked gloomily. 'Darcy – the Strong Man.' The description was added not by way of information, but as a sneer, for Healy, who had a wretched stomach and suffered agonies from it had seen the Strong Man screaming his head off with an ordinary toothache. It had left an indelible impression on his mind.

'Ah, God, Ned, sure Darcy could never handle a lion!' Cloone said in consternation. 'Darcy is too rough.'

'Darcy is too frightened,' Healy said candidly. 'Here, let me fill that for you.'

'Is he any good at all with them?' Cloone asked tensely.

'He's good all right,' Healy replied with a frown, for, though he didn't like Darcy much, he was a fair man. 'He's very conscientious. They don't like him; that's the only thing.'

'But how could they, Ned?' Cloone asked feverishly. 'Lions could never get on with a Strong Man. Lions are sensitive, like women. What possessed you to give them to Darcy?'

'I was damn grateful to Darcy for helping me out of the hole you left me in,' Healy said candidly. 'And I'll never criticize any man that does his best.'

It was like old times for Cloone, sitting in the twilight with his friend, sniffing the thick circus smells all round him and talking to the old hands who came in to ask how he was doing. He told them all about the importance of the army and the danger to the country, and they listened politely but with utter incredulity. It was at times like this that you could see Cloone wasn't really one of them, Healy thought sadly.

When he went off to take the gate, Cloone with a foolish smile nodded in the direction of the big cage and said, 'I'll slip round and have a look at Jumbo and Bess.' They might have been two old sweethearts, the way he talked of them.

'Plenty of time, John,' Healy said. 'They won't be on for half an hour yet.'

From Healy's point of view the main satisfaction of the evening was the number of soldiers who came, officers and all. Healy couldn't help liking a bit of style, and style was something that was disappearing from the Irish countryside. He was only sorry for the miserable show he had for them, and the two lions that were all he had left when the rationing was done. And then their turn came and Darcy stood ready, a huge and handsome man with a self-conscious air.

'Ladies and gentlemen,' the Cockney ringmaster explained, 'owing to Emergency restrictions, Doyle's collection of wild animals – the greatest in the world – has been considerably depleted. But the two lions you are about to see are not just ordinary animals. No, ladies and gentlemen, these two terrible lions are the most savage ever to be captured alive. In the capture of these lions – especially for Doyle's Circus – no less than eight famous big-game hunters lost their lives, as well as an untold number of simple natives.'

Then the band – what was left of it – played; the big cage was rolled on; Darcy whipped the curtain back, and then – after a moment of incredulous silence – came a laugh that chilled Healy's blood. For, inside the cage, with his tunic open and his cap off, was Cloone, sprawled on the ground against the bars, embracing Jumbo with one arm and Bess with the other. The two lions had a smug, meditative air, as though they were posing for a family photograph. At the uproar from the audience, they raised their heads sharply and fresh screams broke out, because Jumbo was seen to be holding Cloone's green gloves in his jaws while Bess sedately held his cane. There was an atmosphere of intense domesticity about the scene that made Healy feel that instead of a cage there should be a comfortable living room with a good fire burning. As a turn, it was superior to anything that had yet been seen, but the circus hands felt it was disaster.

'Oh, my God!' muttered the ringmaster. 'This is awful. This is the end. How could a thing like this happen, Darcy?'

'That's Cloone,' said Darcy with a puzzled frown.

'I know damned well it's Cloone,' the ringmaster said severely. 'I hadn't imagined it was a casual visitor. But how the hell did he get in, and how are we to get him out? Come along now, John,' he called pathetically. 'You don't want to hold up the show.'

But Cloone was too far gone to notice anything except that he had the whole audience to himself.

'Bess wants me to desert,' he announced. 'She says the old war is after going on long enough.'

This delighted the soldiers because, for some reason Bess looked exactly as though she had been saying something of the kind.

'Leave the man go home to his mother,' said a voice.

'Oh, Christ!' said the ringmaster. 'We'll be the laughing stock of the whole country. Darcy, you go in and get him out, there's a good man!'

'Is it me?' Darcy asked angrily. 'How the hell can I go in with him there? They'd ate you, man.' All the same he was a conscientious man, if a bit slow-witted, and after a moment he muttered despairingly 'Where's me hot bar?'

Two policemen who had been sitting near the front approached with their uniform caps in their hands to indicate that this was merely friendly curiosity and that nothing had yet occurred to require their official attention.

'Now, lads, what's the disturbance about?' the sergeant asked amiably. 'Wouldn't you come out of that cage like a good man and not be obstructing the traffic?'

Cloone began to giggle as the humour of it struck him.

'The door is open,' he said. 'Can't you come in and join the party.'

'What's that?' asked the sergeant.

'Come in and meet the family,' said Cloone.

'You're only making trouble for yourself,' the sergeant said sternly.

'Cowardy, cowardy custard!' Cloone said archly.

The sergeant glared at him for a moment and then put on his official cap. It had something of the effect of the judge's donning of the black cap in a murder trial. The younger policeman with a shy air put on his own.

'Someone will have to get him out,' the sergeant announced in an entirely different tone, the one that went with the cap.

'All right, all right,' Darcy said irritably, fetching his hot bar. He opened the door of the cage cautiously and the two lions rose and growled at him. Cloone jumped to his feet.

'Put that down,' he said in an outraged voice. 'Put it down, I say.'

'Get out of my way, God blast you!' snarled Darcy. 'Haven't I trouble enough without you?'

In a moment the atmosphere of domesticity had vanished. It was clear that Darcy hated the lions and the lions hated Darcy. For a few moments they eyed the Strong Man hungrily and growled; they slunk slowly back to the separate compartment at the end of the cage. Darcy, white in the face, slammed the gate behind them, and the ringmaster and the policeman, followed by Healy, entered the other compartment.

'Come home now, John,' Healy said softly.

'That's no way to treat my animals,' Cloone said.

'John! John! Remember the uniform.' A remark that, as he said later, he'd have to answer for on the Last Day because he cared as much about the uniform as he did about the danger to the country. But he was a man-tamer as Cloone was a lion-tamer: each made his own sort of soothing non-sensical noise.

'All right, all right,' Cloone muttered. 'Just let me say goodbye to them.'

'Don't let that man open the gate again or I won't be responsible,' Darcy shouted in a frenzy.

'I'll be responsible, Darcy,' Healy said shortly. 'Go on, John. Do it quick, and for God's sake don't let them out on us. Come on outside, boys.'

And there they had to stand outside the cage powerlessly while Cloone said goodbye to his pets. He opened the gate of the inner cage and stood there for a moment, overcome with emotion. The lions seemed to be overcome as well. After a moment Jumbo tossed his big head as though suppressing a sob and padded up to Cloone. Cloone bent and kissed him on the snout. Bess growled in a way that suggested a moan and came to lick his hand He kissed her as well. 'I'll be back, Bess, I'll be back,' he said with an anguished air. Then he drew himself up and gave them both a military salute. 'Company, present arms!' yelled one of the soldiers, and as Cloone staggered out they rose to cheer him. As Healy said, 'There was never the like of it seen in show business. If you could put it on as an act, you'd be turning them away.'

But for Cloone it was anything but show-business. He strode straight up to Darcy.

'You bloody big bully!' he said with tears of rage in his voice. 'You had to take a red-hot bar to frighten these poor innocent creatures. Like every other bully you're a coward.'

He gave Darcy a punch, and the Strong Man was so astonished that he went down flat on the ground. There was fresh uproar in the audience. The soldiers were getting out-of-hand. Darcy rose with a dazed expression as the two police-men seized Cloone from behind. To give them their due they were less afraid of what Cloone would do to Darcy than of what Darcy might do to Cloone. He was one of those power-ful melancholy men whose tragedy is that they can't have a little disagreement with a man in a pub without running the risk of manslaughter.

Cloone pulled himself away, leaving his unbuttoned tunic in the policeman's hands and then made a dash for the side of the tent. He disappeared under the canvas with the two guards close behind and a score of soldiers after the guards to see that Cloone got fair play. As they were unbuckling their belts for the task, two officers got up as well and rushed out through the main entrance to see that the guards got fair play. It was all very confusing, and the show was as good as over.

They ran Cloone to earth in the kitchen of a cottage down a lane from which there was no escape. By this time he had had the opportunity of considering his own behaviour, and all the fight had gone out of him. Once more he was only a broken-spirited old circus lion. He apologized to the woman of the house for the fright he had given her, and she moaned over him like a Greek chorus, blaming it all on the bad whis-key. He apologized to the police for the trouble he had given them and begged them not to spoil their night's pleasure but to let him surrender himself. He apologized all over again to the two young lieutenants who appeared soon after. By this time he was trembling like an aspen leaf.

'I'm sorry I disgraced ye the way I did,' he muttered. 'I'll never forgive myself. If 'twasn't for the lions I wouldn't have done it.'

At his court martial he appeared on a charge of 'conduct prejudicial to good order and discipline, in that he, Corporal John Cloone, on the 18th day of September of the current year had appeared in public with his tunic in disorder and minus certain articles of equipment: viz. one pair of gloves and one walking stick (regulations).' The charge of assault was dropped at the instance of the President who suggested to the Prosecutor that, considering the prisoner's occupation in civil life, there might have been provocation.

But armies are alike the world over, and whatever their

disregard for civilian rights, they all have the same old-maid-ish preoccupation with their own dignity, and Cloone lost his stripes. Healy asked him what better he could expect from soldiers, people who tried to turn decent artists into megalo-maniacs like themselves. As if anybody had ever succeeded in turning a soldier into anything that was the least use to God or man!


# ACHILLES' HEEL


The Catholic Church has only one weak point which is well known to all the faithful. This is the type of woman who preys on celibates, particularly priests' housekeepers. The priest's housekeeper is a subject in itself, because tests have shown that when transferred to males who are not celibate it pines away and dies. To say that it is sexless is to say both too much and too little. Like the Church it pursues chastity for higher ends, which – in the matter of priests' housekeepers – means the subjection of men in a way that mere wives cannot comprehend. Wives, of course, have a similar am-bition, but their purposes are mysteriously thwarted by love-making, jealousy, and children; and it is well known that many wives break down and weep with rage when they think of the power of priests' housekeepers. *Their* victims, being celibate, have no children, and are automatically sealed off from other women, so that even women who have business to transact with them find they have to do it through the house-keeper.

The Bishop of Moyle was no exception. His housekeeper, Nellie, had been with him since the time he was a Canon, and even then, unknown to himself, he had always been ref-erred to by his congregation as 'Nellie and the Canon'. 'Nellie and the Canon' disliked all-night dances, for instance, so all-night dances simply stopped. There was even a story that Nellie had once appeared on the altar and announced that there would be no eight o'clock Mass because she was keeping the Canon in bed. Even in those days she could not have been very old, and by the time I speak of her, she was a well-preserved woman with a fussy, humble, sugary air that concealed a cold intelligence. In private, her great rival, Canon Lanigan, used to call her 'La Maintenon', but when he visited the Bishop's he was as unctuous as herself, and affected to admire her cooking and even her detestable bottled coffee.

For all Nellie's airs and graces, she wasn't in the least taken in by the Canon; she knew he preferred old French mish-mash to her own simple, straightforward cooking, and she even warned the Bishop against him.

'God forgive me, my Lord,' she said meekly, 'I can't warm to Canon Lanigan. There's something about him that's insincere. Or am I just being silly? I know I'm a foolish old woman, but you knew that yourself the day you engaged me.'

Anyway, Nellie's cooking was not aimed at the Canon but at her own dear simple man – a giant with the heart of a child, as she often said herself in her poetic way. His only real fear was that he might fade away for want of proper nourishment. It wasn't that he was greedy, but that he didn't have much else to worry about. He knew what the appetites of old-fashioned clerics were like, and comparing his own accomplishments and theirs, he couldn't see for the life of him how he was ever going to reach the age of ninety. After eating a whole chicken for his dinner, he would sit in his study for hours with his hands folded on his lap, brooding on it, till Nellie stuck her head through the door.

'You're all right, my Lord?' she would cry.

'Ah, I'm not, Nellie,' he would say despondently over his shoulder. 'I'm feeling a bit low tonight.'

' 'Tis that chicken,' she would cry, making a dramatic entrance. 'I knew it. I said it to Tim Murphy. There wasn't a pick on it.'

'I was wondering about that,' he would say sadly, fixing her with his anxious blue eyes. 'I thought myself 'twas on the slight side.'

'What you want is a nice grilled chop.'

'I wonder, Nellie, I wonder,' he would mutter, shaking his head. 'There's a lot of eating in a chop.'

'Or cutlets, if you prefer them.'

'Well, cutlets make a nice late night snack,' he would say, beginning to relax.

'They do, but they're too dry. What you want is a good plate of nice curly rashers, with lots of fat. Sure, 'twas my own fault. I knew there was nothing in that chicken. I knew there should be rashers along with it, but the way I am, the head is going on me. I'm getting too old. One of these days I won't be able to remember my own name . . . And a couple of chips – sure, 'twould be the making of you.'

The Bishop was anything but a stupid man, but he did tend to take Nellie at her own valuation. He could easily have imagined her in various sorts of trouble. He could have imagined her lending her little savings to the breadman on foot of a proposal of marriage, or getting into debt with a bookmaker. When at last she came to him with her troubles, he couldn't conceive of her having any difficulty with the Revenue Commissioners, and she, it appeared, couldn't either.

'Ah, you said it yourself, my Lord,' she said ingenuously. 'This diocese was ever notorious for slander. But why would they try to fix it on me? I suppose they want to get their own candidate in – someone that would do their whispering for them. It is something I never would do, and I won't do it now, my Lord, even if they do say you are too old.'

'Who says I'm too old?' the Bishop asked with a flash of his blue eyes.

'Oh, don't ask me to tell you things like that,' she said with disgust. 'I'm fifteen years with you, and I never carried stories yet, let Canon Lanigan say what he likes.'

'Never mind about Canon Lanigan,' said the Bishop, feeling he was never going to get to the bottom of it. 'What did this fellow from the Revenue say?'

'Is it Tim Leary?' she asked. 'Sure, what could he say? Ah, 'tisn't that at all, my Lord, but the questions he asked me, the sly rogue! And the things he said! "The biggest smuggler in the whole country" – wasn't that a nice thing for him to say?'

'He called you "the biggest smuggler in the whole country"?' repeated the Bishop, between amusement and rage.

'Ah, how could he call me that?' she replied. 'Sure, the tongue would rot in his mouth. Is it a poor defenceless old woman like me? But that's what he meant all right, my Lord. Sure, I knew well what he had in his mind the whole time. Whiskey, petrol, tea, and things, my Lord, that I declare to you, as if I was going before my Maker this minute, I never heard the names of.'

'Ah, that fellow must be a bit soft in the head,' the Bishop said with a worried air. 'Which Learys does he belong to? Is it the Learys of Clooneavullen?'

In spite of the fact that he had been a Professor of Dogmatic Theology, the Bishop was convinced that you could explain everything about a man just by knowing who his parents were. The grace of God was all very well, but it wasn't the same thing at all as belonging to a good family.

'Aha!' she said, wagging a finger at him. 'Didn't I say exactly the same thing myself? That his own father couldn't read or write, and he accusing me!'

'Never mind about his father,' the Bishop said earnestly. 'Sure, hadn't he an uncle up in the lunatic asylum? I knew him myself. What business has a fellow like that interfering with the likes of me? You tell him to come up here tomorrow, and I'll talk to him myself.'

'You will to be sure, my Lord,' she said complacently. Then at the door she stopped. 'But sure, why would you talk to a little whipper-snapper like that – a man like you that have the ear of the government? You would only have to tell them to send him somewhere else. How well he didn't mind going over your head. Ah, well, I suppose they told him you were too old.'

The Bishop meditated for a moment on that. When she mentioned his getting old she touched on his sore spot because he knew a lot of people thought he was getting old. And he saw her point about people's going over his head, which might, or might not, be the work of clerical opponents like Lanigan. He knew the secrets of power as well as Nellie did, and the most important of these is never to deal directly with your inferiors. Of course, in the eyes of God, they might be anything but inferiors, but nobody knew exactly how they *did* look in the eyes of God, so the best thing was to put them down before they became a menace.

'Very well,' he said in a detached voice that made Nellie's heart flutter. 'Where's my pen?'

It was a voice he used only when some parish priest had been seen drunk in a public place or a gang of young curates had started a card school. 'Give me my pen till I suspend Father Tom,' he would say in a dry voice to his secretary, or else, 'Give me my pen till I scatter them.' It was the voice of ultimate authority, of the Church Militant personified in her own dear man.

In spite of good detective work Nellie never did get to see the Bishop's letter to the Minister, Jim Butcher, but, on the other hand, the Bishop did not get to see the Minister's reply either: Nellie thought it might worry him too much. It ran:

'Dear Doctor Gallogly, how pleasant to hear from you again. Mrs Butcher was saying only yesterday that it was a long time since we saw you. I have had careful inquiries made about the matter you mention, and I am sorry to inform you that the statements of the local Revenue Officer appear to be fully substantiated. Your housekeeper, Miss Ellen Coneely, is the owner of licensed premises on the other side of the Border which have long been known as the headquarters of a considerable smuggling organization, and their base on this side is believed to be the Episcopal Palace. You will realize that the Revenue Commissioners hesitate to take any steps that might embarrass your good self, but you will also realize that this traffic involves a considerable loss of revenue. I should be deeply grateful for your Lordship's assistance in putting an early end to it. *Mise le Meas. Seumas O Buitséir, Aire.*'

Nellie turned cold when she read it. Things were worse than she imagined. It wasn't only Tim Leary she had to deal with but shadowy Commissioners and Ministers in Dublin who might be up to any sort of blackguarding. Nor could she rely on the Bishop himself to deal with them. He was a good, kind man, but the fire had gone out of him. She took up her own pen and wrote:

'Dear Sir, His Lordship, the Most Reverend Doctor Gallogly, Bishop of Moyle, has passed on to me your letter of May 3rd and asked me to reply to it for him. He says it is all lies and intrigues and not to bother him any more about it. He says is it likely he would not know what was going on in his own home, or is it a daylight robber you think he is. This campaign was started entirely by Timothy Leary, and as the Bishop points out, what better could you expect of a man whose uncle died in the Moyle Asylum, a wet and dirty case. The public-house you talk of is only another matter of the lies. It does not belong to me at all, but to my unfortunate brother, a Commandant in the Army of Freedom (how are you?), and now a helpless invalid with varicose veins and six children. How would the likes of him be a smuggler? Timothy Leary will not be allowed to enter this Palace again. What do we pay taxes for? We were better off when we had the English. Your obedient servant, Ellen Coneely.'

There was something about this letter that gave Nellie great satisfaction. Though she did not recognize it, it illustrated to perfection the Achilles Heel of Catholicism, for though Dr Gallogly was entirely innocent of its contents, they left the Minister and his staff with a strong impression that the Bishop of Moyle was now the ringleader of a powerful smuggling gang. No doubt the poor old man was not responsible; old age took people in all sorts of different ways, but it was embarrassing because you couldn't possibly go raiding the Bishop's Palace for contraband. The very thought of what the newspapers would say about that made the Minister wince: the *Irish Times* would report it smugly, with the implication that whatever could be said against Protestant bishops, they drew the line at certain things; the *Irish Independent* would assert that instructions for the raid must have come from Moscow, while the *Irish Press* would compare it to the Casement forgeries.

'For God's sake, leave it as it is, Peter,' the Minister told his secretary. 'This thing is dynamite.'

Nellie, scared by the Minister's letter, worked feverishly and openly to get rid of the contraband in her possession, and Tim Leary knew it and was mortified.

Then one day a man was caught crossing the Border with a keg of whiskey strapped under his car, and Tim was able to trace the keg to Paddy Clancy's liquor store. Paddy had no alternative but to admit that he had sold the keg to the Bishop.

'Give us a look at the Bishop's account, Paddy,' Tim said irritably, and poor Paddy felt it would be safer to produce the ledger. It was an ugly moment. He was never a man to interfere in other people's business, but he knew of old that the Bishop's account was peculiar. Tim Leary looked at it in stupefaction.

'Merciful God, are you trying to tell me the Bishop drinks all that?' he asked.

'I wouldn't know, Tim,' said Paddy. 'I dare say bishops have a lot of entertaining to do – parish priests and that.'

'A gallon a man a night!' Tim cried. He was a rather hysterical young fellow, Paddy thought, and anyway took his job too seriously.

'Now, that's all very well, Tim,' Paddy said severely. 'I'm not in a position to ask my customers questions.'

'Well, I'm going to ask a few,' Tim said, headstrong as ever. 'And unless that man is an out-and-out criminal, he'll answer them, what's more. Give us that ledger.'

Paddy watched him from the door striding off up the street and decided that he wouldn't last long in his job – a young fellow who took things to the fair like that.

At the Palace, Nellie tried hard to head him off. She said first that the Bishop was out. Then she said he was sick, and finally that he had given orders not to admit Tim. Unfortunately for her, she could not get Tim to keep his voice down, and she knew to her cost that with the appetite of a child, the Bishop also had a child's curiosity, and a beggar could hardly come to the door without his peering out and listening. Suddenly, there was a step in the hall and the Bishop came out.

'That will do, Nellie,' he said mildly and came up to Tim with a threatening air, a handsome old man with a baby complexion and fierce blue eyes.

'Now, what do you want, young man?' he asked sternly.

'I'm investigating the smuggling that's going on in this locality and I'd like a few words with you, my Lord.'

'I already wrote to the Minister, young man, and told him I didn't know what I had to do with it.'

'If you'll listen to me for a few minutes I'll soon show you what you have to do with it,' said Tim.

'Aren't you a very saucy young fellow?' the Bishop said in a tone of reproach. 'What part of the world do you hail from?'

'I'm from Manister,' replied Tim, who couldn't be aware of the significance the Bishop attached to heredity.

'I thought you were John Leary's son from Clooneavullen,' the Bishop said in surprise.

'I'm nothing of the sort,' Tim said shortly. 'My father was a schoolmaster.'

'You're not Jim Leary's boy?' the Bishop said softly, resting his old hand on Tim's.

'I am, then,' said Tim, pleased to be identified at last.

'Come in, come in,' the Bishop said, giving his hand a squeeze. 'Your father was Headmaster there when I was a curate. No son of Jim Leary's is going to leave my house without something.'

'I'm on duty, my Lord,' said Tim, following him into his sitting room.

'Ah, sha, aren't we all?' asked the Bishop, going to the sideboard. With shaky hands he produced two glasses and a bottle of whiskey. He put a few spoonfuls in one glass and almost filled the other, which he gave to Tim.

'Now, you can tell me,' he said comfortably. Tim was beginning to realize that he liked the old man, a weakness of his that made him a bad investigator.

'Well, a fellow was caught trying to cross the Border three days ago with a keg of your whiskey slung under his car,' said Tim.

'A keg of my whiskey?' repeated the Bishop with

amusement. 'But what would I be doing with a keg of whiskey?'

'That's what *I* was wondering,' replied Tim. 'You seem to have bought enough of them.'

'I never bought a keg of whiskey in my whole life, man,' the Bishop said candidly. 'I wouldn't know what to do with it. A drop like this just to keep someone company is all I ever see of it. I haven't the constitution for whiskey.'

'If you'll take one look at your account in Paddy Clancy's ledger you'll soon see the sort of constitution you're supposed to have,' said Tim ... 'Or maybe this is the one with the constitution,' he added fiercely as Nellie walked in with a bundle of bills in her hand.

'That's enough of the whispering and intriguing,' she said. 'I admit what I have to admit. 'Twas only to keep my unfortunate angashore of a brother out of the workhouse, a fellow that never did a hand's turn only fighting for Ireland. 'Twas people like me that had to do the real fighting. Not one penny of his Lordship's money went astray. I will go if I'm made but I will not leave this house without my reference.'

'You could keep a houseful of brothers out of what you made on the petrol alone,' Tim said angrily. 'And I suppose you forget the tea and the butter.'

'That will do,' the Bishop said firmly. 'Go away, Nellie,' he added over his shoulder in his dry voice, his episcopal voice.

Nellie looked at him in stupefaction and then burst into a howl of grief and went out, sobbing to herself about 'the fifteen good years of my life that I gave him, and this is all the gratitude I get'. The Bishop waited till her sobs had subsided in the kitchen, and then leaned forward with his hands joined between his knees.

'Do me a favour, Tim,' he said. 'You don't mind if I call you Tim?'

'I'm honoured, my Lord,' said Tim.

'But don't call me Paddy,' added the Bishop, an old joke that did not ring true. 'Tell me, how many people know about this?'

'You might say that, by this time, 'twas common property,' said Tim.

'And what do they think about me?' asked the Bishop.

'You must know yourself they have a great regard for you,' said Tim.

'They have,' the Bishop said dryly. 'They have so much regard for me that they don't mind if I turn my house into a smugglers' den. They didn't suggest what I might be doing with the Cathedral?'

Tim saw then that the Bishop was more affected than he let on to be.

'What will they do to Nellie?' the Bishop added.

'Send her to gaol, I hope,' said Tim. 'Not to mention the fine, that will be worse for her.'

'What sort of fine?'

'It'll have to be calculated,' said Tim. 'But it'll probably run into a couple of thousand pounds.'

'A couple of thousand?' exclaimed the Bishop. 'Sure, I haven't that much money myself, Tim.'

'You may be damn full sure she has it,' said Tim.

'Nellie?' said the Bishop.

'And more along with it.'

'For the love of God!' the Bishop said softly and sat back. crossing his legs. 'And here was I, thinking she was only an old fool! Oh, after this, they'll say I'm not even fit to look after myself. They could put in a coadjutor on me over a thing like this.'

'They wouldn't do that,' Tim said in alarm.

'Oh, indeed they would,' the Bishop said gaily. 'And they'd be fully entitled. And that's not the worst of it. Do you know what's the worst thing about being old, Tim?' he added, leaning forward again. 'I'll tell you. By the time you finish your lunch you start worrying about your dinner. I suppose a man must have something to look forward to. When I was a young priest I didn't care if I never saw a dinner. And if they put Nellie in gaol, 'twill kill me. At my age I'm not going to be able to get another housekeeper like that.'

Tim was a generous young man, and, after all, the Bishop had been a friend of his father.

'Do you think you'd be able to control her for the future?' he asked.

'I do not,' replied the Bishop with his outrageous candour. 'A priest never controlled a woman yet. We haven't the experience, I suppose.'

'Begod, I'd soon control her if I had a free hand,' said Tim.

'Oh, I'll give you all the hand you want,' said the Bishop with an episcopal wave of his hand. ''Tis more in my interest than yours, before they have me married to her.' Then he got up and gave Tim a pat on the shoulder. 'You're a good boy,' he said, 'and I won't forget it for you. Butcher is a good enough fellow, only he's ruined with that wife of his.'

That afternoon the Bishop stood by the window with his hands behind his back and watched while Tim Leary loaded the lorries with commodities the Bishop had thought had gone from the world – chests of tea, bags of sugar, and boxes of butter. Nellie herself did not put in an appearance, but that night when she opened the door and said, 'Dinner is served, my Lord,' the Bishop sat down to a dinner in a thousand – juicy roast beef and roast potatoes with the tenderest of young peas drowned in butter. The Bishop ate his way through it, but he never addressed a word to her. He was thinking of the way he had had to coax and beg for it, an old man with nothing else to look forward to.

After that, he went to his study and took down the history of the diocese that had often comforted him before when he had dreamed of what his own name would look like in future editions, but that night it only made him feel worse. Looking back on the men who had held the see before him he couldn't think of one against whom there had been a breath of scandal, except for one eighteenth-century Bishop who had turned Protestant. He was beginning to think that turning Protestant wasn't the worst thing that could happen to a Bishop.

Then the door opened and Nellie looked in coyly.

'What way are you feeling now?' she whispered.

'Let me alone,' he said in a dry voice without even looking up. 'My heart is broken.'

'Ah, 'tisn't your heart at all,' she said. ' 'Tis that beef. 'Twasn't hung long enough. There isn't a butcher in this town will take the trouble to hang beef. Would I get you a couple of scrambled eggs?'

'Go away, I said!' he retorted, but she heard the tears in his voice.

'You're right,' she said. 'There's nothing in eggs only coloured water. O God, would I fry you a couple of rashers?'

'I tell you I don't want rashers, woman,' he said in a cry of pain.

'The dear knows, they're not worth it,' she admitted sadly. 'What are they only old bones with the hair still growing on them? What you want is a nice little juicy bit of Limerick ham with a couple of mashed potatoes and milk sauce with parsley. 'Twould make a new man of you.'

'All right, all right,' he cried angrily. 'Do what you like but leave me alone.'

Even the prospect of the ham could not lift his sorrow. He knew that whenever a woman says something will make a new man of you, all she means is that it will help to make an old one of you before your time.

# THE WREATH

When Father Fogarty read of the death of his friend, Father Devine, in a Dublin nursing home, he was stunned. He was a man who did not understand the irremediable. He took out an old seminary group, put it on the mantelpiece and spent the evening looking at it. Devine's clever, pale, shrunken face stood out from the rest, not very different from what it had been in his later years except for the absence of pince-nez. He and Fogarty had been boys together in a provincial town where Devine's father had been a schoolmaster and Fogarty's mother had kept a shop. Even then, everybody had known that Devine was marked out by nature for the priesthood. He was clever, docile and beautifully mannered. Fogarty's vocation had come later and proved a surprise, to himself as well as to others.

They had been friends over the years, affectionate when together, critical and sarcastic when apart. They had not seen one another for close on a year. Devine had been unlucky. As long as the old Bishop, Gallogly, lived, he had been fairly well sheltered, but Lanigan, the new one, disliked him. It was partly Devine's own fault. He could not keep his mouth shut. He was witty and waspish and said whatever came into his head about colleagues who had nothing like his gifts. Fogarty remembered the things Devine had said about himself. Devine had affected to believe that Fogarty was a man of many personalities, and asked with mock humility which he was now dealing with – Nero, Napoleon, or St Francis of Assisi.

It all came back: the occasional jaunts together, the plans for holidays abroad that never took place, and now the warm and genuine love for Devine which was so natural to Fogarty welled up in him, and, realizing that never again in this world would he be able to express it, he began to weep. He was as simple as a child in his emotions. When he was in high spirits he devised practical jokes of the utmost crudity; when he was depressed he brooded for days on imaginary injuries: he forgot lightly, remembered suddenly and with exaggerated intensity, and blamed himself cruelly and unjustly for his own shortcomings. He would have been astonished to learn that, for all the intrusions of Nero and Napoleon, his understanding had continued to develop when that of cleverer men had dried up, and that he was a better and wiser man at forty than he had been twenty years before.

But he did not understand the irremediable. He had to have someone to talk to, and for want of a better, rang up Jackson, a curate who had been Devine's other friend. He did not really like Jackson, who was worldly, cynical, and something of a careerist, and he usually called him by the worst name in his vocabulary – a Jesuit. Several times he had asked Devine what he saw in Jackson but Devine's replies had not enlightened him much. 'I wouldn't trust myself too far with the young Loyola if I were you,' Fogarty had told Devine with his worldly swagger. Now, he had no swagger left.

'That's terrible news about Devine, Jim, isn't it?' he said.

'Yes,' Jackson drawled in his usual cautious, cagey way, as though he were afraid to commit himself even about that. 'I suppose it's a happy release for the poor devil.'

That was the sort of tone that maddened Fogarty. It sounded as though Jackson were talking of an old family pet who had been sent to the vet's.

'I hope he appreciates it,' he said gruffly. 'I was thinking of going to town and coming back with the funeral. You wouldn't come, I suppose?'

'I don't very well see how I could, Jerry,' Jackson replied in a tone of mild alarm. 'It's only a week since I was up last.'

'Ah, well, I'll go myself,' said Fogarty. 'You don't know what happened him, do you?'

'Ah, well, he was always anaemic,' Jackson said lightly. 'He should have looked after himself, but he didn't get much chance with old O'Leary.'

'He wasn't intended to,' Fogarty said darkly, indiscreet as usual.

'What?' Jackson asked in surprise. 'Oh no,' he added, resuming his worldly tone. 'It wasn't a sinecure, of course. He was fainting all over the shop. Last time was in the middle of Mass. By then, of course, it was too late. When I saw him last week I knew he was dying.'

'You saw him last week?' Fogarty repeated.

'Oh, just for a few minutes. He couldn't talk much.'

And again, the feeling of his own inadequacy descended on Fogarty. He realized that Jackson, who seemed to have as much feeling as a mowing machine, had kept in touch with Devine, and gone out of his way to see him at the end, while he, the devoted, warm-hearted friend, had let him slip from sight into eternity and was now wallowing in the sense of his own loss.

'I'll never forgive myself, Jim,' he said humbly. 'I never even knew he was sick.'

'I'd like to go to the funeral myself if I could,' said Jackson.

'I'll ring you up later if I can manage it.'

He did manage it, and that evening they set off in Fogarty's car for the city. They stayed in an old hotel in a side-street where porters and waiters all knew them. Jackson brought Fogarty to a very pleasant restaurant for dinner. The very sight of Jackson had been enough to renew Fogarty's doubts. He was a tall, thin man with a prim, watchful, clerical air, and he knew his way around. He spent at least ten minutes over the menu and the wine list, and the head waiter danced attendance on him as head waiters do only when they are either hopeful or intimidated.

'You needn't bother about me,' Fogarty said to cut short the rigmarole. 'I'm having steak.'

'Father Fogarty is having steak, Paddy,' Jackson said suavely, looking at the head waiter over his spectacles with what Fogarty called his 'Jesuit' air. 'Make it rare. And stout, I fancy. It's a favourite beverage of the natives.'

'I'll spare you the stout,' Fogarty said, enjoying the banter. 'Red wine will do me fine.'

'Mind, Paddy,' Jackson said in the same tone, 'Father Fogarty said *red* wine. You're in Ireland now, remember.'

Next morning they went to the parish church where the coffin was resting on trestles before the altar. Beside it, to Fogarty's surprise, was a large wreath of roses. When they got up from their knees, Devine's uncle, Ned, had arrived with his son. Ned was a broad-faced, dark-haired, nervous man, with the anaemic complexion of the family.

'I'm sorry for your trouble, Ned,' said Fogarty.

'I know that, father,' said Ned.

'I don't know if you know Father Jackson. He was a great friend of Father Willie's.'

'I heard him speak of him,' said Ned. 'He talked a lot about the pair of ye. Ye were his great friends. Poor Father Willie!' he added with a sigh. 'He had few enough.'

Just then the parish priest came in and spoke to Ned Devine. His name was Martin. He was a tall man with a stern, unlined, wooden face and candid blue eyes like a baby's. He stood for a few minutes by the coffin, then studied the breastplate and wreath, looking closely at the tag. It was only then that he beckoned the two younger priests towards the door.

'Tell me, what are we going to do about that thing?' he asked with a professional air.

'What thing?' Fogarty asked in surprise.

'That wreath,' Martin replied with a nod over his shoulder.

'What's wrong with it?'

' 'Tis against the rubrics,' replied the parish priest in the complacent tone of a policeman who has looked up the law on the subject.

'For heaven's sake, what have the rubrics to do with it?' Fogarty asked impatiently.

'The rubrics have a whole lot to do with it,' Martin replied with a stern glance. 'And, apart from that, 'tis a bad custom.'

'You mean Masses bring in more money?' Fogarty asked with amused insolence.

'I do not mean Masses bring in more money,' replied Martin who tended to answer every remark verbatim, like a solicitor's letter. It added to the impression of woodenness he gave. 'I mean that flowers are a Pagan survival.' He looked at the two young priests with the same anxious, innocent, wooden air. 'And here am I, week in, week out, preaching against flowers, and a blooming big wreath of them in my own church. And on a priest's coffin, what's more! What am I to say about that?'

'Who asked you to say anything?' Fogarty asked angrily. 'The man wasn't from your diocese.'

'Now, that's all very well,' said Martin. 'That's bad enough by itself, but it isn't the whole story.'

'You mean because it's from a woman?' Jackson broke in lightly in a tone that would have punctured any pose less substantial than Martin's.

'I mean, because it's from a woman, exactly.'

'A woman!' said Fogarty in astonishment. 'Does it say so?'

'It does not say so.'

'Then how do you know?'

'Because it's red roses.'

'And does that mean it's from a woman?'

'What else could it mean?'

'I suppose it could mean it's from somebody who didn't study the language of flowers the way you seem to have done,' Fogarty snapped.

He could feel Jackson's disapproval of him weighing on the air, but when Jackson spoke it was at the parish priest that his coldness and nonchalance were directed.

'Oh, well,' he said with a shrug. 'I'm afraid we know nothing about it, father. You'll have to make up your own mind.'

'I don't like doing anything when I wasn't acquainted with the man,' Martin grumbled, but he made no further attempt to interfere, and one of the undertaker's men took the wreath and put it on the hearse. Fogarty controlled himself with difficulty. As he banged open the door of his car and started the engine his face was flushed. He drove with his head bowed and his brows jutting down like rocks over his eyes. It was what Devine had called his Nero look. As they cleared the main streets he burst out.

'That's the sort of thing that makes me ashamed of myself, Jim. Flowers are a pagan survival! And they take it from him, what's worse. They take it from him. They listen to that sort of stuff instead of telling him to shut his big ignorant gob.'

'Oh, well,' Jackson said tolerantly, taking out his pipe, 'we're hardly being fair to him. After all, he didn't know Devine.'

'But that only makes it worse,' Fogarty said hotly. 'Only for our being there he'd have thrown out that wreath. And for what? His own dirty, mean, suspicious mind!'

'Ah, I wouldn't go as far as that,' Jackson said, frowning. 'I think in his position I'd have asked somebody to take it away.'

'You would?'

'Wouldn't you?'

'But why, in God's name?'

'Oh, I suppose I'd be afraid of the scandal – I'm not a very courageous type.'

'Scandal?'

'Whatever you like to call it. After all, some woman sent it.'

'Yes. One of Devine's old maids.'

'Have you ever heard of an old maid sending a wreath of red roses to a funeral?' Jackson asked, raising his brows, his head cocked.

'To tell you the God's truth, I might have done it myself,' Fogarty confessed with boyish candour. 'It would never have struck me that there was anything wrong with it.'

'It would have struck the old maid all right, though.'

Fogarty turned his eyes for a moment to stare at Jackson. Jackson was staring back. Then he missed a turning and reversed with a muttered curse. To the left of them the Wicklow mountains stretched away southwards, and between the grey walls the fields were a ragged brilliant green under the tattered sky.

'You're not serious, Jim?' he said after a few minutes.

'Oh, I'm not suggesting that there was anything wrong,' Jackson said, gesturing widely with his pipe. 'Women get ideas. We all know that.'

'These things can happen in very innocent ways,' Fogarty said with ingenuous solemnity. Then he scowled again and a blush spread over his handsome craggy face. Like all those who live mainly in their imaginations, he was always astonished and shocked at the suggestions that reached him from the outside world: he could live with his fantasies only by assuming that they were nothing more. Jackson, whose own imagination was curbed and even timid, who never went at things like a thoroughbred at a gate, watched him with amusement and a certain envy. Just occasionally he felt that he himself would have liked to welcome a new idea with that boyish wonder and panic.

'I can't believe it,' Fogarty said angrily, tossing his head.

'You don't have to,' Jackson replied, nursing his pipe and swinging round in the seat with his arm close to Fogarty's shoulder. 'As I say, women get these queer ideas. There's usually nothing in them. At the same time, I must say *I* wouldn't be very scandalized if I found out that there was something in it. If ever a man needed someone to care for him, Devine did in the last year or two.'

'But not Devine, Jim,' Fogarty said, raising his voice. 'Not Devine! You could believe a thing like that about me. I suppose I could believe it about you. But I knew Devine since we were kids, and he wouldn't be capable of it.'

'I never knew him in that way,' Jackson admitted. 'In fact, I scarcely knew him at all, really. But I'd have said he was as capable of it as the rest of us. He was lonelier than the rest of us.'

'God, don't I know it?' Fogarty said in sudden self-reproach. 'I could understand if it was drink.'

'Oh, not drink!' Jackson said with distaste. 'He was too fastidious. Can you imagine him in the DTs like some old parish priest, trying to strangle the nurses?'

'But that's what I say, Jim. He wasn't the type.'

'Oh, you must make distinctions,' said Jackson. 'I could imagine him attracted by some intelligent woman. You know yourself how he'd appeal to her, the same way he appealed to us, a cultured man in a country town. I don't have to tell you the sort of life an intelligent woman leads, married to some lout of a shopkeeper or a gentleman farmer. Poor devils, it's a mercy that most of them aren't educated.'

'He didn't give you any hint who she was?' Fogarty asked incredulously. Jackson had spoken with such conviction that it impressed him as true.

'Oh, I don't even know if there was such a woman,' Jackson said hastily, and then he blushed too. Fogarty remained silent. He knew now that Jackson had been talking about himself, not Devine.

As the country grew wilder and furze bushes and ruined keeps took the place of pastures and old abbeys, Fogarty found his eyes attracted more and more to the wreath that swayed lightly with the hearse, the only spot of pure colour in the whole landscape with its watery greens and blues and greys. It seemed an image of the essential mystery of a priest's life. What, after all, did he really know of Devine?

Only what his own temperament suggested, and mostly – when he wasn't being St Francis of Assisi – he had seen himself as the worldly one of the pair, the practical, coarse-grained man who cut corners, and Devine as the saint, racked by the fastidiousness and asceticism that exploded in his bitter little jests. Now his mind boggled at the idea of the agony that alone could have driven Devine into an entanglement with a woman; yet the measure of his incredulity was that of the conviction he would presently begin to feel. When once an unusual idea broke through his imagination, he hugged it, brooded on it, promoted it to the dignity of a revelation.

'God, don't we lead terrible lives?' he burst out at last. 'Here we are, probably the two people in the world who knew Devine best, and even we have no notion what that thing in front of us means.'

'Which might be as well for our peace of mind,' said Jackson.

'I'll engage it did damn little for Devine's,' Fogarty said grimly. It was peculiar; he did not believe yet in the reality of the woman behind the wreath, but already he hated her.

'Oh, I don't know,' Jackson said in some surprise. 'Isn't that what we all really want from life?'

'Is it?' Fogarty asked in wonder. He had always thought of Jackson as a cold fish, and suddenly found himself wondering about that as well. After all, there must have been something in him that attracted Devine. He had the feeling that Jackson, who was, as he recognized, by far the subtler man, was probing him, and for the same reason. Each was looking in the other for the quality that had attracted Devine, and, which, having made him their friend might make them friends also. Each was trying to see how far he could go with the other. Fogarty, as usual, was the first with a confession.

'I couldn't do it, Jim,' he said earnestly. 'I was never even tempted, except once, and then it was the wife of one of the men who was in the seminary with me. I was crazy about her. But when I saw what her marriage to the other fellow was like, I changed my mind. She hated him like poison, Jim. I soon saw she might have hated me in the same way. It's only when you see what marriage is really like, as we do, that you realize how lucky we are.'

'Lucky?' Jackson repeated mockingly.

'Aren't we?'

'Did you ever know a seminary that wasn't full of men who thought they were lucky? They might be drinking themselves to death, but they never doubted their luck? Nonsense, man! Anyway, why do you think she'd have hated you?'

'I don't,' Fogarty replied with a boyish laugh. 'Naturally, I think I'd have been the perfect husband for her. That's the way Nature kids you.'

'Well, why shouldn't you have made her a perfect husband?' Jackson asked quizzically. 'There's nothing much wrong with you that I can see. Though I admit I can see you better as a devoted father.'

'God knows you might be right,' Fogarty said, his face clouding again. It was as changeable as an Irish sky, Jackson thought with amusement. 'You could get on well enough without the woman, but the kids are hell. She had two. "Father Fogey" they used to call me. And my mother was as bad,' he burst out. 'She was wrapped up in the pair of us. She always wanted us to be better than everybody else, and when we weren't she used to cry. She said it was the Fogarty blood breaking out in us – the Fogartys were all horse dealers.' His handsome, happy face was black with all the remorse and guilt. 'I'm afraid she died under the impression that I was a Fogarty after all.'

'If the Fogartys are any relation to the Martins, I'd say it was most unlikely,' Jackson said, half amused, half touched.

'I never knew till she was dead how much she meant to me,' Fogarty said broodingly. 'Hennessey warned me not to take the Burial Service myself, but I thought it was the last thing I could do for her. He knew what he was talking about, of course. I disgraced myself, bawling like a blooming kid, and he pushed me aside and finished it for me. My God, the way we gallop through that till it comes to our own turn! Every time I've read it since, I've read it as if it were for my mother.'

Jackson shook his head uncomprehendingly.

'You feel these things more than I do,' he said. 'I'm a cold fish.'

It struck Fogarty with some force that this was precisely what he had always believed himself and that now he could believe it no longer.

'Until then, I used to be a bit flighty,' he confessed. 'After that I knew it wasn't in me to care for another woman.'

'That's only more of your nonsense,' said Jackson impatiently. 'Love is just one thing, not half a dozen. If I were a young fellow looking for a wife I'd go after some girl who felt like that about her father. You probably have too much of it. I haven't enough. When I was in Manister there was a shopkeeper's wife I used to see. I talked to her and lent her books. She was half crazy with loneliness. Then one morning I got home and found her standing outside my door in the pouring rain. She'd been there half the night. She wanted me to take her away, to "save" her, as she said. You can imagine what happened her after.'

'Went off with someone else, I suppose?'

'No such luck. She took to drinking and sleeping with racing men. Sometimes I blame myself for it. I feel I should have kidded her along. But I haven't enough love to go round. You have too much. With your enthusiastic nature you'd probably have run off with her.'

'I often wondered what I would do,' Fogarty said shyly.

He felt very close to tears. It was partly the wreath, brilliant in the sunlight, that had drawn him out of his habitual reserve and make him talk in that way with a man of even greater reserve. Partly it was the emotion of returning to the little town where he had grown up. He hated and avoided it; it seemed to him to represent all the narrowness and meanness that he tried to banish from his thoughts, but at the same time it contained all the nostalgia and violence he had felt there; and when he drew near it again a tumult of emotions rose in him that half-strangled him. He was watching for it already like a lover.

'There it is!' he said triumphantly, pointing to a valley where a tapering Franciscan tower rose on the edge of a

187

clutter of low Georgian houses and thatched cabins. 'They'll be waiting for us at the bridge. That's how they'll be waiting for me when my turn comes, Jim.'

A considerable crowd had gathered at the farther side of the bridge to escort the hearse to the cemetery. Four men shouldered the shiny coffin over the bridge past the ruined castle and up the hilly Main Street. Shutters were up on the shop fronts, blinds were drawn, everything was at a standstill except where a curtain was lifted and an old woman peered out.

'Counting the mourners,' Fogarty said with a bitter laugh. 'They'll say I had nothing like as many as Devine. That place,' he added, lowering his voice, 'the second shop from the corner, that was ours.'

Jackson took it in at a glance. He was puzzled and touched by Fogarty's emotion because there was nothing to distinguish the little market town from a hundred others. A laneway led off the hilly road and they came to the abbey, a ruined tower and a few walls, with tombstones sown thickly in quire and nave. The hearse was already drawn up outside and people had gathered in a semicircle about it. Ned Devine came hastily up to the car where the two priests were donning their vestments. Fogarty knew at once that there was trouble brewing.

'Whisper, Father Jerry,' Ned muttered in a strained excited voice. 'People are talking about that wreath. I wonder would you know who sent it?'

'I don't know the first thing about it, Ned,' Fogarty replied, and suddenly his heart began to beat violently.

'Come here a minute, Sheela,' Ned called, and a tall, pale girl with the stain of tears on her long bony face left the little group of mourners and joined them. Fogarty nodded to her. She was Devine's sister, a schoolteacher who had never married. 'This is Father Jackson, Father Willie's other friend. They don't know anything about it either.'

'Then I'd let them take it back,' she said doggedly.

'What would you say, father?' Ned asked, appealing to Fogarty, and suddenly Fogarty felt his courage desert him. In disputing with Martin he had felt himself an equal on neutral ground, but now the passion and prejudice of the little town seemed to rise up and oppose him, and he felt himself again a boy, rebellious and terrified. You had to know the place to realize the hysteria that could be provoked by something like a funeral.

'I can only tell you what I told Father Martin already,' he said, growing red and angry.

'Did he talk about it too?' Ned asked sharply.

'There!' Sheela said vindictively. 'What did I tell you?'

'Well, the pair of you are cleverer than I am,' Fogarty said. 'I saw nothing wrong with it.'

'It was no proper thing to send to a priest's funeral,' she hissed with prim fury. 'And whoever sent it was no friend of my brother.'

'You saw nothing wrong with it, father?' Ned prompted appealingly.

'But I tell you, Uncle Ned, if that wreath goes into the graveyard we'll be the laughing stock of the town,' she said in an old-maidish frenzy. 'I'll throw it out myself if you won't.'

'Whisht, girl, whisht, and let Father Jerry talk!' Ned said furiously.

'It's entirely a matter for yourselves, Ned,' Fogarty said excitedly. He was really scared now. He knew he was in danger of behaving imprudently in public, and sooner or later, the story would get back to the Bishop, and it would be suggested that he knew more than he pretended.

'If you'll excuse me interrupting, father,' Jackson said suavely, giving Fogarty a warning glance over his spectacles. 'I know this is none of my business.'

'Not at all, father, not at all,' Ned said passionately. 'You were the boy's friend. All we want is for you to tell us what to do.'

'Oh, well, Mr Devine, that would be too great a responsibility for me to take,' Jackson replied with a cagey smile, though Fogarty saw that his face was very flushed. 'Only someone who really knows the town could advise you about that. I only know what things are like in my own place. Of course, I entirely agree with Miss Devine,' he said, giving her a smile that suggested that this, like crucifixion, was something he preferred to avoid. 'Naturally, Father Fogarty and I have discussed it already. I think personally that it was entirely improper to send a wreath.' Then his mild, clerical voice suddenly grew menacing and he shrugged his shoulders with an air of contempt. 'But, speaking as an outsider, I'd say if you were to send that wreath back from the graveyard, you'd make yourself something far worse than a laughing stock. You'd throw mud on a dead man's name that would never be forgotten for you the longest day you lived ... Of course, that's only an outsider's opinion,' he added urbanely, drawing in his breath in a positive hiss.

'Of course, of course, of course,' Ned Devine said, clicking his fingers and snapping into action. 'We should have thought of it ourselves, father. 'Twould be giving tongues to the stones.'

Then he lifted the wreath himself and carried it to the graveside. Several of the men by the gate looked at him with a questioning eye and fell in behind him. Some hysteria had gone out of the air. Fogarty gently squeezed Jackson's hand.

'Good man, Jim!' he said in a whisper. 'Good man you are!'

He stood with Jackson at the head of the open grave beside the local priests. As their voices rose in the psalms for the dead and their vestments billowed about them, Fogarty's brooding eyes swept the crowd of faces he had known since his childhood and which were now caricatured by age and pain. Each time they came to rest on the wreath which stood at one side of the open grave. It would lie there now above Devine when all the living had gone, his secret. And each time it came over him in a wave of emotion that what he and Jackson had protected was something more than a sentimental token. It was the thing that had linked them to Devine, and for the future would link them to one another – love. Not half a dozen things, but one thing, between son and mother, man and sweetheart, friend and friend.

# THE WEEPING CHILDREN

Joe Saunders and his wife, Brigid, had been married a year when they had their first baby – a little girl they called Nance, after Brigid's mother. Brigid was Irish, and Joe had always had a feeling that there must be some Irish blood in himself. She was a Catholic, and, though Joe was an unbeliever, he liked it in her, and encouraged her to put up holy pictures and statues all over the house. He even went to Mass with her occasionally, but she said he put her off her prayers with his air of devotion, which made him laugh. She often made him laugh, and he liked it, because he had a natural gravity that turned easily to melancholy and even tears. She had good-breeding as well, and he liked that too, though she sometimes upset him by the way she unconsciously patronized his mother and sisters. They were common, and he knew they were common, but he didn't like it to be rubbed in. Brigid had kept her girlish gaiety and her delight in flirting shamelessly with any man who fancied her. It amused Joe, because for all her charm, he knew the wild, chaste, innocent streak in her, and realized that the smart operators would get absolutely nowhere with her.

After Nance's birth Joe felt that life had done him proud. There were times when he saw everything with a sort of double vision, as though he were not only doing whatever he was doing – like pushing the pram round the estate, or creeping into the back room at night to see that the baby was covered – but watching himself do it, as though he were someone in a film or a book, and the conjunction of the two visions gave the thing itself an intense stereoscopic quality. He was sure that this must be what people meant when they talked of happiness.

But he realized that it was different for Brigid. Though at times she could forget herself and play with the baby like a girl with a doll, she was often gloomy, tearful and irritable. This was not like her. Joe's great friend, Jerry Cross, called it something like post-partem psychosis, and though Joe had no great faith in the long names Jerry liked to give things, he accepted his advice and took Brigid for a week to Brighton. It did her good but only for a short while. Joe – a sensitive man – sometimes thought he knew exactly how she felt – a wild girl with a vivacious temperament, who loved outings and parties, trapped by a morsel of humanity who took everything and gave nothing.

Joe was attentive to the point of officiousness, seeing that she went to the cinema and visited friends. But even to old friends she had changed, and had taken a positive dislike to Jerry Cross. Though Jerry was great at giving women little presents, he didn't seem to like them much, and now Brigid chose to interpret this as dislike of herself. With a sort of schoolgirl pertness that drove Joe to despair she mocked Cross about his over-heated bachelor flat, his expensive gramophone and collection of records, and his liqueur cabinet that always seemed to contain some new exotic drink that Jerry would press on his visitors, rubbing his hands and saying in his anxious way: 'It's not bad, is it? I mean, it really is not bad. You think that, too, Joe.' Twice, to protect Cross, Joe had to reprove her, and though he did it gently, it cut him to the heart to have to do it at all.

'Why can't you be nicer to Jerry?' he asked as they were going home one night. 'He hasn't so many friends.'

'He has no friends at all, if you ask me,' Brigid said coldly. 'He's too bloody selfish to afford them.'

'Selfish?' Joe exclaimed, stopping dead. 'A man who put a cheque for two hundred quid on my mantelpiece while I was out of the room!'

'We know all that,' Brigid said contemptuously. 'Damn well he knew you wouldn't take it.'

'He knew more than I did,' Joe said, resuming his walk. 'Anyway, it wasn't the money that mattered at the time. It was his confidence in me. It gave me confidence in myself. I tell you, Brigid, there are things between men that you'll never understand, not till the day you die.'

But argument had no effect on Brigid except perhaps to give her fresh grounds for spite. One evening at Joe's house, Cross was boasting innocently of some shady deal he had refused to be connected with, and Brigid, with mock admiration, drew him skilfully out. It was one of Cross's little weaknesses that he liked to think himself a really shrewd businessman – 'a bloody dreamer' was how an uncle had described him to Joe.

'You always play it safe, Jerry, don't you?' she asked at last.

'What's that, Brigid?' Cross asked eagerly, too pleased with himself to be aware of her malice.

'Brigid!' Joe said warningly.

'Anyone who had anything to do with you would want to watch out,' she said.

Cross got up and clutched the lapels of his coat as though he were about to make a speech. It suddenly struck Joe that he was a little man who lived in expectation of having to make speeches – unpleasant ones, in his own defence.

'I assure you, Brigid, that nobody who had anything to do with me ever had to watch out, as you put it,' he said over-loudly, speaking as it were to a faraway audience. 'I do play it safe, though. You're right there, I do. And I'll play it safer for the future by not calling here, as I have been doing.'

Then he made for the door, and Joe, holding his coat for him, realized that he was shivering violently. Joe opened the door, put his arm round Cross' shoulder and walked slowly to the gate with him. Cross walked close to him, so as not to break the embrace, and yet Joe knew he did not feel it in a homosexual way. The estate road went uphill to the bus stop on the tree-shaded suburban road, and the two men walked together like sweethearts till they reached it. Then Joe took Cross' hand in his own two.

'Try not to think of it, Jerry,' he said in a low voice. 'She doesn't even know what she's saying. The girl is sick in her mind.'

'She is, Joe, she is, she is,' Cross said with pathetic eagerness. 'I thought it from the first, but now I'm sure. I'm sorry I was so sharp with her.'

'You weren't, Jerry; not so sharp as I'd have been.'

It was only when he had waved goodbye to Cross from the pavement that Joe gave way to tears. He walked slowly up and down the road till the fit had passed. As he entered the house, Brigid was waiting for him in the sitting room, sitting exactly as when he had left.

'Come in, Joe,' she said quietly. 'We have to talk.'

'I'm sorry, Brigid, but I don't want to talk,' he said, feeling sure that if he did he would break down again.

'I want to talk,' she said in a flat tone. 'It may be the last chance we'll get. I'll have to clear out.'

'What's that?' he asked incredulously.

'I have to clear out,' she said again, and he knew that she meant it.

It was at moments like these that all the wise passivity in Joe came on top. In his time he had been humiliated, hurt so that the pain had never left him, but he knew you had to give in to it, let the pain wash over you, if you didn't want it to destroy you.

'Why do you think you have to clear out, dear?' he asked mildly, taking a chair inside the door and joining his hands before him.

'Because I don't want to destroy your life the way I destroyed my own,' she said.

'Well, I should have something to say to that,' he said. 'So should the baby, of course. Unless you're proposing to take her with you.'

'I'm not,' she said with artificial casualness. 'I dare say your mother can look after her.'

'I dare say she could,' he said calmly. 'But it's not my idea of what a child needs.'

'At least your mother won't insult your friends,' Brigid said bitterly. He knew then that she had no illusions about her behaviour to Cross, and his heart softened.

'You mean more to me than any of my friends, dear,' he said. 'Even Jerry – and Heaven knows, he means quite a lot. But why do you have to do things like that? They hurt you as much as they hurt other people. What is it, Brigid? Why don't you trust me? Is it another man?'

For a moment Joe thought she really was going to strike him. Then the humour of it seemed to dawn on her, and she gave a weak grin.

'You have a very poor opinion of yourself, haven't you?' she asked pertly. 'Even that jenny-ass, Cross, wouldn't think of a silly think like that. I never looked at the side of the road a man walked at since I married you.'

There was no mistaking the absolute truthfulness of that, and again he felt the sense of relief, and with it the old tenderness and admiration.

'Naturally, that's what I hoped, dear,' he said. 'And damn it all, nothing else matters.'

'Not even the ones I met before I met you?' she asked mockingly, and her tone struck him cold again.

'I see,' he said. 'You mean there was someone else?'

'Naturally,' she said angrily. And then, as though reading his thoughts, she reverted to her tone of exasperated amusement. 'Now, I suppose you think I'm breaking my heart over him? I am, like hell! I hope to God I never lay eyes on him again. I wish I could say the same thing about his child.'

'His child?' Joe repeated stupidly. Now he felt that the world really was collapsing about him. 'You mean you had a child already?'

'What do you think brought me over to London in the first place?' she asked reasonably.

'I don't know,' Joe said with simple dignity. 'I just thought you might have been telling me the truth when you said you came over for a job. I suppose you're right to think I'm a bit simple-minded.'

'I never thought you were simple-minded,' she retorted with the fury of a hell-cat. 'I thought you were too good to be true, if you want to know what I really thought.'

'And you have this child where? With your people?'

'No, outside Cork,' she said shortly. 'I suppose I wanted her as far away as possible. And, as I'm about it, there's another thing. I pinched some of the housekeeping money to support her. After I left the job I had nothing of my own.'

'You could scarcely have left the child to starve,' he said

lightly. 'That doesn't count beside the other things.'

'What other things?'

'All the lies you've told me,' he said bitterly. 'I didn't deserve that from you. Look, Brigid, it's no use pretending I'm not hurt – not by what you've just told me. That was your business. But you might have told me before you married me.'

'So that you needn't have married me,' she asked bitterly.

'I mean nothing of the sort,' said Joe. 'I don't know what I should have done, but I don't think it would have come between you and me. You were unfair to me and unfair to the child. You might have trusted me as I trusted you.'

'As if the two things were alike?' she retorted. 'I told you I thought you were too good to be true. You weren't, but to get to know you that way I had to marry you first, and to marry you I had to tell you lies. At least, that's how it seemed to me. And a hell of a lot of good it did me!'

Joe sighed.

'Anyway, we have to think what we're to do about this child, and that's something we can't decide tonight.'

'There's only one thing to do, Joe,' she said. 'I'll have to go back to London and get a job.' She said it manfully enough, but he knew she didn't mean it. She was begging him to find some way out for her.

'We don't have to break up this house,' he said with determination. 'Damn it, it's our own. We can still bring her to live with us.'

'But I don't want her to live with us,' she said angrily. 'Can't you understand? It was all a miserable bloody mistake, and I don't want you to have to live with it either. It's just that I feel such a bitch, having everything in the world I want while she has nothing.'

'I see that,' Joe said gently. 'I see it's not an easy question. We'll have to think of something, that's all.'

He thought a lot about it that night, though less of what they were to do with Brigid's child than of the disaster that had overtaken his beautiful world. Again he could see himself acting, doing whatever he felt he had to do, but beyond that he could see it all as though it were happening to someone in a book or a movie. He could almost hear his own voice as if it were in the third person. ' "We'll have to think of something, that's all," he said.' And he supposed that this must be what people meant when they talked of grief.

Yet when Brigid waked him, bringing him a cup of tea in bed, it seemed to have taken nothing out of her. Unburdening herself of her secret seemed to have restored all her native liveliness, in fact.

When he got home that evening, he was astonished to see Cross waiting for him in the front room, and he knew from Cross' manner that Brigid had made her peace with him. At any other time this would have made him happy, but now it merely seemed an irrelevance. As he saw Cross off, Cross said urgently, 'You won't think me interfering, Joe, but Brigid came to the office and told me about your little trouble. I guessed there was something upsetting her. I only wanted to say how sorry I am.' Joe was amused at Cross' delicacy, and touched that Brigid, for all her fierce pride, had humiliated herself so abjectly before him, but this didn't seem to matter either.

'I know, Jerry, I know,' he said, squeezing Cross' arm, but Cross was full of the subject.

'It's going to be terrible, however you arrange things,' he said, 'and I only want you to know that I'll be delighted to do anything. Delighted! Because I have a great admiration for Brigid, Joe. You know that.' Joe realized that by ways that could have been no great pleasure to her, Brigid had at last managed to pierce Cross' defences. Being Cross, he was doing more than interceding for her. He was hiding the cheque on the mantelpiece.

After supper Joe said to Brigid:

'I've been thinking this thing over, dear, and I see only one way out. We have to bring the child here.'

'I've been thinking it over too, and I don't see the necessity for that at all,' she said hastily. 'Cross thinks the same. To tell you the truth, I think 'twould be impossible for everybody.'

Joe could see exactly what she was thinking about. Now that the burden of secrecy had been lifted, she had fled to the opposite extreme of self-confidence. Only a wild outburst of self-confidence could have given her the courage to go to Cross at all. But with self-confidence she had regained all her old devious personality, and was plotting like mad to retrieve as much as possible from the wreck and avoid humiliating herself before the neighbours and before Joe's decent, common working-class family.

'Not impossible,' he said. 'Difficult, I grant you. We've made a good many friends on the estate, and it's not going to make our position here any better. But others have had to do the same and worse.'

'It's easier for a man than for a woman,' Brigid said ruefully.

'It's harder for a woman because she does more to make the position she finds herself in,' said Joe sternly. 'It's not easy for anybody. All the same, it doesn't count compared with a child's life.'

'And there's your mother to be considered,' she said.

'Exactly. There's Mother, and there's Barbara and Coralie, and we know what they'll think and say. They'll make you pay, Brigid, and I'll suffer for it. But that's not the worst. The worst is that we may get the kid too late for her to be able to fit in. Still, bad as that is, it will be easier now than it would be in ten or fifteen years time.'

'I don't know, Joe,' Brigid said earnestly. 'I cracked up on you before because I was trying to handle it on my own. I won't crack up on you again, and I think there are a lot of things I can do without making ourselves miserable into the bargain.'

'Such as?'

'Well, it was really Jerry who suggested it – getting her over here to a decent home where we can keep an eye on her, taking her on holidays with Nance, and seeing that she goes to a good school when she's old enough.'

'And I suppose Jerry offered to help?'

'He did,' she admitted. 'He's damn decent.'

'He is decent,' said Joe. 'All the same, he's wrong. Dead wrong.' Like many gentle souls, Joe had a streak of iron in him, and when he made up his mind about something he could be very obstinate. 'Jerry is a bachelor. He doesn't even know what he's talking about. You can cut off a man or woman as a loss, and feel that maybe they'll keep afloat, but you can't do that to a child. A child is too helpless. And this time, it isn't only you who have to live with them as well, and if anything happened that child, I'd be a murderer as well. I've got my faults, Brigid, but I'm not a murderer.'

A fortnight later they were flying in from the sea over Dublin, and Joe knew that Brigid was losing her nerve. Every moment seemed to leave her more panic-stricken. When they travelled into the city on the tall, bumpy, swaying bus, she kept silent, but in the hotel room she broke down.

'Look, Joe, I can't face it,' she said.

'Now, Brigid, you've done things a great deal more difficult than this,' he said comfortingly.

'I haven't, Joe,' she said. 'You don't understand, I tell you. I can't go down to Cork tomorrow and meet people I used to know, and start inventing excuses for coming back.'

'You don't have to invent excuses,' he said patiently. 'You're just here with your husband on a holiday – what's wrong with that?'

'And with a two-year-old baby in my arms?' she said bitterly. 'I tell you, Joe, I don't give a damn what happens the child. I'm not going down.'

She frightened Joe. It was as though behind this façade of a capital with its Georgian squares and flashy hotels and expensive restaurants there was a jungle of secrecy and panic. But he did not want Brigid to see how he felt about it.

'Very well, dear,' he said patiently. 'I'll go. I dare say your family can direct me.'

'I suppose they could,' she said doubtfully. 'But if you have any consideration for them, you'll keep as far from them as you can.'

He knew it was unsafe to argue with her. She was close to hysteria or he would have said it was rather peculiar to have a foreigner searching in unfamiliar country for a child of this family who had already been neglected for two years.

'Very well, dear,' he said. 'If you say so, I shall.'

The trip on the train to Cork was pleasant, and his only regret was that Brigid wasn't there to share it with him and point out the places of interest: it seemed like the waste of a good excursion. The city itself seemed pleasant enough too, and he had a good view of the river and quays from his bedroom window. Downstairs, he talked to the hotel manager, who was big-boned, deep-voiced and amiable and threw himself into the business of getting Joe to his destination as though he had no other aim in life. 'Throw' seemed the word that suited him, for he literally heaved himself across the desk, looking at a map and studying a timetable, bellowed softly to members of the staff who might help, and even called in casual passers-by. This scared Joe who did not want his business made public too soon. It would be time enough for explanations when he returned to the hotel with a baby – a difficult moment enough, as even he realized.

But the last ten miles of his journey seemed the most difficult of all.

'It's all right, Mr Coleman,' said Joe. 'I'll hire a car.'

The hotel manager glanced at the clock in the hall and said in his deep voice:

'You won't hire any car. I'll take an hour off after dinner and drive you.'

'That's very kind of you,' whispered Joe, 'but it might be better if I did take a car. You see, it's rather a delicate matter.'

'Oh, sorry, I didn't mean to be inquisitive,' Coleman said with a touch of resentment.

'Don't be silly!' Joe said with a laugh. 'You're not being inquisitive. I haven't anything to hide, and anyhow I'd have had to tell you sooner or later. Sit down for a moment and let me explain.'

The two men sat in a corner of the lounge and Joe explained. The hotel manager listened with a vague smile.

'So far as I'm concerned, I can keep my mouth shut,' he said. 'But don't be surprised if a lot of the staff know who you are already. If they don't know tonight they'll know tomorrow. They'll also know who your wife is. This may seem a big city to you, but it's not big enough for those who have to live in it. Mind,' he added with a smile, 'I wouldn't let that disturb me too much either. Will I get a cot into your room?'

'Not tonight,' said Joe, 'I've tried to sort this thing out. It isn't easy for a man, you know, but I don't think it would be fair to the kid to bring her back tonight, particularly with no woman around. Even if Brigid was here it would be a shock. No, I thought I'd go to this house first, and let the kid get to know me before I bring her back.'

'Tomorrow I have the whole morning clear,' said Coleman.

'No, I didn't mean it that way either,' said Joe. 'I can afford to hire a car. Damn it, having come all this way, I can't be stopped by the hire of a car.'

'No reason you should unless you want to,' Coleman said gruffly. 'I think you're wise not to bring her back tonight though. I'll see you in the lounge after dinner. I'd stick to the roast beef, if I were you.'

After dinner the two men set off in Coleman's old car. After a few minutes Coleman spoke.

'This isn't an aspect of life you get much advice on when you go into the hotel business,' he said in his good-humoured way. 'But, if you'll excuse my being personal, Mr Saunders, you seem to me a rather unusual sort of man.'

'Do I?' Joe asked in genuine surprise. 'I should have said in my circumstances most men would have felt the same.'

'Felt the same, I've no doubt,' said Coleman. 'I'm not so sure they'd have acted the same, though. Naturally, the first thing I did when you told me your story was to ask myself what I'd have done in your place.'

'Yes?' Joe said eagerly.

'And I decided – don't think me impertinent now! – that I'd think twice about it.'

'Don't worry, old man,' Joe said with a loud laugh. 'I did. I thought three times about it, as a matter of fact.'

But those few words seemed to have cleared the air between them. They had passed the city boundaries and were driving along a river bank with a tree-lined walk at the other side of the water. The main road led along a smaller river wooded to its bank. Finally they reached a little village with a church and public-house where they went off on a by-road up the hill. They came out of it above the river and harbour, stopped to inquire their way, and drove slowly for some miles along a deserted upland road. It was darkening, and Coleman drove more carefully. There was a cottage on their right and two small children with bare feet were playing in the road-way outside. He stopped the car suddenly.

'I have a feeling this is it,' he said, and bellowed to the children: 'Is this Mrs Ryan's?'

'What's that, sir?' asked a little boy.

'Mrs Ryan's, I said.'

' 'Tis, sir.'

'And is this Marie?' Coleman asked, pointing to the little girl who accompanied him.

'No, sir, 'tis Martha,' said the child.

'Then where is Marie?' Coleman asked, and suddenly a tall, rough-looking woman with rosy cheeks appeared by the white gatepost. Afterwards Joe thought he would never forget that first impression of her with the white gatepost and dark fuchsia bushes, cut out against the sky.

'Is this the gentleman from England I have?' she called. 'Marie is inside, gentlemen. Won't you come in?'

Joe got out first and held out his hand.

'I'm Joe Saunders, Brigid Healy's husband,' he said. 'And this is Mr Coleman, the hotel manager from Cork. He was kind enough to give me a lift.'

'I was after giving up expecting ye,' she said, showing her big teeth in a smile. 'Come in, let ye! I'm afraid the house is in a mess, but 'tis only the children.'

'You don't have to apologize, Mrs Ryan,' Joe said. 'I come of a large family myself.'

But even Joe's large London family had not prepared him for the little cottage, even if the shadows inside gave little opportunity for deciding whether or not it was in a mess. An open door into the bedroom suggested a big bed that had not been made, and the walls of the kitchen were bare but for a grocer's calendar inside the door. Sitting round the open fire were three other children whose faces he could scarcely see, but it was clear that the bare-legged two year old who roasted her feet before it was Brigid's child. Suddenly he wondered what he was doing there.

'This is Miss Healy's little girl, gentlemen,' said Mrs Ryan. 'She's the spit of her mother, but ye can't see. I'll light the lamp. I suppose ye'd like a cup of tea after yeer journey?'

'No, thanks, Mrs Ryan,' said Joe. 'We've only just had dinner. Besides, we won't stay long. We thought we'd come back tomorrow morning for Marie, just to give you time to get her ready ... Hullo, Marie,' he said, taking the child's hand. 'I bet you don't know who I am.'

'Hullo, Marie,' Coleman said with casual amiability and took her hand as well. She looked up at them without expression and Joe suddenly recognized her resemblance to Brigid. That gave him a turn too.

'Run out and play with Martha and Michael,' Mrs Ryan shouted to the other boy in the room. 'And bring Kitty along with you.' Silently the two children got up and went out, closing the half door behind them. It was not as though they were frightened but as though they saw no reason for disobeying, and for some reason this struck Joe as even worse. He felt that a natural child should be curious. Mrs Ryan lit the lamp, squinting up at it.

'Wisha, sit down, let ye,' she said, pulling up two chairs and wiping the seats vaguely with her apron. 'And how is Miss Healy? You'll have to forgive me. I forget her married name.'

'Saunders,' said Joe, sitting down and opening the little case he had brought with him. 'She's fine, Mrs Ryan. She probably told you we have a little girl of our own now. She wasn't well or she'd have been here herself. I don't want to rush you. These are a few clothes I brought, and perhaps you can tell me if they'll fit.'

He passed the frock, overcoat, and hat to her and she held them to the light with a vague smile. Then she peered at the shoes.

'Wisha, aren't they lovely?' she said. 'Aren't you the lucky girl, Marie? Ye're sure ye won't have the tea? 'Twouldn't take me a minute to boil the kettle.'

'Certain, thanks,' said Joe, who only wanted to get out of the house quick. He crossed to the half-door, and again he caught an image he felt he would never forget of the lamp-light on the hedge and white-washed gatepost where four children were crowded together, talking in whispers. 'Better come in now,' he said with a laugh. 'I bet you heard every word we said. Are they all yours, Mrs Ryan?'

'Ah, no, sir,' she replied almost reproachfully. 'We had no children of our own. 'Tis on account of my husband's death I had to take them.'

The four children came in and stood fidgeting by the dresser, two little boys and two little girls, apparently well-fed if not well-dressed or clean, but somehow lacking all the spontaneity of other children. Joe took out a fistful of coins and distributed them. The children took the money meekly, without gratitude.

'Well, Marie,' he asked, stooping over the child on the stool, 'how do you think you're going to like me for a daddy?'

'She's strange,' Mrs Ryan said apologetically. 'Most of the time she have plenty to say for herself.'

'I'll bet she has,' said Joe. 'And in a couple of days she'll be giving me cheek as well. Won't you, old lady?'

They sat and talked for a few minutes longer. Then Joe said good night, kissed Marie and patted the other children on the head. It was already dark on the road, and he was glad of the headlights that made the green banks seem theatrical but concealed his face.

'Well, I don't know how you feel, but I'm ready for a drink,' said Coleman. 'A large one, at that.'

'What I should like is to buy a few toys for the other kids,' said Joe.

'Too late for that, I'm afraid,' said Coleman. 'The shops are shut until Monday. You might be able to pick up a few cheap toys in a sweet-shop, and a couple of bags of sweets. If you mean they won't have the money long I'm inclined to agree with you.'

As they entered the hotel the tall night porter looked up from his evening paper and said, 'Night, sir. Night, Mr Saunders,' and already Joe knew that his business was being discussed. The waiter who brought them their drinks in the lounge seemed to know as well, but Joe had the idea that he approved. He might have been a father himself. He might even have known Brigid and Marie's father. The pair of them might have sat drinking in this very lounge like any of the couples who sat there now. It was only the other side of the picture that he had been looking at that evening in a lonesome cottage on the hills. He felt very depressed.

Next morning he was more cheerful. He woke to the sound of bells. He had never heard so many bells, or else they sounded louder in the hollow of the city. A pious people all right, he thought. On their way out of town he saw the well-dressed crowds on their way to Mass. In the first village they came to there was a large group outside the church and a similar one outside the public-house.

The four elder children were waiting for them in the roadway, and as they approached, two of these rushed in to give warning. They had all been washed and two of them even wore boots. When they went into the cottage Marie was sitting stiffly on a low chair by the door, as though she had been glued there to keep her from soiling her new dress, and she looked up at them blankly and pointed to her shoes. 'Look! Shoes!' she said shrilly, and Joe, stooping to admire them, saw that they were too big.

'We'll get you properly fitted tomorrow, old lady,' he said.

He distributed the few presents he had managed to buy, shook hands with Mrs Ryan, and carried Marie to the car. The other children followed, and he shook hands with each in turn, and then laid his hand gently on each one's head. Over the low wooden gate he could see the tall figure of Mrs Ryan, holding the doorpost and gazing up and down the deserted road.

As the car started he turned to wave to the little group of children. They stood in the roadway, their presents clutched in their hands, and he saw that they were all weeping quietly. It seemed to him that they were not weeping as real children weep, with abandonment and delight, but hopelessly, as old people weep whom the world has passed by. He was the world and he had passed them by. He knew now why he had not dared to kiss any of them. If he had kissed them he could not have left them there. His first thought was to prevent Marie's seeing them, but he realized that he needn't have worried. She was leaning forward, enchanted, trying to touch her beautiful new shoes. Coleman drove with his eyes fixed on the winding roadway over the hills, and his fat sulky face was expressionless.

'I wonder if you saw what I did?' Joe said at last to break the silence, and Coleman stared at him despairingly.

'I'm in dread I'll never forget it,' he said.

## Selected bestsellers

- ☐ **Eagle in the Sky** Wilbur Smith 60p
- ☐ **Gone with the Wind** Margaret Mitchell £1·50
- ☐ **Jaws** Peter Benchley 70p
- ☐ **The Tower** Richard Martin Stern 60p
  (filmed as *The Towering Inferno*)
- ☐ **Mandingo** Kyle Onstott 75p
- ☐ **Alive: The Story of the Andes Survivors** (illus)
  Piers Paul Read 75p
- ☐ **Tinker Tailor Soldier Spy** John le Carré 75p
- ☐ **East of Eden** John Steinbeck 75p
- ☐ **The Adventures of Sherlock Holmes**
  Sir Arthur Conan Doyle 75p
- ☐ **Nicholas and Alexandra** (illus) Robert K. Massie £1·25
- ☐ **Knock Down** Dick Francis 60p
- ☐ **Penmarric** Susan Howatch 95p
- ☐ **Cashelmara** Susan Howatch 95p
- ☐ **The Poseidon Adventure** Paul Gallico 70p
- ☐ **Flashman** George MacDonald Fraser 70p
- ☐ **Airport** Arthur Hailey 80p
- ☐ **Onward Virgin Soldiers** Leslie Thomas 70p
- ☐ **The Doctor's Quick Weight Loss Diet**
  Stillman and Baker 60p
- ☐ **Vet in Harness** James Herriot 60p

All these books are available at your bookshop or newsagent;
or can be obtained direct from the publisher
Just tick the titles you want and fill in the form below
Prices quoted are applicable in UK

Pan Books Cavaye Place London SW10 9PG
Send purchase price plus 15p for the first book and 5p for each
additional book, to allow for postage and packing

Name (block letters) _____

Address _____

_____

While every effort is made to keep prices low, it is sometimes
necessary to increase prices at short notice. Pan Books reserve the
right to show on covers new retail prices which may differ from
those advertised in the text or elsewhere